Readers Love Ashlyn Chase's Dragon an...

"Shapeshifting done ... s a must-read."

—*RT Book Reviews*, 4 Stars, for *Hooked on a Phoenix*

"This fantastic story will enliven your day and keep you smiling."

—*Night Owl Reviews* TOP PICK, 4½ Stars, for *Hooked on a Phoenix*

"What could be better than hot firefighters who shift into dragons and phoenixes? Another great story from the talented Chase."

—*RT Book Reviews*, 4 Stars, for *Never Dare a Dragon*

"Hot and hilarious. This one is a must-read."

—*Night Owl Reviews* TOP PICK, 5 Stars, for *Never Dare a Dragon*

"Readers will enjoy the banter as well as the steamy encounters that set them aflame."

—*RT Book Reviews*, 4 Stars, for *My Wild Irish Dragon*

"Fantastic. How can you not fall in love with this book, sexy firefighters, both male and female, magical creatures that use their powers for good, a snarky Mother Nature, interfering family members, and some charming Irish accents? Seriously, if you haven't read this one yet, I highly suggest you get it as soon as possible."

—*Night Owl Reviews* TOP PICK, 5 Stars, for *My Wild Irish Dragon*

"Dragon lovers, this is the book for you."
— *La Crimson Femme* for *I Dream of Dragons*

"This story has it all: laughter, tears, magic, and sizzling heat."
— *Night Owl Reviews* TOP PICK, 5 Stars, for *I Dream of Dragons*

MORE THAN A
PHOENIX

ASHLYN CHASE

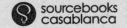

sourcebooks
casablanca

Published by Sourcebooks Casablanca, an imprint of Sourcebooks, Inc.
P.O. Box 4410, Naperville, Illinois 60567-4410
(630) 961-3900
Fax: (630) 961-2168
sourcebooks.com

Printed and bound in the United States of America.
OPM 10 9 8 7 6 5 4 3 2 1

To my extended family. Now that my entire family of origin is gone, you're all I've got.

Fortunately, I like you.

Chapter 1

DEEP IN THE AMAZON RAIN FOREST OF BRAZIL, A GROUP of thirteen men gathered in a circle. All were Caucasian, wearing tattered remnants of old uniforms.

The leader of the white men withdrew a pistol. One of his members shrank back.

"What?" the commandant asked.

"Do you need a weapon to cast a spell?"

"I can use yours, if you prefer…"

The leader's cold blue eyes concerned him. The man shook his head, not trusting some of his companions as far as a blind panther could see.

"Good. Then I'll use this," the commandant said. He raised his Luger P08 pistol in the air and tucked his free hand behind his back. Stepping smartly around the outside of the circle, he spoke in his native language. "May the ancient and powerful gods hear us! May our ancestors who worked tirelessly to become gods hear us! We need you to punish a—"

"No, Commandant! You must not use the word 'punish.' That is considered black magic."

"Horseshit!" he cried. Then he took a few deep breaths and resumed walking. "I meant to say, we need justice!" Glaring at the one who'd had the audacity to interrupt his spell casting, the leader continued.

The man watched with great concern. Would the spell backfire because he'd asked for the ancient gods' help to cause harm? Or did the leader of the white men, who'd been hiding here for three generations, know what he was doing? The lives of his entire group plus the women and children in the compound could be affected. Would their gods punish the innocents among them?

"Perhaps we should do this another time… After we've had a chance to discuss—"

"There is no other time! The stars have aligned to favor this spell. It is the first of May, a sacred holiday. If you want to scare off the developer, this is the time. Or do you want our community discovered? Do you want to be made to answer for the actions of your ancestors? It won't even be legal. We'll be tried and found guilty in the court of popular opinion. Remember how one of our direct ancestors never made it to court? He was assassinated!"

The man hesitated, then nodded for him to continue.

The commandant completed the circle and made a sharp quarter-turn to retake his spot. "There is an unreasonable man calling himself the developer," the commandant yelled loudly, pointing with his pistol in the direction of the Amazon River. "He wants to destroy this peaceful place. He plans to bring many tourists here. He will ruin our way of life—if you do not stop him!

"Stop him!" the commandant cried, and the others echoed. "Stop him! Stop him!"

"This is not his home! Send him back where he belongs!" All the voices took up the chant. "Send him back, send him back, send him back…"

Where had the man who called himself the developer come from? Surely it must be far away. And how would the gods and spirits of their ancestors make him go back there?

Just then, the leader withdrew a poppet—a small, stuffed effigy of a man—held the Luger against its head, and yelled, "Go home!"

Before he could pull the trigger, a spider monkey fell from an overhanging tree and landed smack in the middle of their circle.

"Eep!" The monkey grabbed the doll out of the leader's hand, then scurried away as the stunned men watched.

"Fuck! That damned monkey broke the circle!" the commandant yelled in frustration. Then he bent over and shook his head. "I'm not doing it again."

"But did it work?" one of the men asked.

He shrugged. "Probably." He gazed in the direction in which the monkey had fled. "If the gods don't make him leave, at least the monkey took him away."

They all laughed—except the concerned member.

———∽∽∽———

Mallory Summers was trying to chat with a nice young man about the weather, but couldn't help being distracted by two old biddies sitting on the bus bench, peeking at her from under their umbrellas.

One old woman leaned toward the other and whispered loudly, "Tsk. Tsk. Such a sweet young thing..."

"It's a shame," said the other one.

Shame? Should I be ashamed for chatting up a nice-looking guy and offering to share my umbrella? Just to make sure the gossips knew how unashamed she was, she turned back to the young man and spoke louder. "Yeah, I saw the weather report this morning. It's supposed to rain until about noon."

The guy just nodded. He was a little hard to engage in conversation.

Still, she persisted. "That will probably keep people at home, so my work at the mall will be slow."

Out of the corner of her eye, she spotted one of the women waddling up to a guy in uniform. They were farther away, so she couldn't hear what they were saying.

A few moments later, he approached her slowly. He was a handsome devil. She could only imagine what the interfering old woman had said. Probably warned him not to be taken in by the young lady's flirtatious ways.

"Uh, hi," the guy said, smiling. He had stunning brown eyes, with thick, dark lashes most women would envy. One of the patches on his uniform looked just like the one on her uncle's Boston Fire Department uniform.

She suddenly realized he looked familiar. "Hi. Do I know you?"

The young man paused. His smile turned into a grin, lighting up his handsome face. "I know you. You're Mallory Summers."

"Right—and you are…"

"Dante Fierro, and I'm wondering who you're talking to."

"Huh?" *Well, that's rude. Why should anybody care?* She was about to say as much when she turned back to the guy in question to apologize for everyone else's bad manners—but he was gone.

"Where did he go?" she asked.

"Where did who go?"

"The man… I don't know his name. And—wait a minute… You're the Dante Fierro from high school?"

"Yup. So you do remember me."

"Of course."

"Do you always hold conversations with blank air?"

"What the heck are you talking about?"

"Mallory, these ladies have seen you at this bus stop three times, talking to yourself. They won't call the cops, because you're not doing anything illegal, and they don't want to call an ambulance, which would be expensive, but they're worried about you."

Mallory jammed her hands on her hips and strode over to the two old ladies. "You should be minding your own business."

They leaned away from her as if they might catch an airborne virus.

"Mallory…" Dante gentled his voice. "I don't live far from here. Why don't you come over for coffee and we can talk."

"Because I have to go to work. I take two buses to get to my job at the Union Mall."

"I can drive you."

The weather didn't look like it was going to let up, and a nice warm car sounded good. She shrugged. "I don't want to put you out. You look like you're on your way to work too."

"I'm on my way home, actually. Come on. It's no trouble."

She smiled. "Well, now that I realize who you are, it would probably be okay to accept a ride. After all, it's not like you're a complete stranger."

"Good." He stuck out his elbow like he was escorting her to a fancy ball. "Let's go."

She slipped her hand into the crook of his arm and gave the old busybodies a glare as they passed.

He lived around the corner in a nice two-family house on L Street, a stone's throw from the main drag, which bordered the beach.

"I shouldn't stay for coffee. I can get coffee at the mall. Is that your car?" She nodded toward a black Camaro with bright-red racing stripes down the side.

"Yup. My brother Noah calls it my wife."

"Your wife? Why?"

"Because I named her Joanna, and I take good care of her. He says it's because she eats up half my paycheck."

She giggled. "Okay. Well, nice to meet you, Joanna." As they approached the passenger's side, she realized how talking to an inanimate object might also make her look like a crazy person—and he'd already caught her talking to, what…a dead guy? Maybe someone who stepped in front of a bus many years ago… She still wasn't sure what was going on. Could two old ladies be punking her?

He just smiled, dug the key fob out of his pocket, and opened the door for her.

She settled herself on the comfortable leather seat and looked around. His car was indeed in pristine condition. It didn't have that new car smell, but it looked as if it could have.

He jumped into the driver's seat and pulled out of the driveway. "Where to?"

"I work at the mall in Somerville. I thought I already said so."

He drove in the general direction of the expressway, but stayed quiet for a few moments. At last, he asked, "Mallory, are you sure you should be going to work?"

She reared back and stared at him. What was he

saying? And did she want to know? "Yeah. Why wouldn't I?"

He glanced over at her. "It's just that… Well, you… I mean…"

"Just say it, Dante. You think I'm nuts."

"No, not nuts. I wouldn't put it that way, but maybe… I don't know, stressed?"

"Nope. I'm an artist, and having a creative outlet decreases stress. To pay the bills, I take professional portraits at the mall. Kids' photos mostly. But I like kids, so that's not very stressful either."

"Please don't be offended, but…are you on drugs?"

She burst out laughing. "No. Are you?"

He sighed. "Of course not. Maybe you should think about seeing someone for an evaluation though."

"Like who?"

"Like a doctor. I mean, you're not stressed and not on drugs, so why were you hallucinating? Doesn't that concern you?"

She cringed. "A lot of artists aren't wrapped too tight, but this has never happened to me before. I'm as confused as you are."

"Except for the two other times those ladies saw you."

She took a deep breath. How many times had this happened? If she *had* been hallucinating, how would she know? What if she was seeing ghosts and couldn't tell them from real people? That baffled her. She felt like that poor little kid in the *Sixth Sense* movie.

She remembered that one time the cops came when she was having an argument with someone panhandling. He kept following her and wouldn't listen when she told him to back off. The cops acted like she was the only one responsible. When she got through explaining her side of the story, the beggar was gone. But the cops weren't. One of them tried to take her to his cruiser until she wrenched her arm free and ran down the alley and around to the back of a laundromat.

Oh…and then that other thing happened. She had somehow been able to run up a drainpipe, which clearly shouldn't have held her weight—not that she was heavy. And when she saw herself in a puddle on the roof, she saw a monkey. Just for a second. Then the puddle blurred, and she saw her own face and long blonde hair again. Maybe she *was* losing her mind.

"Mallory, please let me take you to the ER for a quick evaluation," he was saying. "You can call in sick or say you're running late."

"But what if they lock me up?"

Dante looked right at her. "Are you planning to harm yourself or anyone else?"

"Of course not!"

"Then they can't hospitalize you against your will."

At this point, she thought a professional opinion might be a good idea. She let out a deep sigh. "Yeah. I guess you're right. Take me to Boston General."

After several minutes of sitting and stewing about Mallory, Dante heard his brother Noah trudging up the stairs to the second-floor apartment they rented together. He looked like a drowned rat as he let his soggy coat drop onto the floor. Noah was probably expecting him to say something about picking it up. Dante slumped over and said nothing.

"What's wrong?" Noah asked.

"What makes you think something's wrong?"

"Your hair is sticking out in all directions like you've been pulling it out, and you're not annoyingly cheerful. So something is wrong. Or more wrong than usual."

Dante sighed. "Okay, I need to talk about it, but you can't tell anyone."

"Who would I tell?" Noah pulled a chair over, acting like this might be something serious.

"Oh, I don't know…maybe the whole damn family at Sunday dinner. Or the guys at your firehouse."

"What did you do?"

"Nothing." Dante rose and paced the length of the living room. At last, he stopped in front of Noah and asked, "Do you remember Mallory Summers?"

"Homecoming queen Mallory? Prom queen Mallory? The girl you had a massive crush on but were too chicken to ask out?"

Dante folded his arms. "Yeah, that's the one, but I wasn't too chicken to ask her out. I just realized she was out of my league and saved myself a humiliating rejection."

"So now what? You bumped into her, finally asked her out, and got shot down anyway?" Noah rose and trod toward the kitchen. "Why would I tell anyone about something like that?"

"That's not what happened. Will you just listen a minute?"

"I will, if you'll say something worth listening to. You want a beer? I know it's, like, ten o'clock in the morning, but you look like you could use one. I know I could. We had a bitch of a fire in a downtown clothing store last night."

Dante plopped onto the couch. "Sorry to hear that. Getting back to Mallory... I brought her to the hospital this morning. She was hallucinating."

"Shit! Was she on drugs?"

"No. At least she said she wasn't and didn't look or act like it. Like I told her, it could have been due to medical reasons. Very high blood sugar, severe depression... I had to talk her into calling in sick and letting me take her to Boston General for an evaluation."

"Who would've ever thought... She seemed so put-together." Noah continued on to the refrigerator and grabbed two bottles of Sam Adams lager.

"I know. I could hardly believe it myself." *And I'm still not sure what's going on.*

Noah returned to the living room and handed Dante one of the beer bottles. "So, what do you think caused it?"

"I don't know. She was coherent and didn't look depressed. But she kept saying, 'Don't tell my parents. I don't want to worry them.'"

Noah shook his head sadly. "I'm sorry, Bro. I know you liked her. It's really hard to watch the good ones fall. Maybe she'll get up again."

Dante left his beer bottle on the coffee table and paced again. He raked his hands through his shaggy dark hair. "There's got to be something I can do."

"You could get a haircut. Get it cut short so it won't stick out like that."

"Shut up. I don't need anything for myself, just a miracle for Mallory."

Noah dropped into the ergonomic lounge chair and put his feet up on the matching ottoman. "Sorry, Bro.

I'm fresh out of miracles, and I'd steer clear of her, if I were you. It sounds like she's batshit crazy."

Dante's eyes widened, then he paused as if he'd just thought of something. "Wait a minute. Maybe there *is* something we can do to help."

"We? Oh no. I'm not getting involved in this. And you shouldn't either."

Dante's eyes narrowed. "Don't tell me what to do, Little Brother."

Noah snorted. "Yeah. I'm your younger brother, but I'm two inches taller than you, so I'm not your little brother and haven't been since tenth grade."

Dante let out an exasperated breath. "Whatever. Look, maybe if it's a chemical imbalance problem, there might be a chemical solution."

"What? Like an antidepressant counteracts the chemical imbalance of depression? Are you thinking she'll be fine with some medication?"

"Yeah. Why not?"

"I have a bad feeling about this. You're as easy to read as a book. Your energy is returning, and you look excited. You have some kind of crazy idea brewing in your head."

Dante smiled. "She might need a good friend right about now."

Noah just laughed and shook his head at his brother. "I always knew you were the incurable optimist of the family, but I didn't think you were completely insane."

"What do you mean by that?"

"Look, Bro. She's not the girl you thought you knew. Obviously. You need to forget about her."

"Why? Just because she's hit a bump in the road?"

"That bump could be a land mine. I'm just looking out for you."

"I don't care what you think. I'm going to the hospital to check on her." Dante grabbed his keys off the counter and strode to the coat closet.

Noah rose and rolled his eyes. "Fine. I'll go with you. Don't be surprised if she's already locked up in the loony bin."

"Hey, will you cut that out?"

"Cut what out?"

"The insults. Loony bin. Batshit crazy."

"Sorry, Bro. I just think you need to hear it the way others will see it. I know you."

"Then you know I won't just desert a friend in need."

Noah picked his coat up off the floor. "Yeah, and neither will I."

Mallory Summers sat in the hallway, just outside the ER's nurses' station. There had been some kind of multicar crash and people were being brought in on stretchers. She realized bloody victims took precedence over someone who *might be* seeing things that *supposedly* weren't there, but she felt like she'd been waiting for-friggin'-ever.

She had given her insurance card and contact information, filled out the long-ass medical form, and twiddled her thumbs for about as long as she could stand it. When she rose to leave, a nurse popped her head up over the desk.

"We'll be right with you, hon. Just have a seat."

"You said that an hour ago."

"It hasn't been an hour, has it?" She swiveled to look at the large analog clock on the wall. "Oh, wow. It's time for my break."

Mallory dropped the clipboard on the desk and strode out the double doors of the waiting room. When she heard the nurse calling after her, she sped up and finally ran outdoors. She didn't get far. One moment, she was looking over her shoulder, and the next, she smashed into something solid that said, "Oomph," and grabbed her arms.

"Excuse me!"

"Where are you going in such a hurry?"

She looked up into the friendly face of Dante Fierro again. He was with someone else who looked familiar. She thought it must be one of his many brothers.

"I'm…I'm going home. There's nothing wrong with me."

"Is that what they said?"

"They didn't say anything." She struggled to pull her arm away, but he held on tight.

His slightly taller counterpart asked, "What happened? You look upset."

"Who are you?"

"This is my brother Noah. I just thought I'd come down and check on you. See how you were doing."

"Well, I'm fine. The only reason I seem upset is because I sat there in the waiting room for an eon, then after they took my insurance information, they gave me a form to fill out, which took another eon, then I sat in the ER and waited for another eon. Finally, I got sick of sitting around and left."

"You mean nobody actually examined you yet?" Noah asked.

"Exactly. Look. I—I need to go."

Noah glanced at his brother, and they seemed to communicate without saying a single word. "Wait here," Noah said, and he strode inside the hospital building.

"Dante, there's no point in trying to intervene. There was some kind of big accident. There were a lot of people in much rougher shape than I am. In fact, I'm in perfect health. I just *maybe* saw someone who wasn't there."

"There was definitely no one there, Mallory."

"So?"

"Are you telling me it's no big deal?"

"No, but just sitting there wasn't going to help. Look, I was going to tell you later, but if anyone calls you, it's because I put you down as my emergency contact. I found your number in the phone book."

His posture straightened. "Why would you do that?"

"Because I don't want anyone to call my parents. All my friends know how to contact them, but you don't."

He hesitated a moment. "Let me give you my cell. The landline is mainly for my parents and the job."

She listened as he recited the number and programmed it into her contacts.

"I'm not telling you what to do, but don't you think your parents would want to know if something is really wrong?"

She sighed. "Yes and no. My mother would. My father would just be pissed off that I interrupted him in the middle of a big real estate deal."

"Are you kidding? He would get mad at you if you're ill?"

"I'm not ill! This project he's working on is out of the country. If he had to fly home, it would probably take a couple of days to get here. And yeah. Unless I was in a full body cast, he'd be pissed."

Dante shook his head. "Let me see what's keeping Noah." He called his brother and waited. When he didn't answer, Dante held out his keys. "Here. Wait in Joanna. I'll go get Noah, and we'll drive you home."

She took a step back. "I—I can find my own way home."

He tipped his head and looked puzzled. "Oh, you don't know where I parked. It's right there. The black Camaro."

"That's okay. You keep your keys. It's stopped raining now. I'll wait by the car until you come back."

Dante hesitated but finally said, "Okay," and walked into the hospital.

———

He heard rather than saw his brother. Noah's voice sounded angry, and there was a female responding in an equally frustrated tone.

"Oh shit," he muttered. What had his little brother gotten into now?

"Sir, you need to stop here and fill out a form," someone said as Dante strode by.

"I'm fine. Just here to see someone in there." He pointed toward the double doors and kept on walking.

"So, you'd just let someone go on hallucinating rather than trying to help her?" Noah spat.

"If she doesn't want to wait while more critical patients go first, I can't force her to."

"But you should have at least spoken to her. She said she was just left sitting and waiting—in the hall!"

Dante didn't expect to see Noah so worked up about Mallory's situation. He hadn't even wanted to get involved. Why was he all hot under the collar?

Ah. He saw it now. The young woman in the white lab coat was just Noah's type. Long, straight dark hair. Petite figure. The sparks flying were pure sexual chemistry. His tall, trim brother was standing too close and looming over her.

And she wasn't backing down—she met his intense stare with her own. Dante figured he'd better rescue Noah before this woman tied him to a chair with her stethoscope.

He moved closer to the heated exchange. "Come on, Bro."

"Hell no. This doctor has some explaining to do."

"I already explained. We have a triage system. Your friend was going to be seen, but the trauma cases have to come first. It could be a matter of life and death."

"Well, if she goes home and commits suicide, that's on you."

The young doctor gasped. "Oh my goodness! Is she suicidal?"

"Hell, I don't know, but if she is—"

Dante grabbed Noah by the shoulder. "Come on. Mallory's waiting by the car."

Noah glared at the doctor, and she leaned forward, placing her hands on her slender hips as if challenging him to continue his ridiculous tirade.

"Fine. Goodbye," Noah said. "Have a crappy day."

As she strode away, Dante heard her mumble, "Son of a monkey's butt." He rolled his eyes, grabbed his brother's arm, and dragged him away.

By the time they reached the parking lot, Mallory was nowhere to be seen. Dante sputtered a slew of curse words under his breath.

"See, dude? She doesn't want help. And like the doctor said, you can't force it on her."

"Unbelievable. Now you're taking the doctor's side, after chewing her out and wishing her a crappy day." He unlocked the car doors.

Noah chuckled. "Yeah, I stepped in it, didn't I?"

After they both jumped in, Dante answered. "You sure did. I hope you never get brought into that ER for smoke inhalation. She'll probably leave you in the hallway for a month."

"No. She took the Hippocratic oath. That would turn it into a hypocritical oath."

Dante shook his head and drove out of the parking lot.

––––––––

Noah had to do something to pull his brother out of this funk. They had three days off, and he didn't want to spend them watching Dante mope around.

"Hey, how about if we go out tonight? There's a new club downtown."

Dante stretched out on the couch. "Nah. I'm not in the mood to go clubbing."

"Well, I am. I'd like to meet someone, and you're my wingman."

Dante smirked. "Yeah, your wingman with real wings." Being a phoenix meant sometimes you had to make lame jokes.

"Somehow, I don't think you'll need them. Just

distract the girl I don't want so I can swoop in on the one I do want."

"I know how being a wingman works." Dante grabbed the remote off the coffee table.

"Then how about it? Will you do that for me?"

After a long pause, Dante sighed. "I guess so. As long as you don't expect me to get involved with anyone."

"I don't expect anything of you, except that you go with me so I don't look like a total loser with no friends. Tonight is all about me."

Noah knew how his brother would react if he even hinted that he was going to turn the tables on him. His plan was to push Dante toward someone who might interest him. Someone other than Mallory Summers.

Dante was a ladies' man. He couldn't help flirting with a pretty girl, and Noah knew it. He'd even flirted with Gabe's girl, Misty, once. He'd only done it to push Gabe into her arms, and it had worked. Even though it had looked like Dante might get a punch in the nose for his trouble, he'd turned on the charm like a pro.

Hopefully, this club would be full of attractive single women. Noah hadn't had a girlfriend in a while, and thinking about meeting someone *did* appeal to him. But tonight really wasn't about him. It was about Dante.

"Do you have something decent to wear out?"

"What do you mean? I'll wear whatever I usually wear." Dante frowned and clicked on the TV.

"I just thought, you know, maybe we can go out and get something a little newer."

Dante clicked off the TV. "What's going on?"

"What do you mean?"

"You're acting weird."

"I am not. What's wrong with just wanting to look good when we go out?"

Dante sat up. "Are you hoping I'll look good so I'll find someone other than Mallory to focus on?"

Noah shrugged. "You could at least be open to it. Mallory Summers isn't the only girl on the planet. Who knows who you'll meet, if you're not a total a-hole?"

Dante rose, still clutching the remote control. "If this is a setup…"

"It isn't. I swear. I really do want to get out there and meet somebody for myself. I'll admit I wouldn't be unhappy if you found somebody too, but—"

Dante threw the remote on the floor. "I knew it."

"Knew what?"

"I knew you didn't like Mallory. Just because she's having some sort of medical issue or crisis doesn't mean you get to pass judgment on her. She's none of your business."

"That's what I was saying this morning. But no. You had to drag me into it, and frankly, I'm kind of glad you did. It seems like you need some perspective."

Dante raked his hands through his hair. He looked like he was going to explode. Instead, he just dropped back down on the couch. "Maybe it's time to get my own place."

Noah staggered back about a foot. "Your own place? Why? Just so I'll mind my own business?"

"Yeah." Dante picked up the remote and clicked on the TV again.

"Look," Noah said. "We're best friends as well as roommates. And brothers on top of that. There's no way we can stay out of each other's business. If you want to

get your own place, fine. But it's going to be a shithole.
We can't afford anything decent on our own."

Dante ignored him.

Noah had to leave before he said anything more
incendiary. He didn't want his brother to start packing.
Real estate in Boston was ridiculously expensive, even
to rent.

They had a sweet setup here. Dante was able to walk
to work, so there wasn't much wear and tear on the
expensive vehicle he loved and babied.

Noah hadn't been working as long as Dante had, but
he was saving for his own vehicle...a Jeep or something
he could take off-roading on the weekends.

Living in South Boston and working downtown was
plenty convenient. On good days, he could walk, and
when the weather was rotten, Dante took pity on him
and dropped him off at work before going to the South
Boston fire station. It really was a shame he couldn't
shift and fly. But a phoenix with its colorful plumage
would attract way too much attention.

It hurt to think his brother would just up and leave.
Noah needed to give him some space and let him calm
down. So he grabbed his coat and set off on a long walk.

After wandering for a while, he turned toward the
Quincy Market area. Sometimes things were going on
down there, by Faneuil Hall or Government Center.
Who knew, maybe there'd be some sort of protest, or
street performers would be doing something interesting.

It was a Wednesday, so there wasn't much happening. Just the usual tourist buses rolling by, foot traffic
going in and out of shops and restaurants, and the business commerce that took place every day.

Noah spotted an old bookshop on the corner that he'd forgotten about. The place looked like it had been there for at least a century. They specialized in rare and antique books. Feeling drawn to the place for some inexplicable reason, he stepped over the threshold onto wide oak floorboards. Row upon row of bookshelves held any number of leather-bound tomes, torn book jackets, and an impressive amount of dust.

He scanned titles as he strolled by with his hands in his pockets. At the end of one particular shelf, a book leaned precariously. Noah picked it up, only intending to straighten it, until something caught his eye. The gold lettering on the cover glinted in the sun filtering through the windows. He tried to read the title and quickly realized it was in Latin. He'd had to take one year of Latin in school but never saw the point in spending a lot of time or attention on a dead language.

He flipped open the book and found himself fascinated by some of the beautiful scrollwork on the capital letters at the top of each page. It wasn't like a religious text. There were columns that looked like bullet points. Like lists. It almost looked like a recipe book. He frowned at some of the text, but he recognized the word for *gold* and couldn't help being curious.

Dante was better at Latin. He had taken two or three years of it in school, and Noah wanted to show this to him. There was something about this book…

"I think this is alchemy," Dante said as he examined the book a few hours later. "You brought me a book of ancient science experiments, turning lead into gold."

"Seriously?" Noah exclaimed.

"Yeah. From what I can tell…" He got up off the couch. "Let me get my iPad. Maybe we can find some kind of Latin app or downloadable translation software."

"You don't have to do that now."

"I'm just glad to get off my ass and do something. I actually watched the fishing channel, and the only thing more boring than fishing is watching people fishing."

Noah laughed and followed him as far as the hallway.

The whole time he was fetching his iPad from his bedroom, Dante kept talking. "You're the science geek. Maybe you can set up a lab in the spare room."

"Sure. And instead of taking a second job to afford another place, I can just churn out enough gold to stay here."

Dante had just exited his room, iPad in hand, but stopped in his tracks and hung his head. "I'm sorry, Bro. I didn't mean that part about moving out."

"Good. I was hoping that was the case."

"You didn't deserve that. I know you're trying to look out for me, but…"

"But deciding what's best for you is out of line. I know."

Dante nodded. "I'm glad I didn't have to be the one to say it. So, do you still want to go out tonight? I'm willing to wing it for you, if that's really what you want to do."

"Yeah. I'd like to meet somebody. Even if it's not 'the one,' I feel like doing things with someone other than my brother. No offense."

"None taken. I'm still bummed about Mallory, but I can turn on the charm when I need to—as long as we're there for you, not me."

"It's either that or stay home and set up an alchemy lab to keep me busy in my old age." Noah was still planning to turn the tables, but he'd be a lot more subtle about it.

Dante laughed. "Old age. What are you, twenty-three?"

"Yup. And I'll be twenty-four in about two months. I'm getting up there." He aimed a teasing grin at Dante.

"Yeah, and a month later, I turn twenty-six. When are you going to catch up, Little Brother? I keep trying to wait for you…"

It felt good to be kidding around with his brother again. They had been living here for three years, ever since Noah had gotten through firefighter training and his probationary period. They'd had their ups and downs, but neither had ever talked about splitting up and going their separate ways…until today.

Chapter 2

Noah scanned the busy club. The lights were low, but it didn't matter. Having paranormal eyesight was a plus in these situations. "Let's walk the perimeter clockwise and check out the girls facing us, then get something at the bar and go back the other way."

Dante chuckled. "Yeah. If we swiveled to check out the chicks on the other side of the tables, it would be a little obvious what we're doing."

"Exactly."

Noah led the way, making a note of the women Dante might like. Their taste in women differed greatly. That had been a plus, and would continue to be as long as he could find a gorgeous blonde with an athletic build for Dante sitting with a petite brunette for himself.

The guys had passed only four booths when some big lug coming toward them barreled into Noah, knocking him sideways. To his shock and embarrassment, he fell and landed *hard* in the lap of some poor, unsuspecting woman. She squeaked a sound of surprise, but didn't say "owww."

"I'm sorry. Are you okay?" He scrambled to slide off her lap. As he gazed at her face, her beautiful brown eyes widened.

She looked familiar, and suddenly, it struck him. He had met her only that morning. "Dr. Samuels?" He struggled to leave the booth when she placed a warm hand on his arm.

"I'm fine. Are you okay?"

He paused at the end of the bench without getting up. Her voice was soft and kind. This was not the Dr. Samuels he'd spoken to sharply that morning.

She scooted over to make room for him. "I'm sorry about our disagreement earlier. How's your friend?"

The woman on the other side of the table, who looked similar to the good doctor, slid over and patted the bench next to her. "Join us," she said to Dante.

He grinned. "Sure."

There was some kind of twinkle in his brother's eye. Noah didn't know whether that was a good thing or not. Hopefully, he was willing to consider a pretty brunette.

"She's not exactly my friend. Just an acquaintance. Someone we knew in high school."

"I don't even know your name," Dr. Samuels said.

"Jesus. I'm an idiot."

"That's an unusual name and job description…"

Noah laughed and extended his hand. "Noah Fierro, and this is my brother Dante. We're firefighters."

She smiled and shook his hand. "And I'm Kizzy. This is my sister, Ruth. She's a labor and delivery nurse."

"Kizzy? That's an unusual name."

"It's a form of the name Keziah. I used to hate it, but now that the mean kids have grown up, I kind of like being different."

"Mean kids? Did you get teased about your name when you were younger?"

She rolled her eyes. "I've heard them all. Dizzy Kizzy. Crazy Kizzy. And on humid days, even Frizzy Kizzy."

Noah chuckled, then quickly schooled his expression. "I like it."

"Does that mean you like her now?" Dante asked.

Noah wanted to kick his brother under the table, *but that wouldn't look immature at all*, he thought sarcastically. "If she likes me… At least it seems like she's not mad at me anymore."

Kizzy laughed. "I was never really angry. I was just frustrated, and I guess I took it out on you. I'm sorry for my part in that argument. It was a crazy morning. Now that I'm off duty and I've had one of these lovely things"—she lifted her empty wineglass—"I'm feeling more relaxed."

"Let's get you another," Dante said. "What are you drinking?" He pointed to both Kizzy's and Ruth's wineglasses.

The women glanced at each other, as if they could communicate without words as easily as he and Dante could.

Ruth answered. "We both just finished a glass of Shiraz."

Dante rose. "Two more glasses of Shiraz it is. Ruth, would you like to come with me? I'll need someone to carry Noah's and my Coronas."

"I'm getting a Corona, I guess," Noah said to Kizzy.

"It's Cinco de Mayo. Would you rather have a margarita?"

"Nah. You had it right the first time."

Dante shook his head. "He's not usually this much of a smart-ass," he said to Kizzy. "You must bring out the worst in him."

He aimed a teasing grin at Noah. But before Noah

could think of a comeback, Dante had slid out of the booth, taken Ruth's hand, and helped her out as well. Then they disappeared, and Noah was alone with Kizzy.

Her eyes had him mesmerized. They were almond-shaped, enhanced by thick black lashes and eyebrows. Her irises were such a dark brown that they appeared almost as black as her pupils.

Suddenly, he was tongue-tied, and she lowered her gaze shyly.

Oh no. Here comes one of those awkward silences.

At last, she looked up. "I've never had a handsome firefighter fall into my lap before."

He chuckled. "I wasn't really expecting to meet someone that way either." He nodded toward the bar. "I was hoping my brother might find someone to hit it off with."

Kizzy sighed. "My sister is taken, and my future brother-in-law really wouldn't like the competition."

"Oh well. He's kind of stuck on Mallory anyway. It probably wouldn't have been fair to your sister, now that I think about it."

"I understand. You had hoped to find him someone who wasn't hallucinating. Is that it?"

"Exactly."

"You're a good brother. I don't know if you can really influence someone else's choices. I've tried without a lot of success."

"You don't like your sister's choice?"

"Oh, no. He's fine. I'm sure he'll be good to her. She's an L&D nurse, as I mentioned, and he's a surgeon. They have a lot in common. But surgeons... Well, some of them have a god complex."

He had heard that, but hadn't experienced it. "So, another family member in medicine. Anyone else?"

"Yeah. My father. He's a cardiologist."

"Wow. You have a highly successful family." Suddenly, Noah wondered if he was good enough for Kizzy. Sure, he was an EMT as well as a firefighter, but was that enough? If not, that would be a shame. He liked this Kizzy Samuels. *Really* liked her.

———

Kizzy was enjoying the Fierros' company, but too soon, Dante wanted to head home. Noah bid them a reluctant farewell, and Kizzy wondered if she'd ever hear from him again. She hoped so. He didn't ask for her phone number, but at least he knew where she worked.

"He's cute!" Ruth said as the guys walked away.

"Which one?"

"Both of them…but I was talking about the guy sitting next to you. Noah. He seemed—well, after the initial reaction—really into you. Do you think he fell in your lap on purpose?"

She laughed. "No. I'm sure he didn't. He landed pretty hard, and considering how our first meeting went, I'm surprised he didn't run off as soon as he recognized me."

"Yeah, what was that about?"

Kizzy just waved away the question. "Nothing. Just a triage decision he didn't like."

"You must get that a lot in the ER. In L&D, the baby makes the decisions about who goes first. Still, I thought he might ask for your number before he left."

"Oh well." Kizzy tried not to look disappointed. She

was second-guessing everything she'd said to him—not only that morning, but tonight too. Why did she mention her future brother-in-law having a god complex? That wasn't very nice. He might be wondering what she'd say about him behind his back. Not only that, but she had her own god complex to worry about.

"There's something else I need to talk about, and you're the only one who would understand."

"Go ahead."

"I'm not sure we should talk about it here."

Her sister glanced around the busy, noisy club. "I doubt anyone could hear us, even if they wanted to. This might be the best place to talk."

"Okay. Well, it's about our powers as witches. And because of the spell books, and the fact that we only have one of the three, our power to perform the impossible is limited to one save per day."

"Uh-huh. I know all that. What are you asking?"

Kizzy sighed. "You're more psychic than I am. I just wish I knew at the beginning of the day who would be the one to save."

"I'm not sure I'm much more psychic than you are, but okay. How do you decide now?"

She shrugged. "It's hit or miss. Sometimes I think I know, and I guess right. And other times, by the end of my shift, I'm kicking myself. Do I save the kid who comes in at eight in the morning, knowing that some brain surgeon or astronaut might show up in three or four hours? Or is the child more important?"

Ruth took a sip of her wine and set it down, looking thoughtful. "I can see where it would be more difficult for you. For me, it's not that hard, since most deliveries go as expected. If there's one that's really struggling and the child shows signs of stress, that's the one I intervene with. Very rarely do I get two of those per shift, and if I've done the spell with the first one…well, the second one is in the hands of the gods and goddesses. Is that what you're asking? What to do if you've already blown your magical load?" She gave her sister a lopsided grin.

Kizzy chuckled. "Yeah, I guess that's one way to put it. I don't envy your having to go through hours of pain with a person, but at least that's expected. When I see a person in excruciating pain, my heart breaks for them."

"How many cases do you get on an average day?"

Kizzy snorted. "There is no such thing as an average day in a busy city ER. But I guess I can see anywhere from twenty to fifty patients in a shift."

"Yikes. Fifty? No wonder you're confused. You have a lot to choose from."

"Exactly."

"Why don't you ask Dad for advice?"

Kizzy rolled her eyes. "He'll just give me some pat answer like you do your best and that's all you can do."

Ruth shrugged. "That sounds about right to me. What is it you would like to do differently? Eliminate the guesswork?"

"Yes. Exactly. Do you think there's a way you can tell when something major is going to happen, before the patients even show up? Or have a clue as to who's most deserving of a miracle?"

"So far, I haven't been able to train my psychic skills to work that way, at least not consistently. I've been picking up some weird vibes lately, but I have no idea what it's related to. At least not yet."

Kizzy picked up her cocktail napkin and began tearing it. "If only we had the other books. Maybe we'd have complete control over our powers. I know our great-grandma tracked two of them to Boston, which is why we're here, but one went to South America. How the heck are we supposed to find all three without the ability to pinpoint them? And why can't we, by the way?"

"Silly woman. They must be protected by wards, just as ours is. I'm not sure I'd want all three. It's tough, I know. You win some, you lose some. If we won all the time, don't you know what would happen?"

"Yeah. We'd be found out pretty quickly."

"Yep. And then what?"

Kizzy sighed. "And then we'd be interrogated, expected to let everyone in on our secrets, other doctors would publish papers throughout the medical community, and we'd probably be kidnapped by the government and forced to work for the Department of Defense."

Ruth giggled. "You're so dramatic. I doubt the government would utilize us for slave labor, but letting this stuff fall into the hands of certain unprincipled people could spell disaster. We're healers. But we could harm, if we wanted to."

"Are you sure? We've never even tried to harm anyone."

Her sister winced. "I have."

She said it so softly, Kizzy wasn't sure she heard her correctly. "Fudge cake! What do you mean? Did you do something intentionally?"

After a brief hesitation, Ruth said, "We were little. Mom had just told us how we were different from other kids and how we had to use our power *only* for good while still respecting the free will of all humankind. She said if we wished anyone harm, karma would get us eventually…and then she explained what that meant."

"I remember that day."

Ruth picked up her wineglass and swirled the contents. "I wasn't sure if she was telling us the truth, so I had to test it." She set down her glass and clasped her hands. "You won't tell anyone, will you?"

"Of course not. What did you do?"

Ruth's face turned pink. "Remember the brat who used to live across the street? Eddie?"

"Yeah…" Kizzy remembered how the neighbors across the street moved in a hurry. No one seemed to know why or where they went.

"Well, he was teasing me, as usual, and I wished with all my heart that he would go away and never come back. The next day, moving vans came, packed everything up, and off they went. I don't know for sure if that was because of me, but I think it must've been."

"And did karma kick your ass?"

"Maybe. The guilt has weighed heavily on me ever since."

"I wouldn't worry about it. I'm sure they had some kind of plan. People don't just up and move overnight."

"Unless a witch cast a spell on them. What if they just found themselves driving a moving van across the country, no jobs, no home to go to…nothing but questions?"

Kizzy gave that some thought. "I imagine they would have come back. If they hadn't quit their jobs and sold their home, that stuff would still be waiting for them. Right?"

"But I added the words 'never ever to return.'"

"I guess we can't know. Unless you want to try to find them."

Ruth looked sheepish. "Do you think I should? I mean, I'd rather not. There's not much I can do about it seventeen years later."

"You could just look him up on Facebook. If he landed on his feet, you can stop feeling guilty. If not, you can do a spell to help him and his family."

"I already tried a reversal spell. Because they didn't come back, I don't know if it worked or not. Thus the nagging voice in my head for seventeen years."

Kizzy winced. "Man, you were a naughty girl. I just believed everything I was told."

"You were older. I kind of wish Mom had waited until I was a little more mature and could have handled it better."

"I had no idea you were having any problem handling it at all."

"Why wouldn't I? You're having a tough time with it right now. And you've always been the smarter, more responsible one."

"I don't know about that, but being responsible drives me up the wall sometimes. I don't want to be responsible for picking and choosing who lives and who dies. Especially if several family members are involved. Do I save the mom, the child, or the father?"

Ruth's facial expression bespoke pity. Ordinarily, pity wasn't something Kizzy wanted. Tonight, she did.

"Have you ever thought about just not using your power?"

Kizzy hesitated. "I've actually vowed not to and

broken that vow in three days or less. When someone needs my help and medical help isn't enough, I can't refuse to use the power at my disposal. As long as I have enough strength in me."

Ruth reached across the table and grasped her hand. "That's the sister I know and love. So I guess you're stuck with it—the responsibility, the knowledge, and the power to save one human life that never would have made it without you. But only one per day."

Kizzy inhaled deeply and let out a long, resigned breath. "A blessing and a curse. What did I do to deserve this?"

"Hold that pose, sweetie. Oh, what a nice, big smile!" Mallory captured the picture before the squirmy, wormy toddler managed to break free of his mother's death grip again, like Houdini.

"He's a live wire, isn't he?" a baritone voice said.

Mallory glanced over her shoulder and saw the kid's grandfather. He looked just like him—well, a hint of what he'd look like in a few decades.

"A lot of kids seem to have extra energy spurts when they go to a photographer," she said, maintaining her own polite smile.

"Let's get a few more," the young mother said.

"Sure. Would you like one with Granddad?" She indicated the gentleman to her right.

The woman's posture stiffened. "With who?"

She faced the doting man and addressed him directly. "I don't know what you like to be called, sir. Grandpa? Papa?"

"I'm his father. You can call me Mike."

"Oh! Okay, Mike it is."

The woman shot to her feet, almost dropping her two-year-old son. "What is wrong with you?"

Oh no. Here we go again. "I'm sorry. Did I say something to upset you?" She had obviously mistaken a spirit for flesh and bone again. Or maybe the woman was sensitive just because an older man was mistaken for a granddad.

Sometimes, Mallory tried to play dumb while coming up with something else she could have plausibly said. *Let's see. I said, Mike it is. So, talking about photos… Like it is? Tike that he is? Mice… Oh crap. I'm coming up with zilch.*

"Yes, you upset me. Do you always talk to a kid's dead father?"

"Dead father? Oh, I'm sorry!" *Sheesh. I hope you left them lots of money*, Mallory thought.

"If I didn't, it's too late now," he joked.

Mallory had finally figured out she saw dead people. Unfortunately, she didn't know if they were real or not, and occasionally, she made an oopsy, but this was the first one to read her mind! "Oh crap. It's getting worse," she mumbled.

"I'd like to speak to your boss."

Her supervisor was a nice, understanding guy. But this was one misunderstanding he wouldn't know how to smooth over. "There shouldn't be any need to bother him, ma'am. I can offer you a free photo from this sitting and another free sitting if you don't see one you like from today."

"Like hell. I want your boss to know the kind of stunt

you're pulling. Although I'm not sure what your angle is yet. Is this where you tell me you're a medium and my dear departed wants to tell me something, if I'd like to pay you for the information?"

"No! Nothing like that."

Damn. She spotted her boss, Bailey, returning from lunch early, and it looked like he noticed something was wrong. He was picking up his pace.

The woman was struggling to get the squirming toddler into his spring jacket when Bailey arrived.

"Is everything all right here?"

"No. No, it is not." And now the mom had tears in her eyes.

Mallory couldn't help feeling awful about the misunderstanding, but how the heck could she explain it without sounding—well, crazy? "I'm sorry, Bailey. There was a misunderstanding. It was my fault. I told her I'd pay for her son's picture and give her another sitting if she's not happy with the shots I took."

"What was the misunderstanding?"

"I…uh…that is to say, I…"

"She tried to tell me she was communicating with my dead husband."

"I didn't tell her that! I saw someone and thought he was with them."

"She called him by name." The woman crossed her arms and glared. "There was nobody there. She spoke to thin air and asked if he—or whatever she was seeing—would like to get in the picture. Either it was some kind of scam, or your girl here has a screw loose."

He gaped at her. "I don't know what to say except what Mallory already said. We're terribly sorry. There will be no charge for today, and we'll be glad to retake the shoot whenever you like."

"Is she going to be the one taking the pictures?" The woman zipped up her son's jacket, and he started to cry.

Bailey glanced at Mallory. "She's my usual photographer, but I have a part-timer coming on soon."

Mallory didn't know anything about a new hire.

The woman hoisted a huge diaper bag over her shoulder. "I'll set up an appointment after you have a new employee."

Mallory had to make nice with this woman. "When I have the proofs—"

"I'll call you," her boss interjected.

"Fine. I never want to see her again." The woman swung the toddler up into her arms and marched off.

"What the hell happened while I was at lunch?" Bailey asked.

"I…uh…"

"Yeah. You said that a couple of times now. Can you give me a better explanation?"

Mallory fidgeted. "Not really. I saw someone out of the corner of my eye, thought it was the father or grandfather, and spoke with him about how much the kid looked like him."

"And who were you speaking to?"

"Apparently, the father's spirit. When I turned back, he wasn't there."

"Let me get this straight. You spoke to the child's father, who you thought was there in the flesh, and yet he disappeared in the time it took to glance away."

"Yes."

"So were you talking to…a ghost?"

"Apparently."

"Have you seen ghosts before?"

Mallory focused on her shoes and kicked at the floor. "Yes. A couple of times."

Bailey was silent for a while. "And you can't tell the difference between someone who's actually there and a spirit? Like…you can't see through them or anything?"

"No. I mean yes. I mean no, I can't tell. Yes, I can't see through them."

"She said you called him by name. How did you know his name?"

"The man said to call him Mike."

"So you heard as well as saw whatever it was?"

"Yes."

"Can you see him now?"

"No." After a brief hesitation, she filled in what would probably be his next question. "He left with the woman and her child."

"Just now, while I was standing here."

"Yes."

Oh boy. She knew she was in for it. His expression didn't give away much, but he walked to the phone and pushed a button. One button. Probably *Security*.

Dante had pored over the alchemy book, making lists of what they'd need. His brother played on his iPad and seemed oblivious, which was weird, since it was his book and experiment. "Noah, are you okay?"

"Yeah. Why wouldn't I be?"

"You just seem quieter than usual."

"I'm fine. Just doing a little background check on Dr. Samuels."

"Kizzy? Why? What have you found?"

"Just the usual stuff on Facebook. Pictures of her in her cap and gown. Some with an older guy who must be her father. A couple of shots at a lake with Ruth and a couple of other girls. She doesn't post much. There was a charity clothing drive and a 5K she was asking people to sponsor. A LinkedIn and Google search confirmed that she's a doctor at Boston General."

"So basically, she told you the truth. You didn't discover any surprises?"

"Nope. The only thing she didn't tell me is that she likes good causes."

"So, how about if you invite her to the Battle of the Badges basketball game? It's to raise money for the children's hospital."

"Sure, except I'll be on the court, and she'll be sitting alone in the stands."

"She'd probably love watching you play for charity. And who says she'll be alone? She could bring her sister or a friend."

Noah nodded slowly, as if he were thinking about it.

"Not to change the subject, but I was about to go out and get some of the stuff we need to set up our lab," Dante said.

Still not looking up, Noah asked, "Do you really think it'll work?"

"There's only one way to find out, dude. With your science brains and my Latin translation skills and both of us believing in the unbelievable, I wouldn't be surprised if we're rolling in gold someday."

Noah laughed. "Even if we only get a nugget, it'll be more than we had before."

"Do you want to come with? Or would you rather stay here and clean the spare room?"

Noah looked up from his iPad and opened his mouth as if to make a smart remark when Dante's phone rang.

Dante held up one finger. "Hold that thought. Hello?"

"Dante, it's Mallory. I…uh…I need a ride home from work. Would you be able to come and get me?"

"Sure." He thought he heard her sniffle. "Are you okay?"

"Not really. I got fired from my job. The security guards escorted me outside and everything. They don't want me to take the bus. They want someone to come and get me."

"I'll be right there. Where should I look for you?"

"I'll be the loser on the sidewalk across from Lord & Taylor."

"You're not—"

"And don't tell me I'm not a loser!"

"Okay. I'll be there in fifteen or twenty minutes." Dante hung up the phone and said, "Plans have changed, Bro. Mallory needs me to pick her up at the mall."

"Does that get me out of cleaning the back room or shopping for glass beakers and stuff?"

"Hey, this is your baby. I'm just assisting you." Dante grabbed his jacket and keys. "Maybe you can find that lead musket ball you've been hanging on to for some damn reason. We need lead to turn into gold."

"Yeah, I know. I'll see what I can do about that. Maybe I'll even clean up the spare room. Should I wait for you before I make my first million?"

"Nah. I don't know when I'll be back. Mallory might want to talk or something."

"Okay. Go play knight in shining armor."

Dante smiled. Noah was joking, but he'd love to be Mallory's knight.

Chapter 3

DANTE SPOTTED HER. HEAD DOWN, MALLORY SAT ON THE filthy sidewalk with her feet in the gutter. Her business suit must be getting ruined, but she clearly didn't care. It broke Dante's heart to see her like this.

Pulling up beside her, he leaned over and opened the passenger-side door. He thought about parking and coming to escort her to the car like a gentleman, but he figured she'd just want to get out of there as soon as possible.

She looked up. Her makeup had run, and her eyes were red and puffy. *Shit. They left her crying on the sidewalk. How humiliating!*

Stoop-shouldered, she rose slowly and dropped into the bucket seat of his Camaro.

"Jesus, Mallory. What happened?"

She sighed. "You can probably guess…"

"Not really. Did it have something to do with seeing someone who wasn't there?"

"I could have sworn he was real," she said softly. "He even told me his name and that the little boy I was photographing was his son. Cute little kid. Until his mother freaked out, and then her son started crying too."

"Uh-oh."

"Yeah." She sighed. "Of course, it didn't help that I thought I was talking to the boy's grandfather. I guess some guys go prematurely gray."

"Or the woman may have married a much older man."

"True. Men don't shoot blanks until they're, what... fifty or sixty?"

Dante covered a smile by looking the other way as he pulled into the street, merging with traffic. "Where would you like to go?"

She shrugged. "Home, I guess."

"It's almost lunch time. Why don't we get some takeout on the way? I don't imagine you feel much like cooking."

"You got that right."

"What are you in the mood for?"

"I don't know. Strychnine? Arsenic?"

"Hey." He reached over and rubbed the back of her neck. "Don't talk like that. We'll figure out what's going on and fix this."

"How? And why would you want to? I'm a total train wreck."

"Oh, man... Let's put off that conversation for a minute." Dante speed-dialed his favorite pizza place. "Yeah, I'd like to order a large pizza. My lady friend will tell you what toppings to put on it."

Mallory sighed. "Just veggies on half and whatever my man friend wants on the other half." She gave him a weak smile.

"Pepperoni," he said. "I'll pick it up in a few minutes. It's for Dante Fierro."

As usual, the traffic took care of any wait time needed to make a fresh pizza. He picked it up while Mallory stayed in the car. He was glad she didn't offer to pay for it. He'd like to think of this as their first date. *Yeah, what a pathetic date*. Hopefully, there would be others, and he could make those special.

He followed her directions and pulled into a short driveway in front of her two-story white vinyl-sided town house. Nice but boring. The large development made him think of how easy it would be to walk into the wrong place after a few beers—provided anyone left their doors unlocked. Nobody in South Boston would, of course.

A few steps led up to the front door. A far cry from the beautiful brownstone town house he'd grown up in. He didn't know where Mallory had lived in high school. Her father was in real estate, but she could have been raised in a high-rise condo or low-rent apartment for all he knew. There was a lot he didn't know about Mallory Summers. He was anxious to learn more.

She led him up a short flight of carpeted stairs and into an open-concept kitchen, living, and dining room. He thought the house style was called a split-level.

"It's basic, but it's home, thanks to my father. It's his development."

"Nice. Do you own it?"

"Sort of."

Carrying the pizza, he glanced around, taking in the neutral palette and the tasteful decor. She must have kept the place clean and decluttered, since she didn't know he was coming over. That, or it was brand new. The place was pristine.

"Have you lived here long?"

"Not long at all. I still have a few things in boxes in the storage space downstairs."

"That doesn't mean anything. Noah and I have lived

in our apartment for two years, and we still have stuff in boxes."

"Tsk, tsk," she said, smiling. She seemed to be kidding. That was a good sign.

"Do you want this in the kitchen?" he said, lifting the pizza box.

"Just put it on the dining table. I'll get some plates." She paused on her way to the cabinets. "Wine?"

"Sure. I'll have whatever you're having."

"Oh, I don't think you want an entire bottle, since that's what I'll be having."

He chuckled. Even with her life falling apart, she was able to maintain a sense of humor. At least *he hoped* that was an attempt at humor. "Yeah. A glass will do, since I'm driving, and I have to work tonight."

"Oh. Am I keeping you from getting ready for work?"

"I'm as ready as I get. We have lockers, and I always keep a clean uniform there."

She gave him a shy smile as she retrieved two plates and wine glasses, then placed them on the table. "I'd like to see you in action."

He took that as another positive sign. "You can come by anytime. I work at the firehouse on Broadway."

"I might. Lord knows I have nothing else to do." She grabbed the Chianti from the small built-in wine rack above the fridge.

"That's a handy use of the empty space above a refrigerator." He wasn't about to comment on how hard it was to reach anything in a cabinet up there, pointing out her less than dramatic height. She might be five feet six.

"Yup. My father thought of everything."

"Oh yeah. You said he built this place. Is it just this building or the whole street? There are more town houses that look similar."

"Three blocks." She uncorked the wine and poured two glasses half full.

"Wow. Does he charge you rent?"

"Just enough to cover the property taxes and maintenance fees. It's a condo. I get all the perks with none of the mortgage. That's why I really can't afford to move. Who else is going to 'give me' a condo?"

He thought about all the sugar daddies out there who'd probably love to keep her as a side piece. Again, he didn't know her well, but he was fairly sure she wouldn't resort to that.

They ate their pizza with their hands. Apparently, she wasn't the fancy type, or Italian. He had been assured by his parents that using silverware was the only way to consume pizza. His fellow firefighters contradicted that notion, eating it right out of the box. With them, he was lucky to get a paper plate.

"You said you were an artist. Do you have a studio in a spare bedroom or something?"

"Not in a bedroom. I would hate to damage the new carpeting. I asked my father to leave the basement unfinished. I have a washer and dryer down there, as well as my studio. Do you want to see it after lunch?"

"Sure. I'd like that. Your place is so nice and junk-free, if you're not cramming the extra stuff in a spare room where it will all fall out when you open the door."

She laughed. It was a welcome sound. "I have two walk-in closets. I use one for clothes, the other for cramming."

They smiled at each other and swiftly went back to finishing their lunch.

Mallory had one piece of pizza, and Dante had two. He'd have finished his half of the pizza, except he wanted to leave some for her to have later. He imagined she might not want to make dinner either.

The wine seemed to relax her. She stopped at one glass, and he was glad to see she had changed her mind about drowning her sorrows. Mallory wasn't nearly the train wreck she thought she was. At least he didn't think so. Seeing dead people was certainly inconvenient. Maybe he was foolishly giving his high school crush the benefit of every doubt.

She had asked him how he could help her. He really didn't think she was suffering from schizophrenia. He'd read up on it, and she didn't seem to fit the description. It was largely an inherited illness, and she denied any knowledge of mental illness in her family. That would be a hard diagnosis to hide without a relative in the attic.

"Take me to your studio. I'd like to see that artwork of yours."

Dante reached over and covered her hand with his. "Mallory, can I make a weird suggestion? You can tell me to mind my own business if I'm way off base."

Weird? What could he be talking about? Mallory didn't know how much more weird her life could get. "Uh, sure. I'll be honest and tell you if it's too weird for me."

"Okay. Hear me out. A hypnotherapist came to our firehouse to do a relaxation exercise with the guys. He said it was something we could continue to do on our own, and it would help us sleep, stay calm in stressful situations, and get back on an even keel faster after a rough shift. I have his card. Would you be willing to talk to him?"

"Hypnosis?"

"Yeah. Decreasing stress might help. I was even thinking that maybe he can do some kind of post-hypnotic suggestion to help you block out the stuff that's not really there."

She felt like she was grasping at straws anyway, so why not entertain the idea? "I guess I could try it. The only thing is, therapy is expensive, isn't it?"

"He didn't make it sound like a ton of sessions were needed. We only had one, and it helped a lot. If it's just the money, I'll pay for a session."

Dante was so sweet, but she didn't want to take advantage of him. They weren't even dating. Not that she'd mind dating the handsome, brave firefighter, but her history with men was pretty abysmal. He was probably just feeling sorry for her. "I can probably afford a session or two. Maybe a quick chat with a therapist might help."

"Okay. I'll find his number when I get home and give you a call."

"Dante, you probably have better places to be. I'm grateful for your help, but I'll understand if you don't call me after giving me the therapist's number."

He frowned. "Why on earth would you say that?"

"I—it's just that…well, I come with a lot of baggage. I don't expect you to carry my burdens."

"Hey, I'm a big, strong firefighter. I carry full-grown

men over my shoulder. What's a little baggage?" He smiled, but she didn't return it. "Look, Mallory. We all have baggage. Yours is a little unusual, but you act like you're the worst person who ever walked the earth."

"Sorry. I tend to beat myself up sometimes."

"Ya think? Come here." He rose and took her hand.

As he led her to the couch, her nerves kicked in. What was he going to do? Kiss her? Lecture her?

"Have a seat. I want to tell you a story."

"Okay." That was a scenario she hadn't seen coming. She got comfy, and he put his arm around her shoulder.

"Once upon a time, there was this young man—no. A boy. He was still just a boy. He had a great family and lots of good pals. But he didn't have a girlfriend. He was shorter than a lot of girls in his class and on the shy side. Especially around the pretty ones." He gave her a smile, and if she wasn't mistaken, it was meant just for her.

"Well, there was this one girl in particular he had a crush on. But she didn't even know he was alive. She was smart, beautiful, had a great personality and lots of friends. She seemed to have it all. The boy was so sure she was out of his league that he never even spoke to her.

"Then they graduated from school, and everyone went off to pursue their dreams. He never knew what her plans were. Didn't know if she was off to college or some big adventure. He felt as if he had lost her, even though he'd never really known her. And he had no one to blame but himself."

"Does this story have a happy ending? I hope."

His striking chocolate eyes held her gaze. "I hope so too."

Even though her world was falling apart and a lot of

guys would take advantage of the situation, she didn't think he would. If she wanted him to kiss her, she was going to have to initiate it.

She leaned in, and he tentatively leaned toward her but stopped.

"Are you going to kiss me?" she asked.

"Depends. Do you want me to?"

"Yes, please." Mallory mentally rolled her eyes at herself. *Yes, please? Lame.*

She didn't have time to finish chiding herself. He closed the gap and took her lips in a gentle but purposeful kiss. His lips were soft but insistent. He opened his mouth, and she opened hers at the same time. Their tongues stroked each other. Dante tasted like the wine they'd just had, plus something richer. Certainly not the boy he was describing. Something all man. This was the kind of man she could trust—and it scared the hell out of her. Anyone she'd trusted in the past had hurt her—or she'd beaten them to it.

Mallory started to shake and backed off a few inches. "Oh no…"

"What's the matter?"

No, no! Not now! Mallory's only experience with this feeling had been followed by running up a drain pipe and seeing a monkey in a puddle. She had been so scared of the police, she thought the shaking had to do with that. She wasn't scared of Dante. What the hell was happening?

In seconds, she might be swinging from the chandelier in her foyer if she couldn't get herself under control.

"I—I'm sorry…" That was all she had time to say before her arms and legs grew a thick brown coat of hair and she leapt from her spot on the couch—right out of her best black dress pants. She shook off the jacket and was soon running off to the upstairs bathroom wearing nothing but her pink lace bra and pink silk top. Her lace panties had fallen off one leg and looped around the other foot.

After hugging the toilet for a few tense moments, some maturity kicked in.

No. I'm not going to run and hide. I don't want him to think he's losing his mind or seeing things. He'll probably dump me like a hot rock, but it's only fair he should know. It's not him. It's definitely me.

She hadn't heard the front door slam yet, so either he left it wide open when he fled, or he was frozen in shock somewhere.

She crept back down the stairway, her long arms and tail holding onto the railing. He was still where she had left him on the couch, so he must have been scared stiff.

He turned toward her and smiled. "There you are." He seemed as calm as a summer breeze.

She didn't quite know what to do. She hadn't expected this reaction. He patted the couch next to him. "Relax. It's okay."

Her muscles sagged in relief, and her body returned to its normal size with her normal amount of body hair… but without her normal amount of clothes!

He grabbed her slacks off the floor, turned his head away, and held out the pants where she could reach them. She grasped and wriggled into them. Her blouse was still on, but she had to readjust the bra under it.

As soon as she was dressed, she murmured, "You're still here."

"Is that okay? We hadn't said goodbye, so I wasn't sure you wanted me to leave."

"Uh…no, I don't want you to leave. But I can't imagine you'd want to stay. Are you…all right?"

He laughed. "I'm fine. In fact, I have a secret too. I'll share it with you, if you can handle it at the moment, and also keep it to yourself."

"If it's about you being that boy in school, I think I figured that out."

He laughed. "It's not just that, but I'm glad you got the point. My secret is something like yours. Will you believe me if I just tell you, or are you someone who needs to see something with their own eyes?"

"I might need convincing, but I'd like to be warned first. I'm sorry I couldn't give you the same consideration."

"I understand. It looked like you weren't able to control the shift."

"You're right. I couldn't. It's only happened once before—about a month ago. I had convinced myself it was an illusion." She dropped onto the sofa next to him. He held out his hand for her to grasp or leave as she preferred. She laced her fingers with his. "Tell me your secret. If it's anything like mine, I'm dying to know. I feel so alone."

"I'm a shape-shifter too. A phoenix, to be exact."

"Phoenix? Like the firebird that rises from its ashes? I thought that was just a legend."

"Nope. Not legend or fairy tale. We're a race that can be traced back to written histories from ancient Rome. Some say a phoenix came to this hemisphere with Columbus when he set sail from Spain. But the Native Americans have stories about firebirds that have been handed down too."

"Are there many of you?"

Dante tipped his head as if thinking. "It depends on what you're talking about. There are Fierros in Boston and some in Arizona, but I don't think there are a lot of phoenixes worldwide. And I doubt everyone with that last name is a firebird."

"Oh. So, what does a phoenix look like, exactly?"

"Why don't I show you? Think you can handle a short demonstration?"

"You won't set my place on fire, will you?"

His jaw dropped. "Absolutely not. I'm a fire *fighter*, not a fire *setter*."

"Oh. Sorry. I guess that was a stupid question."

"No. Considering the many legends that are incorrect, it wasn't an unusual assumption. Don't worry. We don't spontaneously combust."

"So, what do you do? I mean, is the reincarnation thing real?"

"If we die in a fire, we can reincarnate. It's why my mother doesn't freak out about having so many sons as firefighters. We do our best to avoid dying though."

"Oh, good."

"Where should I undress? I'll give you a brief demonstration. Wait—I didn't mean that like it sounded…"

She chuckled. "I know. Bathroom. Top of the stairs."

"Okay. Before I go, I want you to know what to expect. I'll be aware of who I am and who you are the whole time. I'll look like a bird, about the size of a hawk, but with bright-colored tail feathers.

"I'll only stay in bird form a short time. We age faster as birds, so shifting is highly discouraged. And showing humans the paranormal world is forbidden.

But you've already promised not to tell anyone. Are you ready?"

"Yup. Ready and as curious as George."

He grinned. "Okay then. On that note..." He ran up the stairs. A few moments later, a beautiful bird with colorful tail feathers flew down the stairway, circled the ceiling fan and landed on the back of the couch.

"Wow." It wasn't an eloquent comment, but the gift of speech had deserted her. She reached out toward him slowly, and he walked forward a few steps. Eventually, she patted his head gently with one finger. He didn't flinch.

"I can't believe this. Am I hallucinating again?"

He hopped away and flew up the stairs. A few moments later, Dante walked back down the stairs, fully dressed. "You're perfectly sane. You're just a shape-shifter. And by the way, you should never tell anyone what you are. I probably should have explained that first."

She laughed. "Who would believe me? First I'm the crazy girl who talks to people who aren't there, and now I'm a shape-shifting spider monkey. Your secret is safe with me."

"And you're safe with me." He sat beside her.

She relaxed. "I do feel safe with you. I don't know anyone else who would still be sitting here, talking to me like this. Most guys would have run."

"You haven't shifted in front of anyone else, have you?"

"No. I've been lucky, I guess. You're the first person to see it happen. I don't know what I'd say to anyone who witnessed it. They'd probably think they were going crazy."

"You don't think anyone would be concerned *for you*?"

"I honestly don't. Remember how I said all my friends knew where my parents were and that's why I had to call you?"

"Yeah?"

"Well, all my friends are scattered around the world now, living their own lives, and don't know where I am, never mind my parents."

"Seriously? I remember you having tons of friends."

"Very few of them were close friends. Most were acquaintances."

"You hung out with Marcy a lot…"

"She's in Hawaii."

"What about Belinda?"

"Backpacking across Europe." Mallory sighed. "I feel like you're my only friend these days. I've barely heard from anyone else."

He inhaled deeply and rubbed her back. "Then they're idiots."

"Thank you."

"For what?" he asked, sounding surprised.

She smiled and laid her head on his shoulder. "For being you."

"I wish I could do more. Are you still willing to see the hypnotherapist?"

"I—I'd like to, but what if I shift in front of him?"

"If it happens when you're nervous or afraid, you won't shift. He's going to put you into a deeply relaxed state. You just have to stay calm before that."

She groaned. "I guess if hypnosis helps me stay calm and avoid shifts, it's worth a try. At least if all I turn into is a monkey, I'll have opposable thumbs to turn the doorknob and leave if he's freaking out."

———⁓———

Noah had set up their whole lab by the time Dante returned. It was almost time to leave for work, but he was proud of what he'd managed to accomplish in such a short time. As it turned out, he needed the distraction.

"Check out the spare room," Noah announced proudly to his older brother.

"Okay, but we have to leave in a few minutes." Dante strode down the hall to the last door on the left. When he opened it, he whistled in appreciation.

Noah stepped up behind him and viewed the fruits of his labors. A long collapsible table they'd bought for backyard parties was set up in the middle of the room, with a makeshift tin-foil top. A Bunsen burner had been duct-taped in place. There were droppers, a selection of measuring cups, a wooden rack that held glass beakers, and a few metal instruments for grasping the glass vials and holding them above the gas flame. There was a metal stand to hold a bulbous glass container mounted over the fire to cook for a while.

He felt like a proud papa. "All we need is a propane tank and some lead."

"I'll be damned. You're actually doing it."

"Did you think I was joking all that time?"

"Well, no. Not exactly…"

"What exactly did you think?" Noah asked.

"I guess I thought you needed a hobby. You know… until you find a girl to marry you and have your kids."

"What? So you had no intention of helping me?"

"Of course I did. *I will*. I guess… All you wanted me to do was to translate the Latin for you, right?"

"Hell no. I want you to be here for safety reasons. No one should be alone in a lab. What if something goes wrong and I pass out from chemical poisoning? Or a fire starts? An extra pair of hands wouldn't hurt when handling volatile substances."

"Wait. Volatile substances?"

"You know…fire…chemicals…"

"Shit, yeah. I hadn't thought about that."

Noah shook his head. "Unbelievable."

"Look. I'm sorry. I wish I knew more about this. But don't worry, I won't leave you to blow up our apartment alone."

"Gee, thanks."

Dante left the room and grabbed his car keys. "Are you ready to go?"

"I think I'll walk today."

"Oh, come on. Don't be upset. I said I'd help."

Noah sighed. "It's not you. Or it's not *just* you. I was rejected by Kizzy."

"Huh? I thought she was into you."

"I thought so too. I sent her a friend request on Facebook, and she accepted it. So I sent her a private message. We started chatting, and that was going well, so I asked her out. Everything went quiet for a while, then she came back with a million excuses about being busy and helping her father with something, and her sister needing her, and whatever. The thing is, she turned me down."

"I'm sorry, Bro. I really thought you two hit it off. Did you ask her to the basketball game?"

"No. I figured I'd take her out to dinner some night when neither of us had to work."

"Maybe she's tired at night. The game is on a Saturday. She can't be working every weekend. Come on. Let me drive you to work. We can figure this out on the way."

"No. Thanks though. I really want to walk." Noah grabbed his Boston Fire Department jacket. "I need to think about the science experiment."

"Okay. Call me if you want to talk it over."

"Nah. I'll be fine." He dashed down the stairs and set off for his downtown firehouse. He had avoided the sting of rejection by setting up the lab, and now that he'd had time to process what happened with Kizzy, he wanted to be alone. Obviously, he'd done something wrong, but what?

Noah had dated off and on, but never had a serious relationship.

Just like his brothers, he had to find a woman he could totally trust with his and his family's paranormal secret. That took a special kind of woman. Someone with maturity. His older brothers were lucky to have found their soulmates. The loves of their lives. He wondered if that kind of luck could continue.

Women were a puzzle, and not one as easily figured out as a chemical formula. Relationships could be just as volatile—if not more so.

~~~

Two members of the secret group in Brazil had been sent to Boston. The spell to make the developer leave hadn't produced the desired result, and now their commandant was angry. Unlimited power would be theirs if they could only locate the companion occult books, so Wilhelm and Franz were selected to go. Franz was the commandant's grandson and Wilhelm was a trusted advisor.

"The books are around here somewhere. I can feel it," Wilhelm, the elder, said as they deplaned at Logan Airport.

"Here? In the airport itself?" his younger pupil, Franz, asked. "I sense nothing unusual."

Wilhelm rolled his eyes. "Not *here* here. Somewhere in the area, which is more than I sensed in Brazil using a locator spell."

Franz frowned at him. "We still have no idea how to narrow it down to a smaller area."

"Actually, I do have an idea. I put a spell on us before we left. If anyone is using the power contained in those books, we'll gravitate toward it."

"Huh? You didn't tell me that. So, your plan is to just wander around a city of more than six hundred thousand people, hoping to sense someone using the supernatural power in those books?"

"Do you have a better idea, Franz?"

He shook his sandy-blond head. "No."

"Until you think of something helpful, keep your mouth shut and your eyes open."

His young charge followed him to the baggage claim area.

After collecting their suitcases, Franz dared to speak again. "I wonder how the books got split up in the first place. I figured all the occult texts went to South America with the original elders. I thought using occult knowledge was how they evaded capture and trial as war criminals."

"No one knows exactly what happened. Someone may have had a change of heart and sent them in different directions. At the end of the war, items were seized. Even someone on our side may have feared the power promised if all three books were used together. They could make us gods."

"But the other two went in the same direction," Franz insisted. "The locator spell only found one place."

"Yes. One place. Someone may have stolen two of the three books, *or* one book may have been destroyed and there's only one here."

"So, we may not be able to find all three? Is that what you're saying?" Franz nervously bit his lip. "Our mission is to recover both books and reunite all three."

"No one knows the mission better than I," Wilhelm said. "Your grandfather cautioned us not to come back without them. We could face death if we fail."

Chapter 4

"WHY DID YOU SAY NO?" RUTH WHISPERED FROM HER spot on the buttery-soft leather sofa.

"I didn't say no. I said 'not now.' It's not the same thing," Kizzy explained. Their father would be returning any minute. She had to shut down this conversation.

"It is to a guy. When was the last time you dated?"

Kizzy elbowed her sister in the ribs as their father ambled into the living room, scanning the thick tome in his hands.

"I don't know, girls. I don't see anything in here about who could be looking for the other books or why. We don't even know for sure that there are two more. The story that the three together create unlimited power could be just that. A story. You swear you've felt someone probing, Ruthie?"

"I swear, Dad. I don't know who it is, but the energy feels malignant."

"Holy pickled pig's feet!" Kizzy said. "*Malignant*? Are you sure?"

"Why is everyone questioning my psychic sense? I wouldn't have said anything if the energy was neutral, benevolent, or if I wasn't sure."

"I'm sorry, Sis. Even though Dad and I are less psychic than you are, I would have thought we'd pick up on something like that."

"Well, I don't know about Dad, but *you've* had

something else on your mind." Ruth winked at her. "Besides, you can develop your psychic power, if you're willing to spend the time practicing."

"Oh? You're distracted?" Their father picked up on the one thing Kizzy didn't want to talk about. "Doctors like us can't afford to let that happen. Is everything all right, Kizz?" He set the book on the mahogany coffee table and sat in the adjacent chair.

"Everything's fine, Dad. Nothing to worry about."

"Really? Because you girls know if there's ever anything you need to talk about, I'm here for you. I've been both father and mother for fifteen years, and with the help of a nanny, I think I did a pretty good job."

"You did. And we know you'll always be there for us," Kizzy said. "Don't worry so much. You raised us to be independent women, able to handle ourselves."

"Oh, go on. Tell him," Ruth said.

"Tell me what?" He sounded alarmed. Now, he'd never let it go until she offered an explanation. She gave her sister the stink eye.

"There's nothing to tell. It's okay, Dad. Really. I just met a guy. Nothing may come of it."

"She met a tall, dark, and handsome firefighter. And he asked her out. I hope she'll give him a chance. It's been too long, Kizz."

"A firefighter? Oh, honey. That's not a good choice. The job is dangerous. You'll always be worried about him. And talk about crazy hours... They're on for at least twenty-four at a stretch. I don't see how that's even legal. No one can function after a rough double shift. We both know that firsthand."

"She turned him down," Ruth said.

"Thank goodness."

"Now, wait a minute," Kizzy said. "I only said no for now, because of what Ruth was telling me. It sounded like a bad time. I didn't necessarily turn him down for a date sometime in the future."

Aaron Samuels sat forward. "It *is* a bad time. And so is any time in the future, as long as he's a firefighter. I imagine that won't change. They tend to be adrenaline junkies."

"Come on, that's an unfair generalization." Kizzy knew she sounded defensive, but she didn't care. "Noah's whole family is part of the fire service. Keeping the city safe is a noble profession, and he seems to love it. Plus, he's careful, and he does things for charity. He's a good guy, Dad."

"Noah? That's his name?"

"Yes."

"And he works in Brookline?" her father asked.

"No. Downtown Boston."

"Oh, cra—I mean, crumb bunny."

"What does that mean?" Ruth asked and giggled.

"It means that's a crummy place to work. He probably sees the worst of humanity there. If he were working here or in Chestnut Hill or somewhere in the suburbs, it might not be so bad."

"For crying out loud, Dad. It's the financial district! Not Dorchester or Roxbury. Maybe he'll get a hot stock tip from a grateful broker. Why do you always assume the worst?"

"Dad, Kizzy, we need to focus on the book." Ruth sent her an apologetic look. Clearly, she hadn't expected the conversation to take such a pessimistic turn.

"Yes, you're right, dear," the elder Dr. Samuels said. "I wish I had your psychic powers, but I don't. Male witches in our family have other gifts, but divination isn't one of them. I have to rely on the two of you to keep me informed. Please put your love lives on hold until we figure out what this threat is. Please? Humor an old man, okay?"

Kizzy frowned. "I already did that, remember? I said 'not now,' and Ruth thinks I might have discouraged him altogether—even though I didn't mean to."

"And I'm engaged but without a date set, so I'm all yours for the time being. I'd rather not move back home though. Then I'd have to explain why to Gordon, and I don't think he'd understand."

"Look, I know you're adults, but I'm still concerned for your safety. You'll just have to put up with me being a little overprotective."

"Don't you think it's time to tell Gordon the truth?" Kizzy asked.

"I'm not convinced it's necessary yet," their father said. "Until a date is set. Don't get me wrong, I'm not pushing you to get married. Neither one of you. I'd rather you be one hundred percent sure of the man's love, devotion, and trust."

Kizzy sighed. "I know, Dad. And believe me, I'm grateful I don't have to put up with some of the pressure my friends do. They tell me about parental conversations that include phrases like 'I won't be around forever' and 'you need to get married before the dreaded 3–0.'"

"You have plenty of time, Kizz. I like your sister's idea of developing your psychic powers. Maybe between both of you, the other books can be located.

"We don't know what's coming for us," he continued. "If it's as malicious as you say, we may be facing something truly evil. I never told you this, but on her deathbed, your great-grandmother begged us not to let 'the entity' get all three books."

"The entity? That's what she called…it? Or them?"

"I wish I knew more. We tried to get her to elaborate, but she died moments later." He scratched his head. "You tried the locator spell before, but that was as a lark. We didn't need the other books then. Perhaps now that we do, the spell would carry more weight. Can you repeat the ritual? Sometimes the universe waits until you really mean the words you say."

"Yes. It's in the book, so I'm sure we can recreate it."

"Good. Let me know what happens."

Kizzy began flipping through the book. It was loosely organized and handwritten centuries ago. Monks were said to have penned and illustrated the pages. No one was given all parts of a spell or the book as a whole—until it was finished. Family lore said that some ancient ruler had commissioned the work, and supposedly, Nostradamus had added to it.

The girls pored over the pages. At last, Ruth leaned back and groaned. "You're so much better at languages than I am, Kizz. Can you find it, please?"

Kizzy watched as her sister rubbed her temples and yawned.

"Are you okay, Ruth?"

"Yeah. Fine. Why?"

"You seem tired. More so than usual."

"Really? Are you sure you're okay, Ruthie?" their father asked.

She let her head rest on the sofa back. "Promise you won't get mad?"

Kizzy's eyes widened. "You're pregnant!"

Ruth rolled her head toward her sister. "Is that your psychic detection or your guess, Kizz?"

"Both."

Ruth sighed. "No use denying it then."

The elder Dr. Samuels appeared frozen, as if stunned into silence. Finally, he found his voice. "Have you told Gordon yet?"

"Not yet. Please keep it to yourselves until I tell you it's a safe topic. Okay?"

"Absolutely," her dad said. "But tell him soon."

"He won't hear it from me," Kizzy said.

Dr. Samuels cleared his throat. "I'm not an expert on supernatural females, but I believe you're even more psychic when pregnant. Is that true?"

"I don't know," Ruth said. "Mom and Grandma didn't tell us much about our reproductive systems before they died."

Aaron Samuels shook his gray head. "I wish they were here to help you, Ruthie."

The three of them reflected on the day their grandmother had fallen and broken her ankle just as the train was coming. Their mother had ordered Kizzy to hold onto Ruth's hand and stay on the sidewalk. Then they watched as the oncoming train hit both of the most important women in their lives.

Kizzy pushed the memory to the back of her mind for the billionth time. "The extra psychic power would make sense though—all those hormones will make any woman overly sensitive."

Ruth chuckled. "One of my patients told me that when she was pregnant, she couldn't get almond milk in a restaurant and burst into tears."

Kizzy and her dad laughed.

"Oh, and there's so much more to look forward to!" Ruth added. "Like morning sickness, which can last all darn day; cankles that engulf your entire leg; learning how to waddle like a penguin…and I can't wait to be punched in the stomach from the inside."

"Come on, Sis…the miracle of growing an entirely new human being? That's huge!"

"Speaking of huge, I can't wait to look like I swallowed a basketball, or to find out how Dolly Parton must feel."

The elder Dr. Samuels had wisely stayed out of it, until now. He laughed. "Your mother and I had to plan every trip around knowing where a clean restroom could be found."

"Oh, thanks, Dad. I forgot about having to pee every fifteen minutes."

"But come on," Kizzy insisted. "Deeply loving someone you haven't even met yet…"

The others smiled wistfully.

"Yeah, there's that," Ruth said at last.

Kizzy embraced her sister and held on longer than usual. "I'm going to be this kid's favorite auntie."

"Gordon has no siblings. You're going to be this kid's *only* auntie."

—⁓—

"So, guys, what am I doing wrong?" Noah asked his fellow firefighters as they ate lunch.

His buddy Mike O'Rourke shrugged. "Damned if I know. I've been married for ten years. Dating etiquette has changed."

"Should I have just asked for her phone number and then called to ask her out? Maybe a private message on social media was too impersonal? A telephone call seemed like an unnecessary step."

The other Mike, Mike Diamond, almost choked on his garlic bread. "Dude. That was probably the most impersonal way you could ask. Besides, girls like to think they're worth an extra step or two."

"Shit." Noah frowned. "Have I blown it?"

Mike D chuckled. "If she likes you enough, she'll give you another chance. Do you have her phone number?"

"Yeah. That's why I was surprised when she said no. Maybe she wanted me to text her."

"Jesus, Fierro. She wants to hear your voice," his captain said. "You can't really convey that you'd be excited to see her again with an emoji."

"No? Not even the eggplant emoji?" O'Rourke asked, grinning.

All the guys laughed. "Especially not the eggplant emoji. You're supposed to be interested but not desperate," Captain Merrick said.

"I *am* interested but not desperate." The guys gave him sidelong glances. "Okay, I'm a little desperate."

The whole group burst out laughing. Noah didn't mind having a good laugh at his own expense, but it was time to shut this down before it got out of hand.

"You schmucks don't know what it's like. You've never met a gorgeous doctor and felt like you're reaching way above your station in life."

"I asked out an actress once," O'Rourke said. Everyone quieted down.

"What happened with that?" Noah asked.

"She said she was flattered, but Hollywood and Massachusetts were just too far apart. I said I'd move, but then she cc'd her agent on her next 'thanks, but no thanks' email. I guess she thought she was letting me down easy, in case I was a stalker."

Everyone laughed again, and Noah cringed. That was why he almost hadn't brought it up. He didn't want to be the butt of their jokes. "Forget it, guys. I shouldn't have asked."

The captain stopped on his way to the sink with his empty plate and clamped a hand on Noah's shoulder. "Don't worry, Fierro. We'd help if we could, but who knows what women want? We certainly don't."

"You could ask a female friend—if you have any," O'Rourke said.

Noah took a big bite of spaghetti and chewed on both the food and his predicament. That might not be a terrible idea. He'd be seeing most of his sisters-in-law on Sunday. His mother was too old to understand the social media stuff, but the next generation down should be able to help him figure out what dating etiquette was acceptable these days. *Who can I ask?*

Sandra and Miguel had been together since high school, so they'd never had to deal with it. Two of the others were freakin' dragons. Who knew what dating had been like for them? He needed to ask a normal girl.

Maybe Misty would be able to help him out. She was only twenty-four. Even though she was with their older brother Gabe now, she was single and dating before that—he assumed. And she was a nice girl who would want to be treated with respect, like Kizzy.

"Yeah. I might do that," he said after he finally swallowed.

Just then the tones rang out, and he didn't have time to do much more than toss the leftovers in the trash. Noah was on tower ladder 3. The dispatcher announced the address of the fire in one of the taller but older buildings nearby—probably built in the seventies. Noah secretly hoped it was a false alarm.

A firefighter's worst nightmare was a high-rise fire. His older brother Ryan had been in one before and lost his life. Well, temporarily. Anyone other than a phoenix or dragon caught in a backdraft explosion wouldn't have seen their next birthday. And since it was such a public "death," Ryan had to relocate to Ireland after he reincarnated. His picture had been in the papers and on the news for days afterward.

They all donned their turnout gear in seconds. As the trucks rolled out onto the street, he found himself thinking of Kizzy again. *Get your head in the game, Fierro.* Even a small distraction could put him or his fellow firefighters in peril.

The Federal Street location was mostly offices on the lower floors, then residential condos from there skyward. The fire was reported to have started on a low floor of a twenty-eight-story building. People were still spilling out onto the sidewalk as the trucks arrived. Noah hopped down from his seat behind Captain Merrick.

"I don't know why you guys are here," cried a portly man wearing a white apron. "It was just a small grease fire, and I put it out with a fire extinguisher. I don't even know who called you."

"And you are?" the captain asked.

"Head chef, Roberto Carelli. That's my restaurant." He pointed to the ground floor of the concrete-and-glass corner building.

A small kitchen fire was one thing, but if it spread upward, it could spell disaster. Even though the chef said he'd snuffed it out, Captain Merrick wouldn't take any chances. Just because people couldn't see the flame anymore didn't mean it was out. Fire could hide in the walls only to erupt later.

A woman wearing a bathrobe approached. "Please check the whole building," she said timidly. Her young husband or boyfriend kicked at the curb, hands in his jeans pockets.

The captain eyed her. "Which floor do you live on?"

"Six," she said.

"Fierro and O'Rourke, check the floors above the restaurant. Pay close attention to six."

"Yes, sir," Noah said. He grabbed the irons in case they needed to pry open a locked door with the halligan bar or hack their way through a wall with the ax. The two of them passed the last of the descending residents on the stairwell as they ascended.

The hallway of the second floor seemed deserted, and all was quiet. There was no smoke. They walked along, placing their bare hands against the walls, looking for a change in temperature.

"Nothin'," said O'Rourke as they reached the end.

"Same here. On to the next floor," Noah said.

It was slow and repetitious, but being thorough now could prevent a disaster later. Walking up twenty-eight floors would tire out a human, but shifters had paranormal stamina. As that thought drifted through his head,

Kizzy's face reappeared...thrown back in ecstasy. *Not now, dammit. Pay attention, Fierro.*

"What do you think you're going to do about that girl?" O'Rourke asked as they reached the sixth floor and repeated their inspection.

Noah groaned. He was about to say he didn't know, but then his hand met a spike in warmth. "Whoa. I think I have something." He pounded on the door. "Boston Fire Department!" When there was no answer, he tried the knob. Locked. He used the halligan tool and pried open the door. Smoke drifted through the entry. "Radio the captain!"

O'Rourke reported they had found smoke in a residence on the sixth floor. The captain said he was standing by. They traced the source of the smoke to a small, unfinished room in the condo.

Noah came upon what looked like a bathroom renovation and flames in the pipe shaft. "Shit. Another amateur plumber."

"Captain. We have fire in a bathroom. Looks like they were soldering pipes in here. Some insulation may have caught and spread up the shaft."

The captain's voice crackled over the radio. "Try and hold it until I can get you a line up there."

Noah began hacking down the wall to expose what was burning. Flames licked up the wall to the ceiling and beyond.

O'Rourke had "the can" with him, a two-and-a-half-gallon water-filled fire extinguisher. He had to use his precious water sparingly, yet they blasted water up the pipe shaft as far as it could reach. More sirens screamed in the background. It wasn't unusual to call in a second alarm if a high rise was involved. Noah was glad more help was on the way, even though he dearly hoped it wouldn't be needed.

The small room was filled with steam and smoke. Even though the smog was dissipating, it was hard to see what might still need attention on the higher floors. Noah wished he could send O'Rourke on an errand, shift, and fly up the shaft. Not gonna happen. Ten guys were probably on their way up.

"Let's take a look. There's only a little water left in the can," Noah said.

O'Rourke let up on the trigger. Getting as close to the pipe as he could, Noah faced upward and scanned the darkness for a telltale flickering yellow-orange flame. He saw nothing but black. "I think we got it," he said triumphantly.

O'Rourke whooped. "Thank God. This could have been a mutha."

"I know, right?" He patted O'Rourke on the back.

"It's out, Captain," Noah announced into the radio.

"No, it ain't," the captain answered bluntly. "I'm looking at the reflection of flickering light far above you. If it's not an orange lava lamp, it's fire."

"Shit," Noah muttered. He poked his head back into the shaft and looked skyward again. Way, way up, he saw a tiny flicker of yellow. "Fucker. I missed it."

"Don't beat yourself up, Fierro," O'Rourke said. "Captain? Where do you want us?"

"Wherever the fire is." He didn't say the word *dumbass*, but it was implied.

Noah rolled his eyes. "We're on it."

They charged up the next several flights of stairs,

checking the area above the seat of the fire carefully. O'Rourke kept the captain updated over the radio until they finally felt a hot wall on the thirteenth floor.

"Give me the halligan," O'Rourke said.

What? Am I incompetent now? Noah wondered, but ignored his friend and attacked the door instead. It splintered as he popped it open. Smoke poured out.

"Fire on thirteen," O'Rourke reported.

The captain called loud enough for the guys on the ground to hear, "We'll set up a command center on seven."

Noah felt like shit for missing the fire that had spread up the shaft. It was his own inner paranormal being angry with himself. He had superior vision. That kind of mistake could happen to any firefighter, but not to his father, not to his brothers. And it shouldn't have happened to him. "I feel like an idiot."

"You can feel later. Right now, we have a fire to put out."

Hours later, the blaze was extinguished. Noah, sooty and tired, trudged down the long stairwell to the street. The guys had to be rotated about every ten to fifteen minutes due to the heat and long upward climb taking its toll, but he insisted on staying put as long as the captain would let him.

Dante appeared at his side.

"Hey, Bro. You were in there a long time."

Noah glared at him. "Yeah. And where were you?"

"I took my turn along with everyone else. You were so intent on the fire, you didn't even see me. I didn't think you wanted to stop and chat."

Noah's anger dissipated. "Yeah. Sorry. I guess I took this one personally. I thought it was out. Even told the captain as much. The whole time, he was looking at flames in the windows above us."

"Shit. That's embarrassing."

"No kidding."

"Hey. It's out now. Nobody died. I don't think anyone was even injured."

"Yeah. We were lucky."

The captain overheard them. "Luck has nothing to do with it, Fierro. It's out because we were here, *putting it out*."

Noah felt a little better. Firefighters knew when they could bust each other's chops, but they also knew when not to. Sometimes they needed to hear what they were doing *right*. It was damned important they remember how vital a role they played in the community. Morale had a way of disintegrating fast if a firefighter felt he'd failed. But he hadn't. The captain was right. He hadn't started the fire—he'd put the fire out.

Sunday dinner at the Fierros was a mandatory event—or it might as well have been. Each son had the same schedule, so whenever they all had a Sunday off, they came home to the South End brownstone where they had all grown up. Mama Fierro expected nothing less, and if her expectations didn't bring them home, her good cooking would.

Gathered around the enormous dining room table were the parents of this rowdy bunch, Antonio and Gabriella, their sons and significant others: Ryan and Chloe, Miguel and Sandra, Jayce and Kristine, Gabe and Misty with baby Tony, and finally the three remaining single sons, Dante, Noah, and Luca, who complained that they needed a larger table—again.

Gabriella Fierro, also known as Ma, Mom, and Grandma, gazed around the table with a wistful expression on her face.

"What?" Dante asked her.

The family members around the table glanced between him and his mother.

Gabriella smiled at her fifth son. "You've always been the perceptive one, haven't you? It's like you know what I'm thinking."

"You just looked like *something* was floating through your brain. If I knew what it was, I wouldn't have said anything."

She chuckled. "Okay. I was just thinking about how lucky I am as a mother, mother-in-law, and grandmother. How proud I am of all of you."

"Oh. That's nice," he said. "Can we eat now?"

Gabriella rolled her eyes. "And the moment is gone. Yes, you can eat."

The steaming bowl of spaghetti Bolognese was passed in one direction while a basket of garlic bread was passed the other way. Veggies followed the bread, and salad followed the spaghetti. Each male family member used tongs to pile their plates high. The females ate a little less greedily but enjoyed the rich Italian food just the same.

"So, what's new?" Antonio asked after he'd swallowed his first bite. "Anything exciting happening to any of you?"

The dozen children and in-laws glanced at each other, but no one spoke up. That meant either everybody was waiting for someone else to start, or all the mouths around the table were full. Either way, the unusual silence demanded to be filled.

"Noah almost burned down Federal Street," Dante said.

Forks froze halfway to his brothers' mouths.

"I did not. Don't listen to him," Noah protested.

Dante laughed. "Okay. I exaggerated a little, but he did miss a fire in the walls, and it sprang up again."

"Shit. How did you do that?" asked Jayce, now a Boston Fire Department captain.

"I didn't! Well, I did, but not on purpose. Jeez."

"That could happen to anybody," said Antonio, the patriarch and a retired captain himself. "Not usually to one of my sons though. You didn't smell smoke or see flames anywhere? Didn't feel the heat? Didn't your paranormal senses let you know something was wrong?"

"Oh, he felt the heat, all right," Dante answered for him, smirking. "I think that's why he was distracted. Noah's got a girl on his mind."

"For Christ's sake, Dante. Will you just shut up already?" Noah clenched his fists, wishing he could punch his troublemaking brother.

Gabriella perked up. "A girl? Oh, Noah, that's wonderful. Tell us all about her."

"Not gonna happen. Besides, it's dead in the water. I asked her out and she said no."

Gabriella sat up straight, which was hard to detect since she was a meager five feet three. "Why would anyone turn down my tall, dark, handsome, and intelligent son?"

"Maybe she has classy taste in men."

"Dante Ralph Fierro! Your brother needs your support right now, not your insults."

"Sorry, Ma."

Noah was glad someone chewed Dante out, since he couldn't punch him. At least not here.

Noah sighed. "Look, I was planning to talk to Misty after dinner about what I might have done wrong, if anything."

"Me?" Misty asked. "Why? Is she a friend of mine?"

"No. It's no one you know. I just thought you might be the best one to ask. You're probably the most normal young woman here."

"Excuse me?" echoed three female voices.

"No. Not normal. Just…well, she's the one who has dated the most normally—I think."

"You're not making it better," Sandra said.

"Sorry, Sandra. You and Miguel were high school sweethearts, so you never dated other people at all." He rounded on Kristine and Chloe. "And you two are dragons. I'm not sure how that made your dating experiences different, but I'm sure it did."

"You got that right," Kristine said. "If Jayce hadn't had paranormal hearing, he'd never have discovered my secret."

Jayce leaned back as if he'd been slapped. "Never? You wouldn't have trusted me enough to tell me at some point?"

"That's not what I meant. In the early stages, I wouldn't have told you—and not only that, it's a miracle we made it to the later stages, since I refused to date fellow firefighters."

"I never heard that part," Gabriella said. "I thought it was the long distance you objected to."

"We had a lot of strikes against us," Jayce said. "But I'm glad we overcame them." He leaned toward Kristine, who gave him a peck on the lips.

"So, what's wrong with askin' me, Noah?" Chloe interjected with her lilting Irish accent.

"Ha!" Ryan exclaimed. "You're the worst one to ask. You had a chip on your shoulder the size of the Prudential Building, and it took me months to knock it off. And then there's the interesting fact that you're actual dragon royalty."

"Sure'n you don't mind livin' in a castle, luv."

"Okay, okay," Gabriella spoke up. "Whoever can help Noah with his dating question, please just do it. The only thing I want in this world is for all of my sons to be happy."

"And you know what that means," Antonio said. "If you're not married, you're not happy. And if you're not happy, Momma isn't happy, and when Momma's not happy…"

"Then *nobody's* happy," several voices chorused around the table.

"It can wait," Noah said.

"Don't put it off," Luca, the youngest, said. "Ask her now. This is the most entertainment I've had since spring break. Besides, I might need to know what to do with a normal girl too."

"My dating life is not entertainment," Noah stated a little louder than he should have.

"Darling! Calm down," Gabriella said.

"Whatever you say." Luca smirked and took a big bite of garlic bread.

"All that garlic will help attract the ladies." Noah smirked at Luca.

"At least it will keep vampires away."

Gabriella slapped her hands over her ears. "Do not talk about vampires! I know they exist, but you stay away from them. All of you!"

"And therein lies the predicament of dating a Fierro," Antonio said. "Finding a mortal who's open-minded enough to accept the supernatural—and our powers, double-edged as they may be—is rare. I'm glad four of you managed to do it. If Noah needs help…"

"I do not need help!"

Antonio gave him "the look." The one that said he was the patriarch, not to be interrupted or questioned.

"Sorry, Dad. It's just that none of you know the story. And I don't want to get into it."

"You're right," Antonio said. "It's your business, and maybe we should all butt out."

"Thank you."

"All except Misty," his mother said hopefully. "He actually asked for her help."

"I just said I was thinking about it. I'm changing my mind now."

Misty's brows raised. "Why? Are you worried I might tell everyone? I won't, you know. Not even Gabe, if you don't want me to."

Gabe's forkful of spaghetti paused on the way to his mouth. "Hey, we have no secrets from each other. Right?"

She chuckled. "Yeah…now. You kept a pretty big secret from me for a very long time. Little Tony was on his way before I knew it, and then I had to wonder what the heck I was carrying."

"*What?*" several offended male voices said at once.

"Stop," Gabriella said and pulled baby Tony onto her lap. "She didn't mean it like that. And even if she did, I had the same questions when I was carrying each of you. It's only natural."

"Sorry, Ma," most of them said.

"If only you all knew," Antonio added, shaking his head. "Poor Misty went through hell. If you weren't around to see the whole thing, you shouldn't even express an opinion."

"Damn right," Gabe said. "I take responsibility for making the whole situation worse."

Misty looked up at Gabe lovingly. "We're together, and that's what matters."

All the couples squeezed each other's hands or gave each other a peck on the lips. Noah wanted that, but could he have it with Kizzy? Or anyone, for that matter? How long could the family's luck hold out?

Gabe tousled his six-month-old son's hair. "I think Misty might be the best one to hear you out, Noah. She really was as close to 'normal' as anyone in this room. I won't even ask what you two discuss."

"Okay. I'll talk to Misty, if she's still willing," Noah said.

"Of course. I'm finished with dinner, and Tony seems happy. We should talk now."

Wiping his mouth on a dinner napkin, Noah rose from the table.

"You can use the man cave," Gabriella offered. "We'll stay up here until you finish your conversation."

As he and Misty reached the door to the finished basement, Noah swiveled so he could see everyone still at the table. "Oh, guess what? Dante has a new girl too."

He grinned as he delivered his parting shot and turned everyone's attention to his buttinsky brother.

—∿∿—

"Thanks for throwing me under the bus like that," Dante muttered on their way home.

"Hey, one good dick move deserves another." After a few uncomfortable silent minutes, Noah asked, "Was any harm done?"

Dante remained quiet, then sighed. "No. I had to reveal basic stuff before they'd leave it alone, like Mallory's name and how we knew each other, but not the weird parts, thank the gods." Dante didn't have the energy to elaborate. Instead, he turned the tables. "What did Misty say?"

"Exactly what I thought she'd say. All the stuff about how men and women make assumptions about each other and how so many misunderstandings could be avoided if they'd only communicate openly and honestly."

Dante snorted. "Yeah, because Gabe is so good at that."

"That was her point. Gabe *isn't* good at that, and apparently, it caused problems. She and Mom call him the 'strong, silent type.' Not a good trait, according to modern women."

Dante laughed. "More like stubborn, silent type. It seems like he's getting over it though. I've never seen him so happy."

"Yeah. He actually smiles now. Misty says he's planning to take the lieutenant's exam soon."

"Really? Why didn't we know that?"

"Because he's Gabe, remember?"

He chuckled. "Oh yeah. Well, he'll have to communicate if he's in a leadership position."

"No shit. It'll probably be good for him."

Dante waited a few more minutes, but then curiosity won out. "So what did she tell you to do about Kizzy?"

"She said not to give up. To ask her to the basketball game, and if she says no, ask her if there's something else she'd rather do. She said persistence in itself can be sexy—just don't make it stalker-ish and creepy."

"Ha! And what if she says she'd rather cut her toenails alone on a Saturday night?"

"Then at least I'll know the truth."

"So, when are you going to call her? The game is next weekend. She might have to make arrangements for time off if she wants to go."

"You want me to call her right now, don't you?"

Dante grinned. "Why not? If she shoots you down again, my being here to pick up the pieces of your shattered heart might help."

"Forget it. I'll call her when I get home—and from my own room with the door closed."

"You can have the whole apartment. I have to go shopping. I think we have only beer and Pringles left."

—⁂—

When Mallory answered the phone, a female voice asked, "Ms. Summers?"

"Yes…" *Oh no. It's probably some charity, asking for money when I'm practically a charity case myself.*

"Are you the Mallory Summers who worked at the mall taking portrait photos?"

Uh-oh. Now she recognized the voice. It was the mom

who had freaked out when Mallory saw her dead husband. What could she want? It was bad enough Mallory had lost her job. Did the woman want to sue her for mental distress or something? "Uh. Yeah, that was me."

"I'm glad I found you. I want to apologize. I feel so bad that you lost your job."

"Oh. Well, apology accepted." *I guess…*

"Please let me make it up to you. I spoke to your boss, and even though he wasn't prepared to rehire you, he mentioned you're an artist. My friend owns a gallery and has agreed to take a look at your artwork and possibly arrange a show—provided she thinks your work will resonate with her patrons."

"Really?" Was this a sick joke? A gallery show would be her dream come true. Could the woman be messing with her head, or might karma be through fucking with her at last?

"Well, it's not a done deal. It depends on the quality of your artwork, of course. I understand you went to art school. I figured you must have talent…"

"Well, yeah. I guess so. I hope it's enough."

"What's your medium, or are you only doing photography?"

"No, I also paint."

"That's perfect. Her clientele are looking for one-of-a-kind works. A photo can be duplicated hundreds if not millions of times. A painting or sculpture—an original piece commands a higher price, and rightly so. I know it isn't easy to make a living with fine art, but this might help."

"So, you think I might make up some lost income that way?"

"I hope so. There are no guarantees. But she has discovered some well-known talents who have gone on to show in New York, LA, and internationally."

"Oh." Mallory felt a little stupid. How should she respond to an opportunity like this? Was the woman simply feeling sorry for her? *Well, duh.* She might as well have come right out and said so. But Mallory wasn't about to let her pride get in the way. Would her stuff merit a show?

The lady must have read her mind. "Your boss said you went to Mass College of Art. He said you were overqualified for the mall position anyway."

"He did? I mean, yeah. I went to Mass Art, but he said I was overqualified? Most artists have to do something else to pay the rent. I figured photography was more creative than pouring coffee."

"Yes, you're right. And it may be your creative mind that allowed you to speak to my husband. I really wish I hadn't been so upset that day. I thought you were talking to my father-in-law, and we didn't have a good relationship. I don't know why I thought he'd care enough to watch over us. My husband, however, would have naturally been interested in our well-being. Despite certain family members thinking of me as a gold digger, it was a genuine love match. I miss him so much. You may not think of it this way, but you have a gift."

Ah. Now I see what's in it for her. She wants me to play "medium" and channel her dead husband.

"I'm afraid that may have been a one-time thing. I have no control over who comes through or why. It hasn't happened very often, and that was the first time a spirit spoke to me."

"Don't worry. I won't ask you to contact him. I'm just really sorry I ruined your life, and for such an unfair reason."

She felt like she should protest the statement that she had ruined her life. That was a bit strong. So what if she couldn't get a job taking photos of kids? She could do other things. She could learn to use those espresso and frothing machines and become a barista. Pouring coffee was a perfectly acceptable way to make an honest living. If worse came to worst, she could always ask if customers wanted fries with their fast-food orders. She wouldn't starve.

"So, are you interested in a show of your work?"

"Hell—I mean, heck yeah! What do I need to do?"

"Just bring a few examples to my friend's gallery. The paintings aren't too big to transport easily, are they? I'd suggest a portfolio, but she likes to see the actual work when possible."

"I paint all different sizes, and my boyfriend can probably help me get them there. How many do you think she'll need to see?"

"Just bring your best two or three. The gallery is on Newbury Street, near Berkley. Do you know the area?"

Did she know it? That was just Boston's premier address for designers, art galleries, and other expensive stuff. She couldn't afford to get her hair done there. *Holy crap*. She had to take a breath in order to play it cool.

"Sure. I'm a native. Just give me her name, the name of the gallery, and if you have it, the phone number. I'll call her and arrange a good time to bring some things over."

"Oh good. Don't put it off. She has a hole in her schedule she's trying to fill. Some artist flaked on her and made plans to go to Paris a week before his show."

Mallory silently thanked the absent-minded artist. Or maybe it was an excuse to cover the fact that he wasn't ready. That would be the only way she'd miss her own gallery opening. Or panic. She always had to be on guard for her own self-sabotaging fear.

Mallory's self-esteem wasn't great, but she couldn't imagine throwing away such an opportunity.

Now the pressure was on to make the most of this lucky break. She couldn't let anything get in the way. Not dead people. Not male distractions, however pleasant. Nothing. *Oh shoot*. She had already told Dante she'd go to the Battle of the Badges basketball game. Well, it might not even be an issue if the woman thought her paintings sucked.

But maybe she'd love them! Showing in a major gallery was her long-term dream. Well, that and traveling to other bigger cities to do the same thing. She'd never thought it would come to fruition early like this. Mallory had to remind herself to breathe.

Chapter 5

NOAH HAD BEEN LETTING KIZZY TAKE OVER HIS BRAIN long enough. He wondered if her rejection had anything to do with her being out of his league, and he had worried about it before. She was probably making three times his salary. Kizzy didn't seem the type to be attracted to money and power, but then again, he didn't know her that well yet.

The alchemy idea had intrigued him from the start, and if her reluctance to date him was a matter of salary, well, being able to turn lead into gold would go a long way to proving or disproving that theory. It was time to put his old chem class skills to the test.

He had picked up the last of the items he'd needed on Monday, and he would have all of today to experiment. Then it was back to work on Wednesday.

Finding sources of lead wasn't the hard part. He'd learned all kinds of things contained lead—bullets, paint, artificial turf, toys, and even candy! Yikes! Yet the amount of pure lead was often negligible. Even reclaiming lead shot resulted in about five percent actual lead after all the other metals and alloys were removed. He had an old Revolutionary War musket ball he'd bought on eBay for some damn reason. That must contain a lot of pure lead. Maybe its use was finally revealing itself.

The heavy pellet sank quickly to the bottom of the chemical bath, and he swirled the beaker around to remove any grime that had attached itself to the lead ball over the centuries. After a quick rinse and a few minutes in the evaporating dish, he determined it was as clean as he could make it.

He transferred it to the crucible, which already contained a few ingredients mentioned in the Latin translation. As a modern science nerd, Noah realized pure gold was not something that could be manufactured. All the gold on earth had been formed billions of years ago when a star went supernova. To think of recreating the big bang in a spare bedroom would stop anyone from attempting the impossible. At least, *it should*.

However, Noah had seen the impossible with his own eyes many times. He and his entire shifter family were scientifically "impossible." And this book didn't look completely scientific. It spoke of magic too. So here he was, armed with a few chemically unstable ingredients, the proper "magical" formula, and his own lunacy.

He had mixed feelings about doing this with his brother in the room. Sure, having another person there for safety was a good idea, but what if they both got hurt?

Just as he lit the Bunsen burner under the clay triangle, the front door opened and Dante's chipper "I'm home" echoed through the hallway.

With the decision having been made for him, Noah exhaled in relief and leaned back in his chair. "In here!"

Dante appeared in the doorway, holding two grocery bags. His eyes widened as he took in the scene.

"You should put on your safety goggles," Noah said.

"You should have your head examined! Are you doing what I think you're doing?"

"Probably."

"Is this your first attempt?"

"Yup."

"And you were going to do it without me? Fuck, Noah. We discussed this. What if everything blows up in your face?"

He swiveled on his metal stool, pointing toward the closet. "We have a fire extinguisher."

"Yeah, a lot of good it will do if you're dismembered in an explosion."

"So, what am I supposed to do? Forget the whole thing? That doesn't sound like me."

"No. It doesn't. Just let me be here to watch your back."

"I guess you want to be blown up too?"

"Hell no. Ma would kill us both…if we survived. Let me just take another look at the Latin text and make sure you've done everything right up to this point. Don't. Move."

"Okay. I. Won't."

Dante hurried to the kitchen to drop off the groceries. When he came back, he picked up the legal pad, scanned Noah's notes, and scratched his head. "Wouldn't you have to force lead to give up a couple of protons to make it turn to gold? I don't see how only the heat from a Bunsen burner can do that."

"There's magic involved."

"Magic? Like the kind in the *Teenage Witch* book you had in high school?"

"Maybe. Some of that stuff was handed down over the centuries."

Dante didn't snort, snicker, or even crack a smile. He just nodded and picked up the Latin text again.

"I think I've got it covered, but knock yourself out. If I'm going to blow us both up, I need a sandwich first." Noah was actually grateful for a second pair of eyes to check the formula and the order of the steps in the "spell." If even one item was off…who knew what kind of "big bang" might occur?

In the kitchen, he put away all the groceries but the items he needed and began building a deli-worthy sandwich. As he spread mustard and mayo on the top piece of rye bread, ready to close up the whole Dagwood special, Dante entered the kitchen.

"About your notes… Did you use chlorine or liquid chloride?"

"Since pure chlorine is a toxic gas and needs to be combined with a negative ion to create matter at all—"

"Oh, fer Chrissakes. You know what I mean."

"I'm just explaining what the difference is, but if you want the short answer…"

"Please."

"Sodium chloride."

"Salt?"

Noah lifted the salt shaker as if showing where he'd obtained it.

"Are you sure that will do it?"

Noah shrugged. "I don't see why not."

"Awesome." Dante returned to the spare room, and Noah chomped into his sandwich.

BOOM!

"You're saying your brother blew up the house?" the fire chief asked.

"No. Hell no. *I* blew up the house," a slightly crispy-looking Dante insisted.

His buddies from his own firehouse snickered in the background. Jay Mahoney said, "You just missed us on your day off, didn't you, Fierro?"

"Nobody blew up the house," Noah explained. "It was just the spare room."

"Oh. *Just* the spare room… Well, that makes it okay," the Southie captain snapped sarcastically.

Dante's counterparts on the B shift rotation smirked and shook their heads as they walked by. The smoking second floor didn't look too bad from the outside. The window had blown out, and whatever was smoldering had been extinguished. Noah's quick response was to shut off the gas and grab the fire extinguisher from the kitchen while Dante went for the one in the bedroom closet.

"The landlords are going to be furious when they hear about this," their first-floor neighbor whispered to his young wife.

"There's no damage to your unit at all, right?" Noah asked. "No smoke or scorch marks anywhere?"

"Uh, not that we can see. I mean, some plaster fell… and who knows what's going on behind the walls, right?" the wife asked.

"Behind the walls?" Her husband's thick eyebrows shot up, and he stared at the house.

Noah began to walk toward the building, but Dante stopped him with a hand to his chest. "There's no fire behind the walls. No smoke anywhere. It's out." He turned to the couple and said, "I emptied two fire extinguishers. Anything that *might* have caught was bathed in foam before the trucks got here. They did a thorough sweep. They wouldn't be packing up if there were any danger."

"I've seen stuff on HGTV," the female neighbor said. "The support beams are probably really old and could have been knocked out of place."

"You're sure it'll be okay to live in?" the man asked.

"A structural engineer will be called," Dante said.

"We'll patch the plaster if the landlord will let us," Noah added. "Your unit should be fine. If you find any smoke or water damage, let us know. We'll get both our places checked out and fixed as soon as we can."

The wife glanced at her husband. "I always thought sharing a house with firefighters would be safer. Who would have thought they'd be the—" Her husband quickly placed his hand over her mouth, then whispered something in her ear.

She stared at the Fierro brothers with her eyes growing wider, as if her husband had just told her they'd set off a bomb on purpose.

"I'm calling the landlord," the male neighbor said.

"No need." Dante dug his cell phone out of his pocket. "It was my fault. I'll call him."

The couple looked at him and Noah skeptically, then returned to their apartment without another word.

"Yeah, and I'm fine, by the way," Dante muttered as soon as they were out of earshot. He got the landlord's voicemail and left a message.

"Hey, Bro. Did the book make it out of there in one piece?" Noah asked.

Dante looked sheepish. "Maybe. I tossed it out the window."

"You what?"

"It seemed the fastest way to save it *and* the apartment at the same time. On my way to the fire extinguisher, I threw it out the broken window."

Noah scrambled to the side where the window was and searched the adjacent narrow strip of grass. He spotted it in the hedge, pages open, a little damp, but not much more tattered than it had been when he'd brought it home.

"Whew." He hugged the ancient text against his chest.

"Is saving that book really a good thing?" Dante asked as he joined him.

Noah looked like he didn't know what to say. He probably knew the right answer was no but couldn't give it to him.

Dante was worried. He thought about telling him to let it go, but that would be like telling Niagara Falls to stop falling. If his brother thought he had a good idea, he'd go back over it a million times, figuring out what had gone wrong. Eventually, he'd try again.

He knew what Noah would get out of it if they succeeded. A chance to impress Kizzy. He suspected his brother was worried about living up to the reputation of medical professionals the young doctor rubbed elbows with on a daily basis. Being a firefighter was nice and all, but it wouldn't support a family in any costly Boston neighborhood—and that's probably the style Kizzy was accustomed to.

Kizzy was hard at work, and it was one of those days when business was steady—not fits and starts. She was on her way to give a patient discharge instructions when her phone rang.

She peeked at the number and was surprised to see it was Noah. Maybe her sister was wrong. Perhaps he understood "not now" meant "probably later." She hoped so. She diverted her course and found a quiet corner as she answered it.

"Noah?"

"Hi, Kizzy. I just wanted to ask you one thing, then I'll leave you alone."

"Leave? No need to do that. Please ask your question." *Maybe he did misunderstand.*

"I was hoping you were sincerely busy and not just blowing me off. If it's the first one, I'll keep calling until we settle on a date. If not, I'll slink away sucking my thumb, but I won't call again."

She laughed. "Thumb-sucking isn't good for your teeth—and please keep asking. I wasn't blowing you off."

"Good!"

He sounded surprised.

"Did you think I just gave you an excuse and wouldn't want you to call again?"

"Kind of, yeah."

"I'm glad you checked. My sister said you'd think that. I really didn't mean it that way."

He let out an audible exhale. "I'm glad I talked to my sister-in-law then. She said that checking would be the only way to know."

"You spoke to your sister-in-law about me?"

"I—well, Dante couldn't keep his stupid mouth shut. He brought up the situation at Sunday dinner."

"Sunday dinner? I was the subject of discussion at your family's dinner table?"

"Sorry. Like I said, it wasn't my intention."

"No. It's okay. How many people hate me for turning you down?"

He laughed. "Nobody hates you. It was *me* they were talking about. I was thinking I must have done something wrong. I decided to ask my sister-in-law about it privately. Dante opened his big mouth before I could do that. It probably wouldn't have been a topic at all, except that my mother wants all of us to settle down. Be happy. Now that the older ones have, she's pressuring us younger guys. Nothing to worry about. We're used to dealing with pressure."

Kizzy chuckled. "I guess I know what you mean— sort of. I've had that kind of pressure in reverse. 'There's plenty of time for that, Kizzy. Concentrate on your career, Kizzy.'" She did her best to imitate her father, but her low, gruff voice just sounded comical to her ears.

He laughed. "We might be able to get them both off our backs if we date infrequently."

She smiled, knowing he couldn't see it. "I suppose so. But don't worry about that. I'm not letting other people run my life."

"I'm not either."

That was dumb, Kizz. Why don't you just call him a mama's boy? "I didn't think you were."

Fortunately, he cleared his throat and changed the subject. "I'm playing in a charity basketball game called the Battle of the Badges to benefit the children's hospital. I know I'll be on the court, but I'd like to take you out afterward."

"Won't you be expected to go out for beer and celebration with your teammates—provided you win, of course?"

"I can do that if you're not interested. I'd rather take a quick shower and go out with you though. Or if you don't feel like watching a basketball game, we can just—"

"No!" She wasn't about to make that mistake again. "I'd love to go to the game and watch you play, then see you after, as long as I don't have to work… When is it?"

"This Saturday."

"Great! Yeah, I can go Saturday. What time?"

"One o'clock. I have to be there early. Would it be okay if I have Dante drop me off and then pick you up at noon? If you want me to come and get you, I'll pick you up, but it would be early, and I'd have to borrow his car anyway—and then he'd have to be in it, because he wants to come…"

She laughed. "It's perfectly okay to have him drop you off and then come get me. Or I can meet you there."

They chatted a few more minutes to pin down the plan, and when she hung up, she was happy. As a parting joke, he'd said "Have a crappy day" and chuckled. She giggled and wished him a crappy day as well.

He was a little younger than she was. He didn't have his own car. He lived with a roommate. But all that didn't matter. It was Noah she was interested in, not his age, car, or apartment.

There were plenty of guys at the hospital with larger salaries and more possessions, and as much as her father would probably like to point that out, she didn't think he'd be that rude. He might not like her dating a *mere* firefighter, but he'd have to suck it up. This was *her* life. Or at least her love life. Her destiny may have been decided before she was born. That in itself presented a dating challenge. "*Hi, my name is Kizzy. I'm an ER doc. Oh, and by the way, my family is rather unique. We're witches. I hope that doesn't bother you...*"

She had a sixth sense about Noah. She didn't know for sure, but she thought she recognized a like-minded soul—or at least a trustworthy one. If she were a betting woman, she'd bet he had a secret too. It would be nice to have that level of trust with someone, eventually.

She returned to the patient who'd been waiting for their instructions and found she was able to deliver them with a smile on her face and a spring in her step.

Her sister was right. She needed this.

Dante had cleaned up the spare room, filled out his land-lord's paperwork for insurance, and done all he could do to take care of his own stupid mistake. Noah was staring at the book, comparing it to a translator app on his computer, because Dante had refused to translate any more Latin from this book.

Not that he didn't care about what had gone wrong, but if there was nothing to be done about it, why not just let it go? They had always been different in that way. Noah needed to understand things, and Dante could just take an outcome at face value—even if the answer was one he didn't like. He could say, "Yup. That didn't work," and move on. Noah had to know *why* it didn't work, and he wouldn't give up until he was sure he was beat.

It would have concerned Dante more, but Noah had promised he wouldn't try another experiment without someone around for safety reasons, and if researching kept Noah occupied, Dante could spend more quality time with Mallory.

Lately, she had been excited about a new project. He was happy to hear the optimism in her voice when they spoke on the phone. But he wasn't about to let her forget about the hypnotherapist either.

Checking his watch, he saw that if he left now, they could stop for coffee on the way and maybe spend a little more time together.

Staring at his brother, who was zoning out on the couch with his iPad, he asked, "Hey Noah, Joanna and I are going out. Do you need anything?"

"Hmmm… Nah."

Noah's preoccupied answer was what he'd hoped to hear. "I'll be gone all afternoon. Try not to get into trouble without me."

Noah just nodded.

The weather had been getting steadily warmer and sunnier. But even so, May in New England was unpredictable. Dante grabbed a light jacket and jogged down two sets of stairs to his Camaro. He tossed the jacket into the back seat and roared off to Mallory's town house.

When he got there, her front door was open, but the screen was closed. He would have panicked if both doors were standing wide open. Apparently, she had been watching for him. As soon as he pulled into her driveway and shut off the engine, she appeared on her doorstep. She had on a pair of skinny jeans and a pretty green sweater that made her eyes even brighter.

With her purse hanging from her shoulder, she locked the front door and walked confidently to his car. "Hey, handsome," she called out.

She made him smile whenever he saw her. Not just because she was beautiful, but because she genuinely seemed to like him and think he was plenty good enough for her. He wondered why he'd ever felt inferior to her before. She wasn't the "perfect" girl he had thought she was in high school. They were just two people, now adults, with a bit of shared history and at least one oddity in common. That was enough for a start. More than what a lot of people started with.

She fell into the seat beside him and leaned over to give him a peck on the lips.

"You seem cheerful today," he commented.

"I am. I'm a little nervous about this appointment, but I get to see you, so it won't be a total waste."

"A waste? Is that what you expect hypnosis will be?"

"Well, no. I'm just trying not to get my hopes up. If he can cure me, that would be fantastic, but it seems like a long shot—to both of us."

He frowned as he backed out of her driveway.

"I guess we won't know unless we try," she continued.

The word *we* pleased him and made him nervous at the same time. He was involving himself in her treatment. It wasn't as if that had happened by accident. He had deliberately inserted himself into her life against advice to the contrary. Had he done the right thing? What if the hypnotherapist uncovered the fact that she was actually half monkey on her father's side or something... His suggestion could backfire.

But she hadn't even talked about using hypnotherapy to get to the root of the shape-shifting. She just wanted to know why she was seeing dead people and if she could make it stop. A totally human therapist could wrap his mind around that much. Probably not shape-shifting.

"So, how is the project coming?" he asked, hoping to change the subject in his own mind to something more pleasant.

"I'm not sure. I cruised past the gallery, thinking she'd only sell stuff she herself liked, but our tastes must be wildly different. There was nothing I liked at all."

"She's probably not concerned with liking the stuff so much as she is with selling it. I wouldn't worry about what you see there. Just show her what you can do. If she thinks there's a market for it, she'll let you know."

"Or if there isn't, she'll tell me that too."

"Come on now. People are going to love your stuff. I thought what you showed me was brilliant." He turned toward her and gave her what he hoped was a reassuring grin. She seemed to relax as she smiled back.

"I think you're prejudiced, but I'm glad someone's on my side."

"Does it feel like anyone is against you?"

"Not personally. It's just the way the world works. Whoever has money seems to have the most value. An artist can be wildly talented and die penniless. It seems like all creativity is subjective, and an artist is at the mercy of whims."

"It's a gamble, for sure. So is life."

She was quiet. Had he said something wrong? They rode in silence for a while.

When he suggested they stop for coffee, she checked the time and said, "No. I just want to get there. The Southeast Expressway could make us late. I don't want to miss this."

"You sound excited. I'm glad you're open to the whole hypnosis thing. I didn't know if you would be."

"What other options do I have? I can't think of anything. I don't care if it's a long shot. I'll take *any* shot right now. The last thing I need is to chat up a bunch of invisible buyers at my first and possibly last gallery show."

He reached over and squeezed her hand. "Don't worry. We'll figure this out."

She was quiet for a few moments, then faced him squarely and asked, "Dante, are you sure you want to get involved with a woman like me?"

He glanced over and took in her serious expression. He desperately wanted to put a smile back on her beautiful face.

"Why wouldn't I?"

"Well, some people might think I'm unstable and dangerous."

"Don't worry." He flashed a grin. "I love unstable, dangerous women."

She leaned back against the leather seat. "Well then, you've met your dream girl."

"What brings you here today, Miss Summers?"

"Didn't Dante tell you?"

"I spoke to Mr. Fierro about the problem, but I'd like to hear it in your own words. Also, I want to know what you're hoping the outcome of our session will be."

"Okay. I see dead people. I think. At least I see and can speak to people who others say aren't there. It's confusing, because I don't know who's real and who isn't.

For all I know, it's all an elaborate hoax and everyone is in on it but me."

"That must be disturbing."

"Yeah, for everyone involved. Except for Dante. He seems really cool about it. I don't know why."

"Maybe he really cares about your well-being. Is that not true?"

"No. I mean, yeah. That's true. I'm sure that's it."

The therapist let it drop. "And what would you like our work here to do?"

"Make the spirits go away. I only want to see and speak to real people. Can you make that happen?"

"We can certainly work toward accomplishing that. Will you be all right if someone shows up during our session?"

"You mean, will I freak out? I haven't yet. Most of the people are quite nice."

"Good. The reason I ask is that if someone arrives, you'll know for a fact that no one is here but you and me. The door is closed."

"True." Mallory's stomach fluttered with nerves as she put her sanity in the hypnotherapist's hands. The guy seemed nice enough.

"First, I want you to know you'll be in control the whole time. If at any point you want to come out of hypnosis, simply raise your hand. I'm here to keep you completely safe and comfortable."

She would have felt safer if Dante was in the room, but she had insisted she'd be fine. Now she was sarcastically chastising "five-minutes-ago Mallory." Dante said he'd go and browse through a bookstore nearby and come back in an hour, so she really had no choice but to get comfortable with this stranger.

"You won't make me cluck like a chicken, will you?"

He frowned. "No. What purpose would that serve? I'm a hypnotherapist, Miss Summers. Not the type of hypnotist you see on stage."

"Okay. Good."

"Besides, remember how I said you'd be in control? All you have to do is tell me you're uncomfortable, and I can change the script or end the session altogether. I'm here to help you, not entertain myself."

She figured that would be his answer. He probably wouldn't have much of a business if he didn't do what he said he was going to do. "So, I'll be able to talk to you, even under hypnosis?"

"Yes. You will. Have you been hypnotized before?"

"No."

He smiled. "I'll bet you have. Ever been driving down a highway and suddenly your exit comes up, even though you thought it was several miles away?"

"Yeah. But that's because I tend to daydream."

"A lot of your daydreaming is probably hypnosis. You don't need a hypnotist to be hypnotized. Actually, all hypnosis is self-hypnosis. If you allow your mind to drift from its conscious beta state to a subconscious alpha state, you're experiencing hypnosis."

"Oh." After thinking about it for a second, she added, "That sounds like it could be dangerous."

"As long as you don't fall asleep at the wheel, it's perfectly safe. You can bring yourself back from alpha at any time."

"Alpha? Beta? Do I need to know this?"

He laughed. "There won't be a test, if that's what you mean, but it's always good to know what's going on. Every part of your body vibrates to its own rhythm. Your brain has a unique set of brain waves. In neuroscience, there are five distinct brain wave frequencies, namely beta, alpha, theta, delta, and gamma. We'll only go from beta to alpha and back."

"What are all the other states for?"

"Well, theta is that twilight state between sleep and barely awake. Deep sleep is a very low frequency called delta. We won't even approach gamma.

"Just remember that you can bring yourself back from alpha to beta at any time. I'll put you into a very relaxed alpha state called a trance. From there, we can access your subconscious mind. Do you have any other questions?"

"No. Do you?"

He smiled. "Not right now. When we begin, I want you to remember you're completely safe. If anything makes you uncomfortable, all you have to do is raise your hand, and we'll stop the session immediately. But let me bring you back gently. Don't jolt yourself back to full consciousness, even though you can."

"Okay. I think I'll be okay." She surprised herself when she realized she meant it.

"Good. I want you to find a comfortable position. You can recline in the chair or sit up or lie on the floor. Whatever is most comfortable for you."

She glanced at the carpet, not because she was actually thinking of lying down, but because she wondered if anyone did. It looked clean, but yuck. It could be full of ground-in dirt from people's shoes, dropped cookie crumbs, or who knew what else. "Nope. I'm good."

"Okay. Let's begin. Take three deep, cleansing

breaths, and let them out slowly. Breathe in, hold it for a few seconds, and relax as you exhale." He spoke softly. "Simply breathe deeply and relax a little more each time you exhale. Inhale…and exhale. You can close your eyes or allow them to drift closed on their own as you relax." His voice had already taken on a dreamlike quality.

He asked her to breathe normally while he counted her down to an even deeper relaxed state. Other than feeling boneless after a good orgasm, she didn't know how much more relaxed she could get.

"*Seven, six…* Even more relaxed. *Five, four…* Deeper and deeper. *Three, two…and one.* You're completely relaxed."

Soon he was describing a beautiful, safe, calm place. He led her along the grassy banks of a slow-flowing river. He told her to feel the sun on her shoulders, smell the freshness of the pine-scented air, and listen to the birds as they chirped in the distance. He let her spend a few moments just enjoying the peacefulness of the place as his voice trailed off.

Suddenly, she wasn't alone. A beautiful woman who looked like her grandmother but many years younger than she remembered her walked out of the woods.

"Grams?"

"Hello, darling."

"Is it really you?"

"Yes. My soul is here with you."

"Just your soul? Because I see you. You look different, but I know it's you."

"I'm in my prime and completely healthy."

"Is that what I've been seeing? People's souls? Why aren't they all as young and healthy as you are?"

"Sometimes, spirits resist moving on. It's usually due to a reluctance to leave loved ones or because of some unfinished business."

"Is that why this is happening to me? Do the spirits want me to help them finish their business?" *Wait, that sounds wrong.*

Her grandmother laughed. "I knew what you meant."

"Ack! You can read my mind?"

"Only if you project your thoughts, as if you want them heard."

Shit. This is weird.

"Not really. We're connected in a different way. Our souls communicate with each other in the spirit world."

"Is that where I am? In the spirit world?"

"No. You're in a therapist's office."

Well, duh. Her grandmother didn't comment. Either because she didn't hear what Mallory didn't want her to hear...or she forgave that particular thought.

"I'm glad you're here, Grams. I have so many questions. But cutting to the chase, is there a way to stop the spirits I don't know from bothering me? Or can you tell me how to tell real people from the spirits?"

Suddenly, she was alone.

"Grams?" No one answered. "Grams? Can you come back?"

Again, there was no answer. Maybe her grandmother would have crossed some kind of line if she told her more. Maybe she'd already crossed a line and was dragged off by the heaven police. *Shit, Mallory. You sound nuts now. Or more nuts than usual.* It was time to come out of this trance and make sense of what she'd been told.

She raised her hand.

—✺—

Dante arrived five minutes before the hour, and the door to the inner office was open. *They're done already?* He peeked in.

"Ah, Mr. Fierro. Come in. We were waiting for you. Have a seat."

Dante entered and sat in the empty chair. "Is everything all right?" He glanced at his watch. "I thought I was early."

"Yes, everything's fine," the therapist said. "We had a breakthrough today. I'd like to see her again, but she wanted to speak to you first."

Mallory squirmed in her seat as if she couldn't wait to tell him what happened—or get out of there. He wasn't sure which.

"I'll let Mallory share with you what she wants you to know."

"First off, I'm not crazy!"

Dante laughed. "I didn't think you were."

"Well, you were more certain of that than I was."

Dante waited, then prompted her to go on. "What else?"

"I found out the spirit world is real, and I'm talking to souls that haven't moved on."

"Wow! That *is* a breakthrough." He wondered how this new information came to her, but following the therapist's lead, he was letting her tell him what she wanted him to know.

She frowned. "Unfortunately, my grandmother left before I could understand the difference between a real human and an uncrossed-over soul."

"So, you had a chat with your grandmother?"

"Oh yeah." She slapped herself upside the head. "My Grams showed up and told me what was happening."

"I'm glad you got some answers. Do you think you'll get more with another session?"

Mallory looked toward the hypnotherapist. "Will I?"

"You might. Especially since it won't be new to you next time. You can enter the trance state more easily when you know what to expect and trust that you'll be completely safe."

"What I really want to know is if we can stop the spirits from visiting except when I want them to."

"I can add a posthypnotic suggestion to that effect."

"You can? Why didn't you?"

"We didn't discuss it. I wouldn't add something like that unless you were completely aware that that's what I was going to do. Mental health is trickier than hypnosis for losing weight or giving up cigarettes."

"I thought you said I wasn't crazy."

He leaned forward. "You're not. Mental health is different than abnormal psychology. Everyone wants mental health. I know it's just semantics, but the difference is important. I wish more emphasis was put on that difference. Society hears the words 'mental health' and automatically jumps to the conclusion that the lack of it is being discussed."

"Oh. So, I'm mentally healthy?"

"Until proven otherwise."

"All of this is good news," Dante said, "except for one thing. *Why* is she being haunted, for lack of a better word? Is there a proper word for what's happening to her?"

The hypnotherapist took a deep breath and looked as if he had to take a moment to think. At last, he said, "Not that I can think of. I haven't had a case like this before, but mediums might have a better handle on the lingo. If she were schizophrenic, that would be one thing, but I don't think she is."

Mallory shot to her feet. "You don't *think*?"

"Relax. I'm quite sure, but I have to allow for the fact that I'm human. I believe in a spirit world, even though my education is rooted in science. I could be wrong, even though I'm confident."

"Oh. I was almost confident too. Confident that I was crazy," she said with a frown.

Dante quickly changed the subject to making another appointment.

Mallory looked at him imploringly. "I'd need a ride. Would you be willing to bring me, Dante?"

"Of course I will," he said. He rose and held out his hand. This relationship was still new and undefined. He'd be thrilled when he could say she was his. Happily, she placed her hand in his and didn't let go.

"If it's any consolation," the therapist said as they were leaving, "the spirits haven't given you any commands. They seem to be benevolent."

"Well, crap. I never thought about what would happen if they told me to do something evil. What if one of them tells me to run into traffic?"

"Would you run into traffic?"

"Of course not."

"Then I wouldn't worry about it."

Dante sucked in a deep breath. How frightening would it be if a voice told someone to run into traffic and that person believed they had to do it? He was grateful Mallory was well aware of the difference.

Chapter 6

AT LAST, THE DAY OF THE BATTLE OF THE BADGES basketball game had arrived. Dante promised to visit his brother a few minutes before the game started and point out Kizzy's location. Noah seemed more nervous about her being there than he did about the game. He'd do well on the court. There was no doubt about that. He'd been playing since he was ten. His older brothers had taught him as soon as they realized how tall he'd be.

Mallory had arranged to meet Dante there. She said she had to finish her paintings first. She'd been working diligently to get her gallery submissions just the way she wanted them and could take public transportation to get to Boston Garden when she was finished. Dante understood her anxiety but couldn't wait to see her relax and have a little fun.

He guessed his brother felt the same way about Kizzy needing a break. Dante's motto was: *Everybody works too hard and takes themselves way too seriously*.

"There she is, Bro," he said to Noah, who was on the bench waiting for the game to start. His brother's eyes followed Dante's finger, pointing at the pretty brunette doctor. He looked relieved when Kizzy smiled and waved.

Grinning, Noah waved back. "Thanks. I owe you for bringing her here."

"No problem. You're taking her out afterward, so I'll take Mallory home in Joanna."

"Dude, that just sounds wrong."

The announcer welcomed everyone and introduced the singer of "The Star-Spangled Banner."

"Well, I'd better get to my seat."

"Yeah. Oh, hey! I see Mallory coming."

Dante glanced up in the stands and beamed when he saw her. She was always so cute. Today, she was wearing a short plaid skirt. A white blouse completed the Catholic schoolgirl look. He didn't know if that's what she was going for or not. Since they didn't go to Catholic school, she may not have even realized it was *a thing*.

He waved and began climbing the bleacher stairs to meet her and guide her to their seats. She didn't stop at the row he'd told her they'd be sitting in. Instead, she kept walking down the steps until she could throw her arms around his neck and kiss him fervently.

Wow. Her lips were warm and insistent. Her whole body was molded against his, and he felt a certain part of his anatomy stir to life.

As soon as "The Star-Spangled Banner" finished, a wolf whistle and a few chuckles made them spring apart.

"I've never made out to the national anthem before," Mallory said.

He laughed. "You're adorable."

"Thanks. You are too."

"Adorable?"

"Sure. Why not? I adore you."

His brows spiked in surprise. Uncharacteristically speechless, Dante simply escorted her to their seats on the bleachers. A smiling Kizzy scooted down to make room for both of them, and he introduced the ladies to each other.

"Kizzy, this is my girlfriend, Mallory Summers." He had wondered how to introduce her to people, as his girlfriend or friend or date, but that kiss pretty much sealed the deal. He must've been grinning like an idiot. "And Mallory, this is Noah's date, Kizzy Samuels."

As they shook hands, Kizzy cocked her head and said, "Mallory Summers? Where have I heard that name before?"

"I don't know," Mallory said. "I don't think I've met anyone named Kizzy."

Kizzy laughed. "That doesn't surprise me. Neither have I."

Dante pointed to the floor. "Noah is one of the centers."

Kizzy sat forward and watched as Noah in his red basketball uniform faced someone in a blue basketball uniform. The ball was between their ready hands, and Noah jumped, batting it first. Dante cheered him on as he rushed toward the basket. He passed it to his right guard, who got close to the basket. Unfortunately, the guy covering him was good and ready for him. He threw the ball but didn't score. When the ball was recovered by one of the blue uniforms, everyone ran like mad to the other end.

"Do you girls like sports?" Dante asked.

"Would you think less of me if I didn't?" Mallory asked.

Kizzy snapped her fingers. "I know where I've heard your name," she said. "I think you were a patient at Boston General. I work in the ER there."

Mallory froze.

Uh-oh. Dante hadn't thought about the two of them remembering that day. He didn't think they had ever met.

"Um. Yeah. I think I was there. That is…I mean, yeah. I've been there. Once." Mallory began to shake. She rose suddenly and said, "Please excuse me for a minute. I have to go to the ladies' room."

Before Dante could ask her if anything was wrong, she had fled up the stairs.

"I hope she's okay," Kizzy said. "I didn't mean to upset her."

"I hope so too." Dante followed her with his eyes until she rushed past the exit and out of sight.

He turned back to the game in time to watch the cops score. "Damn! Oh, sorry. I didn't mean to swear."

Kizzy smiled. "No worries. I've heard much worse."

Just then, a brawl broke out, but it was quickly shut down and paled in comparison to the ruckus toward the back of the bleachers. When Dante turned to see what was going on, he couldn't believe his eyes. A monkey wearing a white blouse with a crossbody purse hanging from its shoulder was swinging from the rafters. People were pointing and laughing.

The game continued as if nothing was wrong until the monkey reached the scoreboard. The players must've noticed the crowd pointing at it and halted the game. There was no use trying to play basketball with the whole audience looking away.

Everyone's attention was riveted on this wild animal, wondering how it got there. Dante heard people in the crowd commenting that it must've been someone's pet that got loose.

"Why would someone bring a pet monkey to a basketball game?"

"Some people are idiots."

"Someone should call animal control."

"Or the cops."

Their annoyance was smothered by the laughter of the crowd.

Dante shot to his feet. He wished he knew what to do. He knew it was Mallory, of course. He recognized her purse, blouse, and alternate form. But shape-shifters didn't exist according to humans—all paranormals had been warned not to blow their covers, and the game was being televised! How could he help her?

He ran down to the sidelines. Dante skidded onto the floor, stopping just under the scoreboard. Holding up his arms, he called out, "Here, babe. Come to me."

"This is your monkey?" one of the firefighter players asked.

"Yeah. What of it?"

"Dude. That's weird."

Dante didn't care how weird it was. He continued to hold out his arms in supplication. "Come on, babe. Jump. I've got you."

Mallory climbed the rafters and swung around the area above his head. Either she was confused or afraid—or both.

One of the other players said, "Well, I'll be a monkey's uncle." Then he laughed and added, "Or maybe that's Noah's title."

Dante looked askance at the firefighter and noticed it was Noah's buddy, O'Rourke. He tuned him out and concentrated on getting Mallory down.

"C'mon, now. I'll catch you."

"It's all right, babe." One of the other firefighters called to her. He must have thought that was her name. "You can let go, babe. He'll catch you."

She let go with one hand and swung by the other arm.

"You can do it. I *promise* to catch you," Dante pleaded.

At last, she nodded, then let go and fell into his arms. He pulled her into a tight hug, and she wrapped her arms and legs around him, holding on for dear life. Dante hurried up the stairs but paused next to Kizzy, not knowing what to say.

"I…ah…"

Kizzy seemed less confused than he would've expected. She smiled. "Yeah. I can see you need to go. I'll wait for Noah."

Dante let out a deep sigh of relief. And then he noticed the security guards coming toward them.

———※———

Mallory had no choice but to make her escape and meet Dante at his car. She wanted her skirt, but where had it fallen off? She tried to scramble out of his arms and go back for it, but he held on tight.

"Now, settle down, everybody," Dante said.

"What kind of dumbass brings a monkey to a basketball game?" one security guard asked the other.

"Damned if I know. What do you have to say, dumbass?" He was squinting at Dante. "Maybe you can answer my friend here."

"Sorry. I'll get her right out of here if you'll just step aside."

The guards regarded each other. "Step aside? So we're supposed to just trust you to take this menace back to the jungle?"

Dante shrugged. Mallory wriggled harder, but he clamped down tightly on her shoulder and held her fast.

"I think it's illegal to own a monkey, isn't it?" one of the guards said to the other.

"Is it? I have no idea."

"Hmmm. Maybe we should call the captain and find out."

As they were hemming and hawing about what to do, Dante calmly said, "Excuse me, gentlemen."

"Where do you think you're going?" the larger of the two guards asked.

He fixed that one with an angry glare. "I'm taking her to where she lives. Unless you want to invite us to *your* house, so your family can adopt her."

"Are you saying you don't own this chimp?"

"She's not a chimp. She's a spider monkey, and no, I don't own her. I can make sure she gets home safely though."

"Spider? Shouldn't she have eight arms and legs or something?" one guard asked the other.

Dante just sighed and tried to dodge their body blockade.

"You *do* know where it belongs? Is that what you're telling us?"

Dante let out a deep breath in a frustrated whoosh. "I'm not telling you anything except 'please excuse me' while I take care of this problem for you." He outma-neuvered the stunned guards and ran off in the direction of the parking lot.

—vvv—

At least Dante wasn't in trouble because of her. Mallory would have to forget about her skirt. Right now, she was lucky Dante was there for her. Lord knows what the guards would have done otherwise. Shot her? Called animal control? She shuddered. *I have to get control over this shifting thing!* If only she knew why it was happening.

When Dante arrived at his car, he opened the passenger-side door, and Mallory hopped in, then crawled over the center console into the backseat. He slammed the door shut and jogged around to the other side.

He had to be furious. She would explain how extreme anxiety affected her, and maybe he'd understand that this didn't happen on purpose. But would he want to hang around until it happened again? She wouldn't blame him if he dumped her in her driveway and never came back.

She took a couple of deep breaths and relaxed until her body grew, and she found herself sitting bare-assed on the back seat.

Dante opened the door, jumped in, slammed it shut, and glanced in the rearview mirror. "You're back."

"Um, yeah." Her voice sounded like an embarrassed little girl's.

After a brief, uncomfortable silence, he asked, "Are you okay?"

"Yes… No. Are you?"

He scratched his head. "I guess so."

A lump was forming in her throat. She spoke before it

became too large to talk around. "I wouldn't blame you if you never want to see me again after this."

He sighed. "That's not gonna happen."

"But I'm nothing but trouble. Don't you see that?"

He turned around and faced her. "You know what I see? I see that I was living half a life before I met you. I didn't even realize how tedious and boring everything was becoming. I'm never bored with you. But I wouldn't mind worrying a little less."

She gazed up at his eyes. They shone with sincerity. She didn't know how she got so lucky. Any other guy would've run for the hills by now.

"Maybe we should go. You can drop me at home and get back to the game."

"I'll take you home, but only so you can put on some more clothes and come back with me."

She smiled shyly. "I wasn't wearing anything else besides the skirt, you know."

His brows shot up. "No panties?"

She shook her head and grinned.

"Screw the game. I'm inviting myself to your place." The engine turned over, and they peeled out of the parking lot.

The game ended with the firefighters winning by a few points. Kizzy had to wait for Noah to take a quick shower and change, so she stayed in the stands while the crowd exited the arena.

She was surprised to see an older couple coming toward her. They were smiling and holding hands, so nothing set off warning bells. She didn't recognize them, but maybe she had treated one of them in the ER. She couldn't possibly remember every face, but sometimes grateful patients remembered *her* for the help she gave—especially the ones who would have been goners without her one magic save per day.

When they reached her, the gentleman stuck out his hand. "We just wanted to introduce ourselves. We're Noah's parents, Antonio and Gabriella Fierro."

"Oh! I—" She was so surprised, she almost forgot her own name. "Uh, I'm Kizzy Samuels. Noah's friend."

Mrs. Fierro's expression looked a little crestfallen, then she quickly put on a happier face. "We're delighted to meet you. It's not often my sixth son speaks so highly of a young lady."

"He's your sixth?"

Antonio grinned. "Yup. Six out of seven. Five are firefighters."

"Wow! That's impressive."

"Not as impressive as what you've accomplished," Gabriella said. "My goodness. A doctor! So how did you meet our Noah?"

Kizzy thought about their argument in the ER, but decided to forgo that story and tell his parents about the much more pleasant re-meet. "He just sort of fell into my lap. Literally."

The Fierros cracked up. Antonio's laugh was big and hearty, like the man standing before her. Gabriella's had a musical ring to it. They seemed like wonderful people. No wonder their son turned out so well—as far as she knew.

"Do you mind if I ask you a personal question?" Kizzy asked.

Antonio and Gabriella glanced at each other, and then Noah's father answered. "Sure. You can ask..."

In other words, she might not get an answer, but they were still smiling, so what the heck? She'd ask.

"I've treated many firefighters in the ER. Usually they come in for smoke inhalation or heat exhaustion, but occasionally severe burns. With so many firefighters in the family, how do you do it? How do you keep from worrying about them constantly?"

"I think that's a question for Gabriella," Antonio said.

If Kizzy were a more psychic witch, she might be able to read her mind. The mother of seven gave her a look of sympathetic understanding. Mind reading was unnecessary.

Gabriella smiled softly. "My Antonio was a firefighter too. When we first met, I worried much more than I do now. That may sound callous, but it's only because I know how well-trained all firefighters are. There are also plenty of policies in place to prevent unnecessary risks. The officers are greatly concerned about their men and women's safety as well as the safety of the public. There's no room for glory or grandstanding."

Kizzy understood. Sometimes she wondered how anyone could do a job like that, but then she remembered how rarely she saw firefighters as patients. Far more frequently, she saw patients they had saved. "It's a noble calling. I imagine families like yours must be committed to the community they serve."

Antonio smiled. "At first, it pays the bills. Then after a few successes, it becomes more. Don't get me wrong. There are situations that can be scary as hell, and then we remind ourselves it's not just our job, it's a calling. Not everyone can do it." Then he chuckled. "And it still pays the bills."

Kizzy couldn't help admiring the many brave men and women who worked for the fire department. If it were her, she'd probably have to be a secretary. No way would she run into an uncontrolled fire! Witches were *not* fans of burning alive!

"You should come to one of our Sunday dinners," Gabriella said. "I'll ask Noah to invite you."

"Oh! That's very kind, but I couldn't impose…"

"It's not an imposition at all. I love to cook for our family gatherings. I enjoy meeting the boys' friends, so my motto is 'the more the merrier.'"

Antonio laughed. "She's not kidding about that. We just had to knock down a wall to expand the dining room table."

Just then, Noah emerged from the locker room. He had a duffel bag of equipment over his shoulder, and his hair was damp, but he still looked good enough to eat. His brows tented as if surprised to see his parents talking with her, but then he grinned. Kizzy loved that wide, pearly-white smile.

When he reached them, he shook his dad's hand and bent down to give his mother a kiss on the cheek. Then he draped an arm around Kizzy's shoulder.

"Great game, Son," Antonio said proudly.

"But that monkey!" Gabriella said. "I wish Dante were here to explain what he had to do with it and where it came from. Do you know, darling?"

Noah shrugged. "You'll have to ask him."

Kizzy smiled and tried to think of something

intelligent to say. Anything to change the subject. She was pretty sure the monkey was wearing Mallory's blouse and crossbody purse, but she wouldn't swear to it.

"The game looked like a close one," she said.

Noah chuckled. "Yeah, the cops weren't as tough this year. Last year was the first year I played them, and we got beat."

"Wait till next year when Luca is playing against you," Gabriella said.

Antonio groaned. "Did you have to remind me we're going to have a cop in the family?"

Noah smirked. "Every family needs a blue sheep."

"Stop it, you two," Gabriella said and swatted her husband. "I was just telling Kizzy you should invite her to Sunday dinner some time, Noah."

He glanced down at her with raised eyebrows as if to ask what she thought of that.

"We can talk about it later. I'm sure Noah must be starving after all the energy he expended."

Gabriella reached for her hand. "You're right. Thank you for looking out for my son." The women squeezed hands, and Gabriella looked up at her much taller husband. "We should be going."

"You mean we should let *them* get going." Antonio winked at her.

Kizzy didn't quite understand what he meant by that, but she was relieved to be getting out of the spotlight. She barely caught it, but she thought Noah rolled his eyes. Something was going on with this family.

~~~

By the time they got back to Mallory's place, Dante had decided not to pressure Mallory, even if she'd planned to seduce him. That was before "the incident."

There was plenty of time to play with Mallory, even though she had seemed willing earlier. He had a war going on inside his head—both heads. Was this really going to happen eventually? Was he finally going to go all the way with his high school crush? Should he grab the opportunity in case he didn't get another one?

Things were different now. He understood her as a person. Despite her challenges, she hadn't lost her sense of humor—or hope. Plus, he knew things about her he never would have guessed. Like her poor self-esteem. How the hell did she wind up like that when most of the boys in school wanted her and she had friends galore?

He pulled into her driveway and shut off the engine. "I'll get you the blanket I keep in my trunk. Hang on a sec."

He hopped out of the car and opened Joanna's trunk, then moved the first aid kit to grab his blanket. The one he kept for emergency purposes, and that included impromptu picnic seductions. He hadn't considered needing it to cover a shape-shifter who had lost half her clothing.

She waited patiently and exited the back seat when he held up the blanket so she could step behind it without being seen from the street. He'd unfolded it only far enough to cover the bottom half to just below her knees. He also turned his face away.

"Thank you," she said. When she was wrapped up in the blanket, she rushed around the town house corner toward her back door. "Would you mind getting my key out of my purse?"

"Yes, of course. Wait. I mean no, I wouldn't mind."

She smiled, and he was relieved to see it. She hadn't smiled at all in the car, even when she was safely away.

"There's the happy expression I love."

Her face turned pink. "I'm not exactly happy, more like embarrassed."

He dug the key out of her purse. "You don't have to be embarrassed around me. I understand. Well, sort of... Do you know why you can't control the shifts? It seems to happen when you get nervous. Have you noticed a pattern or any trigger that might be a clue?"

"No. I don't know anything about this. It's all new to me. I didn't even know shape-shifters existed until I became one!"

Dante unlocked the door and held it open for her. She hurried inside and let out a breath of relief.

They stood staring at each other for a few seconds. Finally, Mallory let go of the blanket, and it dropped to the floor. Her lower body was as shapely as he had imagined. However, he hadn't dreamed the area at the apex of her thighs would be shaved into a heart.

"I take it you were planning a seduction."

"Are you okay with that?"

"Yeah, but are you? I wouldn't blame you if you wanted time to process what just happened."

"I—I think I processed it as much as I can. Right now, I'd like to be close...to you. Is that all right?"

"Oh, yeah. It's fine. You're fine. Very, very fine." *Stop babbling, Fierro.*

She giggled. "I'm glad you think so." She began unbuttoning her blouse.

He walked toward her and placed his hands over hers. "Let me," he said.

She glanced down shyly, then, as if making a firm decision, she straightened and looked him in the eye, letting her arms fall to her sides. He carefully unbuttoned the shirt, revealing creamy skin and no bra. His breath hitched when he finished with the last button and the blouse hung open.

She looked pleased with his reaction. "May I return the favor?"

"Absolutely."

She grabbed the hem of his red T-shirt and pulled it off over his head. When she reached for his belt, he asked, "Do you want to do this right here in the kitchen?"

She chuckled. "I guess I'm a little anxious. But you're right. We can finish this upstairs."

He followed her up the carpeted stairway and into the large room on the right. Her bedroom was a bit girly but not over the top. There were about a dozen pillows on her bed, but they were solid coordinating colors and plain for the most part. The smallest one in the center was embroidered with an M and trimmed in lace. The other furnishings were wood, painted white to match the headboard.

Dante removed his belt and draped it over the rocking chair. As he stripped off his pants, she removed her blouse and folded it over the back of the chair.

Her breath caught when she spotted his impressive hard-on. At least he'd been told it was impressive. He was so turned on, it may have been even statelier than usual.

He stepped closer and held out his arms to her. She eagerly embraced him. He could feel her heart beat. It was a little fast, betraying her anxiety.

"Mallory, I really care about you. I want you to know that. This isn't just about comforting you."

Her lashes hid her eyes, but her cheeks pinked. "I know. I feel the same way."

He swept her hair behind her ear so he could see her face. She was smiling, and there was a soft glow in her eyes. *Yup. She means it.* He cupped her cheek and kissed her soundly.

She responded immediately, opening her mouth and seeking his tongue. Their kiss deepened, and Dante's skin heated. Mallory Summers could drive him to the point of spontaneous combustion.

He walked her backward to the bed, and they both tumbled onto it. Without a word, they resumed the kiss to end all kisses—at least in Dante's experience. She writhed beneath him and he tried to ease off her, but she stopped him.

"Are you uncomfortable?"

Holding his hip, she said breathlessly, "I like you right where you are."

He smiled, knowing what she needed. He rocked against her core, creating erotic friction.

"Oh God!" She arched into him and moaned.

Without breaking his rhythm, he kissed her cheek, jaw, and neck. She was so sensitive and responsive. He suspected she was close to climaxing, and if that were the case, he'd keep going until she came apart in his arms. Later, he could treat her to more.

She cried out, shaking and gripping his shoulders. He kept going, letting her ride the wave. At last, her body relaxed, and her breath came in deep pants.

"I'm sorry," she whispered.

"Sorry? What for? Enjoying yourself?"

"No. Not that. I really needed the release, but I didn't give you anything in return."

He laughed. "I'll let you make it up to me after you've rested a bit."

She grinned up at him, linking her fingers behind his neck. "I will. I promise."

He stared into her eyes. He had been warned by Noah not to fall in love with this girl. He'd called her a train wreck. Well, it was too late. Dante was already falling. And he didn't care if she was a train wreck, a shipwreck, or a fender bender. *No one comes through life unscathed*.

Kizzy and Noah decided to drop in at the bar where the firefighters would be gathering to celebrate, and afterward, they'd go out by themselves for their very first real date.

As they entered the bar, Noah was greeted with many hard pats on the back. It was difficult not to crow about their victory, but with Kizzy right next to him, he decided to take a humbler approach.

"It wasn't just me out there, guys. We were a team. A great team."

"Well, let me be the first to buy a beer for our team leader," O'Rourke said.

"I can't stay. I just wanted to drop in, say hello, and thank everyone for a great game."

"You can make time for one beer and whatever your lady would like," O'Rourke insisted.

He smiled at Kizzy. "Would you like a glass of wine, Kiz? You like red, right?"

"Uh, sure."

Another firefighter strolled over and said, "Hey, Noah. Wasn't that your brother Dante under the scoreboard, catching the monkey that fell?"

Noah had been afraid of this. Many of his fellow firefighters knew his brother too. Dante worked in the station closest to his, and they backed each other up whenever the need presented itself. The family resemblance was pretty close, so it wouldn't take a genius to put them together.

"Yeah. He's always been an animal lover." Hopefully, that would be enough of an answer.

"That monkey is all anyone can talk about," his buddy Paul said as he and his girlfriend, Kim, joined them. "What the hell was that?"

Noah shrugged. "Don't ask me." He glanced down at Kizzy. She remained quiet with a pleasant smile on her face, but he sensed something uncomfortable behind her expression. It seemed plastered on.

"This is Paul Forte and his girlfriend, Kim Kelly. Guys, this is Kizzy Samuels."

"Nice to meet you," Kizzy said, and they all shook hands.

She seemed to be warming up to his friends. At least he hoped so. These people were important to him.

Just then, another buddy, Jeff, and his wife, Maria, strolled over. "Hey, Noah. Are you doing that hot dog eating contest next month for charity?"

"Yeah. I just signed up. Are you?"

"Wouldn't miss it." Just to emphasize the point, Jeff rubbed his belly and burped.

"Kiz, maybe you should be on hand in case anyone

chokes. Kizzy's an ER doc at Boston General," Noah explained.

"Cool," Jeff said. "We could have you on hand for all our hockey games too, in case anyone swallows some teeth."

"Yeah," Paul added. "You should talk to the coach when he gets here."

She fidgeted and dropped Noah's hand. *Uh-oh. She's uncomfortable.*

Noah quickly shut down the conversation, saying, "We just stopped by. I'm taking my lady out to dinner."

He didn't know if he was being rude by not introducing her to every firefighter in the bar, but if they were ever going to get out of there... Since she didn't seem like she wanted to chat, he hoped he was reading the situation right.

"Yeah, yeah. We have eyes," O'Rourke said as he brought over their drinks. "If I had a beauty like that, I'd rather spend my time with her too." Several of the guys within earshot joined in with some good-natured ribbing and laughing.

Kizzy's smile returned, and her olive skin pinked. She reached for the wine, and as soon as he had his beer, she held his free hand again. Noah picked up their clasped hands and kissed her knuckles. Then he turned toward the gathering and excused them.

Walking a few feet away, he asked, "Are you okay? You seem kind of shy."

"That's because I am kind of shy. I've always been an introvert."

"Really? I wouldn't have pictured you that way. But it's fine. Don't get me wrong, I can be a little shy in unfamiliar circumstances too."

She loosened up during the time it took them to finish their drinks and was actually laughing and tossing back zingers when the guys were cracking jokes. Finally, he escorted her to the door and opened it for her, placing his hand on her lower back. He realized belatedly how possessive he was feeling. Hopefully, if she picked up on it, she didn't mind.

"I didn't make reservations for dinner, but it's early, so most restaurants probably aren't busy yet. Are you hungry?"

"I could eat."

"Good. I'm famished."

They reached the corner, and he hailed a taxi. When he had her safely inside, he sprinted around the back of the cab and got in.

"Is there any type of food you prefer, or anything you'd rather stay away from?"

"No. I can eat just about anything. I'm not especially adventurous though. No chocolate-covered bugs, please."

He laughed. "There's a nice American restaurant I like called Blu in the theater district. Do you know where it is?"

Kizzy said no, and the cab driver said yes.

Noah grinned. "Perfect. Let's go there."

Kizzy whispered, "I'm glad your friends didn't think I was with Dante, since I was sitting next to him. Who knew he was going to talk a monkey down from the ceiling today?"

Noah didn't know how to respond to that. "Yeah, that was pretty crazy. But hey, if anyone can charm the pants off anybody, even a monkey, it's Dante."

She laughed and let it drop. *Thank the goddess*.

When they arrived at the restaurant, he paid the cab driver, jumped out, and jogged around the back of the cab to open her door for her. His father had taught them all old-fashioned manners, and they seemed to be appreciated by refined women—like Kizzy.

"The restaurant is on the second floor."

She preceded him up the stairs, and he couldn't help staring at her perfect ass. How he wished he could cup those globes. Not yet, though. It was too soon for anything like that.

Their table was right next to the window, which looked out onto the neon lights of the various theaters and restaurants.

"This is a nice view," Kizzy said.

"Not as nice as mine," Noah said, and then he groaned. "Sorry. That sounded like something cheesy my brother would say."

She laughed. "Yeah. That didn't sound like you."

"It's not. But sometimes I wish I had all the smooth lines and cockiness to pull them off."

"You don't need them. In fact, I'm glad you don't resort to that."

They glanced at each other shyly. It was their first awkward silence, but it wasn't horribly uncomfortable. He just chalked it up to two bashful people on their first date. Then they both started talking at once. And chuckled.

"You go first," Noah said.

Kizzy took a deep breath. "I…I'm not sure how to begin. I think we should take things slow."

"How slow?"

"Sloooooow."

A waiter chose that moment to introduce himself and ask for their drink order. Noah ordered a vodka tonic. Something in Kizzy's expression said he might need it.

After Kizzy had ordered a glass of wine, the waiter left, and Noah just stared at her.

She reached across the table and grasped his hand. "It's not you."

Noah groaned. "Oh great. Here comes the 'It's not you, it's me' story."

"No, it's not me either! I'm afraid there's some family drama going on right now. It's a really, really bad time to start a relationship."

Noah sat up straighter. "Is there anything I can do to help?"

"That's kind of you, but no. It's one of those things that has to stay among family members."

"I understand." And sadly, he did. "We have family drama sometimes too." *Like when one of my brothers burns to death and reincarnates.*

She tipped her head. "Drama? Like why your brother has a monkey who wears his girlfriend's blouse and carries her purse?"

Noah's jaw dropped. When he could speak again, he said, "The monkey was wearing Mallory's top? And that thing around her neck was Mallory's purse?"

"Mm-hmm."

"Are you sure?"

"I was admiring her JanSport crossbody bag when she sat down with us, and I noticed her blouse had cute little pin tucks. The girl has good taste. I guess the monkey does too."

Noah closed his eyes and took a deep breath. "I don't know what to tell you. I didn't see any of that."

Kizzy was quiet, but he could sense her mind spinning. "So, what happened to Mallory?" she asked.

Noah leaned back and frowned. "Damned if I know. Oh—sorry about the swearing. I know you don't like it. If it weren't rude as heck, I'd pull my cell phone out and call Dante right now."

"Don't. I'm sure there's a good explanation, but I'm just as sure I won't hear the truth even when you know it. Like we were saying before, family drama should stay within the family."

He sighed. She was probably right.

And she was right about taking their relationship slow too. Both of them had family stuff going on. But he doubted she would understand his family stuff no matter how slow they took things. Sometimes, he wanted to fall on the double-edged sword of being paranormal.

Chapter 7

As Mallory was cuddling, Dante took a deep breath and said, "This may not be the most romantic topic, but I just thought of something."

Oh well. The afterglow had to fade sometime. "What's that?"

"The symptoms you're experiencing, you said they only started recently, and you don't have any weird family history. What if they're the result of a curse? Or some kind of spell that backfired?"

"A spell? Like actual magic?"

"Yeah."

Mallory sat up and the sheet slipped off of her. Dante's eyes bugged out, as if he'd never seen breasts before. *Is he salivating?* She'd better get him back on track before he forgot what he was saying.

"Is there such a thing as a real curse?"

"Yeah, I think so. I know a couple of witches and a wizard. From what I understand—which isn't a lot—curses are really frowned upon in magic today. Unfortunately, some people are unscrupulous—or sociopathic—and don't care what happens to others."

"What people?" Mallory asked. "Who could do something like that?"

"I guess there are a few who know how to dabble in black magic."

"Seriously?"

"Yeah. It's pretty nasty. It can backfire on the sender, but that's not our problem. I think what we need to do is find someone who could identify and remove a curse if there is one."

Speechless, Mallory just stared at him. The idea that someone would put a curse on her had never even crossed her mind. Why? She hadn't done anything really terrible in her whole life. Who could wish her ill?

"I know it's a long shot." He cleared his throat and sat up. "I'm thinking of a wizard I've heard of. He has a good reputation as someone who knows what he's doing and has high principles. Would you accept his help?"

"That depends. What if he's nuttier than I am? A wizard? I'm pretty open-minded, especially now, but that doesn't mean anything if I freak out over his abilities."

"Don't you want someone who has mind-blowing abilities? I'd want to know he can accomplish what needs to be done."

She didn't answer, because she wasn't sure.

"Say something," Dante pleaded.

"I'm thinking."

"Look, I may be grasping at straws, but I want to help, and this possibility just popped into my head. You don't have to…"

"I guess it would be worth looking into." Before she chickened out, she said, "Call him."

Dante bounded out of the bed. "I left my phone in your kitchen."

As he pulled on his jeans, she had a good look at the well-muscled Adonis she'd just slept with. *Now I'm salivating!* She fetched her red satin robe from the closet and put it on as she followed him downstairs.

When Dante grabbed his phone off the kitchen floor, she was reminded of the passion they'd shared the moment they got in the door. She had never fallen this fast or this hard for anyone. It should have scared her, but it didn't. She trusted Dante. She didn't know why, but she did.

Dante pressed a couple of buttons on his phone, and moments later, he was speaking to one of his brothers. "Hi, Jayce. I'm looking for Kurt. Do you have his number?"

Jayce must've asked what he needed it for, because Dante frowned and said, "It's kind of personal."

He listened for a few seconds and then let out a deep sigh. "I need one of his special skills, if you know what I mean."

He glanced at Mallory. "Yeah, I'm with my girlfriend. But she's cool. She's the one who needs his help."

Dante glanced around the kitchen frantically, as if looking for something. Mallory guessed it might be pencil and paper. She pulled a notepad and pen out of her junk drawer. He smiled and took them.

"Can you repeat that number?"

He jotted down the phone number and said, "Thanks." After a brief pause, he grinned at her, but he was still speaking to his brother. "Yeah, you'll probably meet her at Sunday dinner sometime."

Dante laughed and hung up. She wondered what his brother had said but figured it was none of her business. If he wanted to tell her, he would.

"I have the number, and Jayce thinks he'll help us— especially if I mention that I'm his brother. Apparently, he hangs out at a tearoom on Charles Street. We can ask to meet him there."

"A tearoom?"

"Yeah, I've never been there…or to any tearoom for that matter," Dante said. "Is there anything I should know if we go there? Do I need to stick out my pinky finger while I'm sipping tea?"

She laughed. "I don't think so, but I'd like to see that."

———∿∿∿———

Bored, Noah figured he'd rebuild his lab and try the alchemy formula again—only this time, he'd ban Dante from touching anything until he was completely ready and there to supervise. Going through the box of vials and beakers that had miraculously survived the blast, he wrote down the items he needed to replace.

No matter how he tried to distract himself, however, Kizzy kept returning to his mind. He couldn't help wondering if his being a "mere firefighter" was working against him. Or if he might be too young for her. He had never asked her how old she was. He thought that was some kind of politically incorrect question these days.

Kizzy must be a little older than he was. She had to go to school for at least eight years out of high school, so that made her at least twenty-six. She was probably closer to Dante's age. Unless she was one of those genius kids who graduated at fifteen. Even if she was still paying off student loans, she had the potential for making a lot more money than he ever would.

Glancing at his watch, he realized she'd be getting out of work soon. Did she really have family issues she had to take care of? The fact that she wouldn't elaborate on what they were set off his inquisitiveness, and he needed answers when his curiosity was aroused.

He had to go out anyway to resupply his lab, so he had an excuse to nose around a bit…but he didn't want to stalk her. At least, he didn't want to *get caught* stalking her!

The answer was simple but not easy. Shift and fly above her. Most people never look up, but just in case, he'd need to disguise his red and yellow tail feathers. He could shop for supplies anytime. Right now, if he could catch sight of her leaving the ER, he could—ahem—tail her.

The apartment had a fireplace that hadn't been used in years. The landlord made them sign an addendum in their contract, saying they wouldn't light fires in it. He and Dante had already checked the inside and found it was full of creosote. Very flammable but perfect for covering colorful tail feathers. The dark gunk would stick like glue.

Noah opened the flue and stripped down naked. "Up the hatch." Then he shifted and flew up the chimney, dragging his tail feathers against the filthy wall. Fortunately, being a paranormal and not a real bird, the extra weight on his feathers didn't matter. He was stronger and could still fly, even bogged down with extra weight.

Thus disguised, he sailed over the Boston rush-hour traffic, wishing he could commute this way all the time. If paranormals were out of the closet, he could even carry his uniform in his powerful beak. Wouldn't that be a sight to see!

Finding his way easily to Boston General, he perched

in a tree by the staff parking lot. She'd said she com-
muted with her sister whenever possible. Hopefully,
they'd come out together and get into one of these cars.
Since her sister was a nurse, he bypassed the doctor's
exclusive parking spaces up front. He didn't think she'd
stand on ceremony and insist she'd earned the right to be
there if she were riding in her sister's car.

About half an hour later, Kizzy and Ruth emerged
from the hospital and got into a Prius. Ruth was in the
driver's seat and Kizzy on the passenger side. Happily, it
was a nice day, and they rolled down the windows. Now
he could easily eavesdrop as well as follow them. *Score!*

"I just don't understand why Dad wants us both to stay
in his house until this threat has passed."

That was Kizzy's voice. Noah realized how little he
knew about her. Where did she grow up? That house in
Brookline where Dante said he'd picked her up? What
schools did she go to? Were there others in her family he
just hadn't heard about yet? Their relationship had barely
begun, and now it seemed to be on hold for the unforesee-
able future. *Damn. I finally found someone I can't get out
of my head, and something is wrong.*

Was he really doing the right thing by following her?
What if he slipped up later, and something came out of his
mouth that she had told her sister—not him?

Ruth was speaking now. "Dad's always been a worry-
wart. You know that. Besides, I really do think we'd be
safer there with all the wards in place."

Kizzy worried her lip. "Is there something you're not
telling me? Is everything okay between you and Gordon?"

"Oh yes! Totally." Ruth sighed. "I may have down-
played the danger a bit. But he was fine with it. He said if

I wanted to stay with my dad a few days, he could occupy himself with a new hobby."

"What new hobby?"

Ruth shrugged. "I don't know. He hadn't mentioned anything before that. I was just grateful he didn't mind my leaving, so I didn't ask."

After a long silence, Kizzy spoke again. "Yesterday, you said someone was after the book. Are they gunning for us too?"

"I can't be sure, but the malevolence and determination are there. I have the feeling they would stop at nothing to get that book."

"Fudge!"

The women remained silent again for several minutes. Traffic was terrible, and Ruth may have been concentrating on driving rather than talking. He wished they would speak again. And he wished this traffic was moving faster. Circling above their car made him feel like a vulture.

When they picked up their conversation, he wanted to get close again. Landing on the roof gently, he was able to hear every word perfectly. He wanted to hear more about this danger.

"I hope this threat doesn't last forever. I want to be able to relax in my own home."

That was Kizzy talking. He wondered where her real home was. Dante had picked her up for the basketball game at a house in Brookline, someplace he described as a big brick house. Perhaps she had an apartment in someone else's home. It struck him as odd that he didn't know, but he'd have to let it go—for now. He wanted answers about this threat first.

"And I hope I don't have to stay more than a day

or two. My dear fiancé can't boil water. He'll miss my cooking."

Kizzy chuckled. "I'm sure Gordon would miss you for more than that."

"Oh yeah. I'll miss him for that too."

They laughed.

The traffic finally moved again. They made their way through Kenmore Square, heading toward Brookline. He imagined that being the daughter of a doctor, she may have grown up in one of the pricey mansions on the elite side of town. A big brick mansion.

Finally, just over the Boston-Brookline town line, they headed down a tree-lined side street with beautiful old homes. Some brick, some stone, all traditional. None were palatial or on acres of property. Pulling into the driveway of a modest brick colonial with pristine landscaping, they shut off the engine and got out. It was a home—probably three or four bedrooms, in contrast with some of the huge mansions he'd seen farther from the city.

Instead of going to the front door, they walked down the driveway and entered a side door. There was some kind of panel beside the door, and Kizzy poked a few buttons. Probably an alarm or keyless entry—or both.

After checking the perimeter, Noah perched in a tree overlooking the back porch. He hoped they'd take advantage of the beautiful weather and sit outside so he could eavesdrop some more. He wanted more information about this threat.

Almost as helpful, the kitchen window was open about halfway, and they gathered there. A man joined them with a hearty greeting.

"How are my girls?"

Unless he was Charlie and they were Charlie's Angels, he guessed the guy must be their father.

"Hi, Daddy," Ruth said.

"Kizzy? Are you all right?"

"Yeah. Just a little preoccupied."

"I hope you're not still mooning over that firefighter. Did you break up with him like I told you to?"

A moment later, the sound of a car stopping out front drew his attention, but he wasn't moving from his spot until he heard what she had to say.

"Not exactly."

"What do you mean, not exactly?"

"I told him I had a family situation and that I wouldn't be available for a while."

Sounding frustrated, Kizzy's father said, "I told you a firefighter is not a good choice." Then after blowing out a deep breath, he added, "At least you put him off. That way, you can let him down easy."

"What if I don't want to let him down?"

Silence followed, and Noah tried to picture what his old man's face would look like when one of his brothers defied "orders." *Ugh. Not good.*

"Speaking of *the real threat* here," Ruth interjected, "they're still in the area, but our wards and shields are holding them off."

"Can you detect their presence when you're inside the wards, Ruth?" their father asked.

"No, I can't. The wards are strong enough to shield us from them, but they could be at the front door this minute and I wouldn't know it."

Noah flitted to the roof where he could still hear the

people inside and peeked over the top of the house to see what was going on out front.

"I'm thankful for the wards doing their jobs, but I'm a little nervous about your being here, since they're shielding your power," the elder Dr. Samuels said. "I've been thinking of your safety and the safety of the book while I'm at work, and I'm seriously considering hiring a bodyguard for both of you."

"A what? How in the world is that not going to attract attention?" Kizzy asked.

"I thought about that too, of course. You can each take a leave of absence. Ruth, since you're more psychic and can sense danger approaching, you can go home, but you need to stay put. You'll also know if someone is poking around, and maybe you can call and tell us where they are."

Noah spied two men getting out of a white sedan. They were eyeing the home but not walking up to the door. What could they want?

"And me?" Kizzy asked.

"You'll stay here. I need you to protect the book. I've heard of a shifter PI I'd like to hire to protect you, just in case."

"A private investigator? I thought you said I needed a bodyguard?"

"Ah! Here's the genius of my plan. The guy is a wolf shifter. Now hear me out. This is a bit unorthodox, but desperate times call for desperate measures."

"A werewolf! How desperate are we?"

"You can fake temporary blindness, and *if* you have to go anywhere, he can be your seeing-eye dog."

"Dad! Are you kidding me?"

"No. I'm not. Kizzy, he comes highly recommended. He used to be a Boston PD cop. At the same time, if anything raises red flags, he can investigate. And, if absolutely necessary, he can rip the schnitzel out of an assailant."

Noah had one eye on the guys out front, but they didn't look very threatening. *What assailant would require a werewolf for protection?* He took a closer measure of the men strolling up and down the sidewalk, gazing at the house. And did Dr. Samuels mention a shifter? That meant he knew of such things.

Ruth laughed. "A seeing-eye wolf. Who'd believe that?"

"He isn't an arctic wolf with a thick coat. He could pass for some kind of German Shepherd mix. His name is Nick Wolfensen, and he'll be over later to meet you."

"So, I guess this is a done deal," Kizzy said.

"Not yet. I'll let you meet him first, but if you don't want me to stick to your side like glue all day, you'll give him a chance. Any questions?"

"Would it matter if I don't want any part of this?"

"And do what? Just go on vacation and leave us here to fend for ourselves?"

Kizzy let out a long sigh. "No. Of course not."

"Then I would ask you to keep an open mind."

The conversation ended when Ruth decided to head home. When the side door opened, the two unidentified guys jogged back to their car and got in. They pulled away from the curb and headed down the street before Ruth backed out of the driveway.

⁓

Dante and Mallory walked hand in hand down Charles Street, admiring the old Beacon Hill neighborhood. They glanced up when they saw a teapot hanging from a sign. There was even steam coming out of it. That in itself seemed paranormal.

"We're meeting the wizard here?"

"Yeah. Shhhh…" Dante glanced at the people up and down the sidewalk, but no one seemed to pay them any notice. He opened the door for her, and Mallory walked in hesitantly.

Once inside, she whispered, "I don't see a big curtain hiding a bald guy and lots of levers. How will we know who he is?"

A guy with close-cropped black hair approached them.

"I think he's finding us."

The man stuck out his right hand and introduced himself. "Hi, I'm Kurt. You're the ones who called me."

It wasn't a question. He obviously knew who they were. *How* he knew was anyone's guess. Hopefully he was just a very good wizard. That's what she needed right now.

Dante shook his hand. "I'm Dante Fierro. Nice to meet you, Kurt. And this is my girlfriend, Mallory. She's the one who needs your help."

Kurt stepped back as soon as he looked at her eyes. "Oh shit," he muttered.

Mallory hoped he was struck by her beauty and not some gross aura all over her, but she guessed it was the latter. Could he see her curse?

"What's wrong?" Dante asked.

Kurt folded his arms. "I think we'd better go

somewhere private to discuss this. The owner is a good friend of mine and said he'd let us use the unoccupied apartment upstairs. Follow me."

He led them back outside to a separate entrance, unlocked it, and they traipsed up to a second-floor landing where he unlocked another door. He preceded them inside and held the door as they entered the sparsely furnished living room.

As soon as he locked the door behind them, Mallory asked, "What did you see?" She couldn't wait until they sat down and got comfortable.

"I'm not sure yet. Something… Have a seat. I have a few supplies in the kitchen to get."

She and Dante sat on the gray L-shaped couch. She took his hand.

"Don't worry. It'll be all right." He squeezed her hand and smiled.

Of course he would try to reassure her, no matter what was wrong, but that wasn't exactly what she needed right now. She needed the truth. She hoped the wizard would give her answers.

Kurt returned with a couple of glasses of water and set them on the coffee table on top of coasters. *Wait a minute*. Had those coasters been there a moment ago?

Crap. I'm having a Twilight Zone *moment.*

While Kurt returned to the kitchen, Dante put his arm around her shoulder and rubbed her upper arm soothingly. "Are you as nervous as you seem?"

"Probably. As long as I seem like I'm barely held together with Scotch tape."

Dante gave her a side squeeze. "Don't worry. We'll turn that Scotch tape into duct tape. You'll be okay."

She couldn't help chuckling. She might settle for the secure feeling of being duct-taped together right now.

Kurt returned with a bowl and a duffel bag. He set the bowl on the coffee table in front of himself. It appeared to contain plain water.

"What's all the water for?" Dante asked.

Kurt looked up. "Well, this"—he pointed to the bowl—"is for scrying. The two glasses are for you to drink. I'd offer you a glass of wine or a soda, but there's nothing in the fridge."

Mallory wasn't sure if she should drink the water. Could she trust the wizard?

Dante picked up his glass and took a sip. She waited a few beats and when he didn't choke or keel over, she figured it was just regular old water. *Okay, Mallory. Your imagination is running away with you.*

Kurt opened his duffel bag and pulled out a few items. A candle, a bell, a few sticks, and some sparkling dirt. What was he was going to do with all that? He put the duffel bag down next to his chair. "Stick your finger in the bowl of water, Mallory."

She glanced over at Dante, and he nodded. So she stuck her finger in it, and Kurt scooted forward, staring at the ripples.

"Is that it? Can I take my finger out now?"

"Not just yet."

He just stared at the water, like he was mesmerized by it. She couldn't help wondering what he was looking at or searching for. She scooted forward and tried to see something in the reflection of her finger and hand. The movement caused a few more ripples.

Kurt sat back and muttered, "Hmm…"

"What did you see?"

He narrowed his gaze at the water. "I'm afraid you're cursed, all right. I witnessed a ritual. Definitely a group I'm not familiar with. Is there any reason someone might be angry with you? I saw a jungle-like setting. The people looked Northern European, with light hair, skin, and eyes, but wearing brown wool clothing, and they seemed hot and sweaty, like their clothes were out of place."

"Mallory... Did you go on safari recently?" Dante asked.

Horror replaced confusion in her brain. "I didn't, but maybe my father did. He's in South America, building a huge resort right on the banks of the Amazon River."

"That's where your parents are? That's why you didn't want them to know about any of this?" Dante asked.

"Yes. This deal is my father's baby. He wants to offer Amazon adventures to people with lots of money who want to pretend they're roughing it, and then when it's all over, they'll go back to his five-star hotel. Of course, there will be plenty of spouses who want nothing to do with hacking their way through a jungle, or whatever, and will gladly wait at the resort and spa."

"He must've pissed off someone," Kurt said.

"There could be activists in the rain forest that my father's cutting down. As if the place hasn't been ruined enough." Mallory sighed.

"Can you break the curse?" Dante asked.

Kurt scratched his head. "I don't know. If I knew what sort of curse they put on her, I could definitely undo it. As it is, I'm just flying blind."

"Would it help if you knew the weird things that were happening to her?"

Mallory bolted upright. "That's kind of personal."

Kurt looked from Dante to Mallory and back. "It might help, but I don't want to make the lady uncomfortable."

Mallory felt silly for overreacting. It wasn't as if she was bleeding green during her periods. "I'm sorry. Of course. I'll tell you. It's just going to sound crazy."

Kurt laughed. "I married a vampire. Crazy is my middle name."

Dante didn't blink. Surely, he couldn't believe in vampires... *Oh crap.* The back of her neck prickled. Were vampires real too? She suddenly felt light-headed.

One crisis at a time, Mallory.

She tried to take slow, easy breaths and calm the hell down. "Okay. Here goes. I see dead people. And I turn into a spider monkey sometimes. It started about two months ago, I think."

Kurt didn't seem at all shocked. He just nodded and said, "Turning into a spider monkey makes sense if a South American jungle is the origin of the curse. That's their habitat. Dead people? That could be from anyone anywhere, but I get the sense that there's only one curse, and it's only from this group. The two symptoms must be related."

"So what do monkeys and dead people have to do with one another?" Dante asked.

Kurt shrugged. "I wish I knew. At least I know more now than I did five minutes ago. I think I can try a general curse-breaking, and hopefully it will work—at least partially."

"Hopefully?" Dante repeated.

"If I knew more, I could be sure. All I can guarantee is I'll do my best."

"Of course," Mallory said. "I'm so grateful for your help. I hope you know that."

Kurt laughed. "Your money is gratitude enough."

Mallory hadn't realized there was money involved. She felt like a doofus. Of course there was money involved! Who did this out of the goodness of their heart? Had Dante offered to pay him? How much did this kind of service cost? She leaned in closer to Dante and whispered, "How much does he charge?"

"Your firstborn," Kurt said, deadpan. A moment later he laughed, hard.

Mallory must have been holding her breath, because it came out in a whoosh.

"Jesus, Kurt," Dante said. "Way to freak out a young lady."

"Sorry. I couldn't resist teasing her. And don't worry about the money, Mallory. Dante told me you lost your job."

Maybe Dante had wrangled a discount. Or perhaps the wizard *did* have a big heart—along with a weird sense of humor.

Kurt poured a mound of sparkly dirt in the middle of the water bowl. Then he stuck a few sticks in the middle of it. "Now, close your eyes and concentrate on your breath. Try to empty your mind and just follow your breathing as if it's the only thing you need to think about right now."

"Is that because I might stop breathing if I don't think about how to do it?" Mallory asked.

"No." Kurt chuckled. "I just don't want you putting

any crap from your brain into my spell. You could inadvertently do that because you're so closely tied to this curse. Thoughts are very powerful things. Emotions follow thoughts. If you think about your breaths and nothing else, there's less chance of your affecting the outcome. Make sense?"

"Yeah. I think so."

"Then do it."

Something about this guy seemed military. She wanted to say *Sir, yes, sir*, but instead she just closed her eyes and did as he directed. *Breathe in. Breathe out. Breathe in. Breathe out…*

A few moments later, she smelled something burning. Fortunately, she was sitting next to a firefighter, so she wasn't too worried. Dante would say something if the guy was about to set the place on fire.

Kurt was mumbling something in another language. She had no idea whether it was Latin, Spanish, or some indigenous language. She began to wonder how he would know that, then redirected her thoughts back to her breathing and just hoped it worked.

Suddenly her brain felt weird. She took her head in her hands. "Ohhh…"

Dante grabbed her shoulders to steady her. "Are you okay?"

She opened her eyes. "Yeah. Something just made me really dizzy. It didn't hurt. I'm okay. Sorry if I scared you."

Dante let out a deep breath. "Don't be sorry. I'm just glad you're all right." His attention snapped to Kurt. "Does that mean it worked? Is the curse broken now?"

Kurt shrugged. "Maybe."

"When will we know?" Dante asked.

"When nothing happens to her for a long, long time."

"It sounds like you're saying wait and see."

"Yup."

Mallory wanted to utter something sarcastic, like "awesome," but this guy was trying to help. Waiting would be hard, but she really had no choice. She could hardly criticize him, even if the effort turned out to be futile. He did say he was flying blind... Maybe the bargain price was a "guinea pig" discount.

Noah and Dante were eating a hasty dinner before leaving their apartment for their next twenty-four-hour shifts. They were in their uniforms and ready to go.

Noah had to work up his courage to confront his brother—it was now or never. "Look, Bro. I know you think you love her, but you've got to be kidding me... She's cursed! Hasn't it occurred to you that maybe everyone close to her will be cursed too?"

"I'm fine."

"So far."

Dante leaned back and crossed his arms. "What are you suggesting?"

To avoid a hasty answer, Noah shoved a bite of his chicken pot pie into his mouth. He thought it was going to burn a hole in his tongue, but he was a phoenix. He could always grow a new one in his next incarnation.

"I'm not saying you don't have a right to your opinion," Dante continued for him, "but I'd prefer it if you'd keep it to yourself. Telling me what you think isn't going to make a damn bit of difference."

"I was afraid of that," Noah said.

"Afraid? What are you afraid of? Do you think you're going to *catch it*?"

"I'm not afraid for myself. I'm afraid for you, dick-head."

Dante picked up the remainder of his chicken pot pie and tossed it in the garbage. "I said I was fine," he ground out between clenched teeth. "Maybe you're just jealous because I have a relationship and you don't."

"For fuck's sake… Stop thinking with your dick! Dante, the only hope for Mallory is professional help, and you shouldn't enable her to avoid it."

Dante whirled on him. "You know what? I don't think this living arrangement is working. We're too close and can't stay out of each other's business. At least, *you* can't stay out of *mine*."

Noah recoiled as if he'd been slapped. He didn't have a chance to do anything about it, since Dante stormed off, slamming the door. Hopefully, twenty-four hours on his own would help him calm down and see things logically.

Noah groaned. Who was he kidding? Dante was the emotional one—he saw with his heart. He admired the fact that his brother was in touch with that side of himself, but also found it frustrating as hell. When Dante didn't want to see something, he was capable of ignoring reality.

Maybe he was right this time. Maybe they were getting a little too close for comfort, and it was time to find their own places. The thought saddened him.

As Noah put his leftovers in the fridge, he thought about that alchemy formula. He almost had it all worked out. He was about to substitute the more volatile ingredient with a benign one, but hadn't replaced it before Dante touched something and set it off. Next time would be different.

The neighbors had just moved out. With his and Dante's paranormal hearing, they'd discovered the people thought they might be cooking meth and that's what led to the explosion. If Dante left, he wouldn't have to worry about anyone messing with his process. Before someone else moved in, he should give that experiment another try—without Dante's dubious help. But that would mean no safety backup either. His whole family was close. Anyone would stick out their necks for one of their own. It was the same with the fire service. Maybe that's why he and Dante hadn't recognized that getting mixed up in each other's love lives was a problem.

Noah pushed those thoughts aside and focused instead on whatever Kizzy was going through.

He'd heard bits and pieces of her conversation with her father after Ruth left. Mostly work related. He didn't hear any more about Kizzy's feelings for him, but he didn't expect her to discuss that in depth with her father. He would have liked more than a mere mention—or maybe not. The elder Dr. Samuels seemed to have his mind made up. Noah just wished he knew why.

The only thing he really got out of eavesdropping on the three of them was that their father was definitely in charge. He would have to win over her old man. If the guy knew Noah could take care of his little girl, that would go a long way.

And that meant he needed money. If that's what was *really* motivating her father's disapproval, he could have an unlimited supply with alchemy gold. He'd try the procedure with iron next time. All that lead exposure made him nervous. He could get loads of shavings at the ironworks. He'd go right there after his shift. Chances were Dante would be spending every spare minute with Mallory, but he hoped they'd have a chance to talk at some point.

He didn't dislike Mallory. Who could? She seemed like a nice enough girl, if you didn't know she shape-shifted into a monkey at inopportune times and couldn't tell the dead from the living...

Chapter 8

THE GROUP DESCENDED FROM NAZI WAR CRIMINALS WAS meeting in secret. Observing the developer from a distance, the failure of their spell and continued major development in the area was infuriating them.

For this group, the forest had been a safe haven. Their parents and grandparents had fully indoctrinated them with the message of the SS. They believed at some point they would rise again. They would purify their race and—with the secrets contained in the occult books—they would become gods.

If tourists invaded the area, it would only be a matter of time before members of *the entity* were discovered. If anyone realized what their mission was before they obtained the other two books, they wouldn't stop until there was no chance to realize their destiny.

"I don't know why he hasn't left," the commandant groused. "His child must be suffering. Maybe he just doesn't care about her."

Another member frowned. "I cannot imagine a man who could avoid our curse. Who would be so callous to his children—besides maybe us, if sacrifice were absolutely necessary? He must be a monster. He must be stopped."

The group glanced at each other and spoke among themselves quietly.

"This developer is becoming more than a nuisance," the commandant said.

His second-in-command nodded. "I wish I could feed him to the crocodiles."

"My trusted advisor and grandson will find the other books, and then the interlopers won't matter. We will renew our commitment to world—no, *universe*—domination."

"Have they reported any progress on their mission?"

"Apparently, they tracked one book to a neighborhood just outside the city. They cannot pinpoint its location unless it's in use."

"What does that mean? Is one of the books in use and the other not?"

"I believe the books are in the hands of someone who knows nothing about how to use them."

"Or perhaps the books are not together. If one party has one book, and a totally separate party has the other book, they cannot be very useful. The ingredients were put in one book and the words of the spells were put in the other."

"Yes. And we need them all. All we have is the index and some bits and pieces the elders remembered before they died. We know what the contents of all three books can do. We need those other books!"

"I was thinking about the code. I believe the page numbers refer to the words that go with the correct ingredients, and that is only known to us. If they guess incorrectly and put the wrong pages together, they will either get nothing—"

"Or get the surprise of their lives." The second-in-command laughed out loud.

"Even that would be helpful, as long as the books aren't destroyed. If they use the books at all, we can find them."

"Are you sure they can't be tracked down unless the books are being used, Commandant?" one of the younger members asked. "How did we find the area they are in?"

"And how do we know both books are in the same area if we've only sensed one in use?" asked another.

"*We* did nothing. *I* traced the books with a special locator spell," the second-in-command said and rolled his eyes. "It is a spell only an occult master can perform. I was able to narrow down the location significantly before sending the commandant's advisor and grandson there. I wouldn't send them on a futile errand."

"Of course not. Forgive me," the young man said.

"So... Have they reported in?" the other young man asked.

"They have. As I mentioned before, one of the books has been used, and they have tracked it to a neighborhood. The exact home is eluding them. How would I know that if they hadn't checked in?"

The doubter seemed satisfied for the moment, although the commandant was hoping their agents would have made better progress by now.

"Perhaps you can help them with another locator spell?" someone else suggested.

The commandant snorted. "If that were possible, don't you think I would have instructed one of my SS to do so?"

"Of course, Commandant. I apologize. It's just very frustrating to watch what's going on around us, knowing our ultimate mission could be in jeopardy."

"We are doing everything we can."

He didn't like being questioned or having demands

put upon him. It was the price of leadership, and he would not give up his seat of power, but the uncertainty was stressful.

"Why are you all sitting around?" he demanded.

The other members jumped to their feet and scattered.

Power felt good. No, power felt *wunderbar*. He couldn't wait to become a god!

Sunday dinner at the Fierros' was always a big deal. But this was Luca's graduation day! So many people would be gathered around the huge dining room table that two leaves had to be inserted to accommodate everyone. Their entertaining space had become so cramped, Antonio had finally taken down the wall between the living and dining rooms.

Mrs. Fierro was in the kitchen—correction: *two* of the Mrs. Fierros. Misty was helping Gabriella cook. Kristine had to beg off because her mother was in labor. Being present at the birth of her little brother or sister was all she'd been talking about for months.

"I hear Dante is bringing someone today," Misty said.

Gabriella smiled broadly. "Yes. He has a new girlfriend. He said to set another place for a young woman named Mallory. Apparently, he's known her since high school."

"Mallory? Not Mallory Summers."

"Yes, I think that was her name. Why? Do you know her?"

"Yeah. I think everyone we went to school with knew Mallory, or at least knew *of* her. She was homecoming queen *and* prom queen one year. And she was nice. Not stuck up like a lot of the popular girls."

"I can't wait to meet her," Gabriella said.

The sound of the front door opening and greetings from the living room reached Gabriella's human ears. A paranormal would have heard them coming up the steps.

Gabriella wiped her hands on a kitchen towel. "Can you take over for me here, Misty dear? I need to say hello and meet Dante's young lady."

"Of course. I'll stir the sauce. Don't worry."

Gabriella strode to the living room and was struck by the beautiful blonde standing beside her son Dante, gazing at him adoringly. Nothing could have made Gabriella happier than to have that look be her first impression of Dante's girl.

Dante ignored all the men in the living room and strolled over to his mother, holding the girl's hand. "Ma, I'd like you to meet Mallory Summers. Mallory, this is my mother, Gabriella." He dropped her hand but stayed close.

Mallory shook her hand. "It's nice to meet you, Gabriella."

The girl's blue gaze met her own without blinking, and Gabriella was relieved that the young woman seemed sincere. She could read people well and spot a phony a mile away.

"I'm delighted to meet you too, dear! Usually, I have to tell people to call me Gabriella after they call me Mrs. Fierro a couple of times. I'm glad you felt comfortable using my first name. We're very informal around here."

"Yes. Dante said you were."

Misty called out from the kitchen, "Gabriella, is the oven supposed to smoke like this?"

Everyone in the room snapped to attention. With so

many firefighters in the family, you couldn't say the word *smoke* without several ears perking up.

Antonio was first into the kitchen, with Gabriella right behind him. Following her were Miguel, Jayce, and Luca. Misty opened the oven door, and a billowing cloud of smoke poured out.

Gabriella spotted last night's Pyrex baking dish with blackening Alfredo sauce. "Oh my goodness. How did that dish get in there?"

Luca grimaced. "Um…you know how you asked me to clean up the kitchen last night, Ma?"

Gabriella grabbed her oven mitts and scowled at her youngest son. "Yes. I do remember. And I remember you saying you would."

"Well, the game was about to start," he admitted sheepishly. "I just put the leftovers in the fridge and stuck the dish back in the oven so that the kitchen would look clean, but I'd planned to get to it later."

"And you forgot until I preheated the oven," Gabriella said as she extracted the burnt baking dish, still smoking. She set it on the counter and opened the back window to air out the room.

"Sorry, Mom," Luca said.

She sighed. "Well, be careful when you're living on your own. I don't want one of your brothers to have to respond to a fire in your apartment building."

"Jeez, Mom. I'm not ten. You don't have to worry about me setting my apartment on fire."

"You're getting your own apartment?" Dante asked.

"Yeah. After graduation from the police academy." Then with an embarrassed grin, he added, "Or when Mom and Dad kick me out, whichever comes first."

Gabriella almost teared up. This was her youngest son, her baby, about to graduate from college with a degree in criminal justice. How could all of her sons be so grown-up now? Soon, her husband would be bugging her to move to a warmer climate again.

She wanted to wait until *all* her sons were happily married before moving so far away, and Antonio had been patient. Well, as patient as an impatient man could be. But now she didn't want to move at all. They had a grandson, and hopefully more would come along. What if anyone needed her to babysit? She couldn't do it from the Caribbean.

She suddenly noticed her kitchen was full of faces she loved: Antonio, Jayce, Miguel, Sandra, Misty, Gabe, holding six-month-old Tony, and twenty-one-year-old Luca, even if she was a little miffed with him at the moment.

The only two she couldn't see were Mallory and Dante. Unless she missed her guess, they were probably still in the living room, stealing kisses. The chemistry between them was obvious. She'd bet money another wedding would take place before long. *What beautiful babies those two could make!*

When the oven had stopped smoking, she placed the huge casserole dish of lasagna in it. She could tell by smell when something was done, but just to be on the safe side, she set the kitchen timer for sixty minutes.

"Gabriella, why don't you go sit down and get to know Dante's new friend," Sandra said. "Misty and I can finish up here."

Misty had the salad halfway prepared. The French bread was on the counter.

"I guess there's no reason not to. Thank you, darling. Maybe I will. If you could slice the bread and get it ready to warm in tin foil… You just mix together garlic butter and a little salt—"

Sandra chuckled. "I've seen you do it a hundred times. I can handle it."

Maybe Gabriella wasn't as essential to this family as she had previously thought. "All right." She removed her apron and joined the others who had traipsed back into the dining room. "Let's all sit and have a glass of wine while we wait for dinner," Gabriella said.

Nobody argued, and she didn't expect they would. She brought a bottle of Chianti and a corkscrew to the table and then retrieved glasses from the hutch. Antonio opened the wine bottle and set it aside to breathe.

"Hey, Dad, when did you knock down the wall between the living and dining room? And why didn't you go all the way to the kitchen?" Dante asked. "I think they call that 'open concept,' and it seems everyone wants that now."

"I did it about a month ago. Your mother didn't want open concept, where everyone could look at a mountain of dirty dishes, and you know how she is about people in her kitchen when she's trying to cook. Besides, we had to leave the structural wall alone. Otherwise, the ceiling would be on your head now. You haven't been here for a whole month?"

"Nope. Didn't you miss me?" Dante said with a smirk.

The patriarch smirked right back at him. "I can't keep my sons straight. You all look alike to me."

Everyone around the table laughed, except Gabriella. His teasing was meant in fun, but any of her sons could take it as an insult. Oh well. As long as it was *Antonio* talking, they'd know it was just a joke.

The man was rarely serious now that he'd retired from the fire department. All job stress suddenly removed was good for some firefighters, not so much for others. Thank heavens Antonio was enjoying his retirement fully. There were some alarming statistics about retired firefighters passing away after only five years away from the job.

Each of her boys was very different from the rest. Her firstborn, Ryan, was...well... He was supposed to be dead and couldn't visit often just in case anyone caught sight of him, but he'd be popping in later to congratulate Luca on his graduation. He'd been reincarnated and was living in Ireland with his dragon queen, in a castle.

Jayce, now the eldest, was lighthearted and social. The others respected him, knowing he'd be leading this family someday. But just to be on the safe side, Antonio co-appointed Miguel to take over.

Miguel, next in line, was serious and a rule follower.

Gabe was all quiet strength. Loyal beyond question.

Dante, well—he was a little bit of everything. More like Jayce than anyone else though. A little flirty with the girls, but definitely a man's man.

Noah was curious and smart. She might worry about his gentleness, except that unlike her other quiet sons, he had no problem speaking his mind when he wanted to.

And Luca... Ah, Luca. Her youngest. They called him the baby—and now *the blue sheep*; however, he was anything but. He'd been asserting himself ever since deciding to buck the family tradition and become a cop, maybe to overcompensate and prove himself an adult. She hoped not. He could get into a lot of trouble trying to out-macho all the men around the table and prove he wasn't "the baby" anymore.

As she gazed around the table, she realized someone was missing. "Where's Noah?" Antonio wasn't the only one who messed up occasionally and missed a son, although it rarely happened to her. Noah hadn't called to say he wouldn't be coming, so maybe he was just delayed.

"Dante, did Noah say anything about being late?" Antonio asked.

"Not to me."

Something about his too-casual shrug set off her warning bells. "Is everything all right between you two?"

Dante heaved a big sigh. "Jeez, Mom. I swear you're psychic."

She would have chuckled if she weren't so concerned. "What's going on?"

He glanced at Mallory, but before he could respond, she said with eyes downcast, "It's my fault."

Dante was quick to disagree. "No, it isn't."

Gabriella wondered at that. Was there competition for Mallory's affections? She was certainly beautiful enough to inspire male rivalry.

Then Jayce, thank goodness, put it into words. "Is he jealous?"

"No. Nothing like that. He just can't keep his nose out of my business."

"Well, it's no wonder, honey. You've been best friends since you were little, and now you're roommates," she began. She didn't quite know where she was going with the conversation, so she couldn't help being grateful when the phone rang. "I'll get it," Gabriella sang out. Hopefully, it was son number six, explaining his absence.

The phone was on the wall in the kitchen, where it had been for a couple of decades. She grabbed it without looking at the caller ID. "Noah?"

"No, it's Kristine."

"Oh, Kristine! Did your mother have the baby?"

"Yes! I have a little sister!"

"Oh, that's so exciting!" Gabriella stuck her hand over the mouthpiece and poked her head around the doorjamb. "We have an announcement! Amy's had her little dra—I mean, baby! It's a girl!" *Oh my goodness. I almost let the word dragon slip out in front of a human stranger!*

"Congratulations, Kristine!" many voices yelled at once.

"So, are mother and baby doing well?"

"Yes," Kristine said. "Tell everyone both are healthy and my stepdad is thrilled beyond belief. Also, please tell Luca I'm sorry I couldn't be at his graduation. I'll try to stop by in a few hours."

"Oh, don't worry, darling. Everyone understands."

They exchanged a few more good wishes and then hung up. Before Gabriella made it back to her seat, the phone rang again.

"I'll get it." She spun around and went back the way she came. "Hello?"

"Yeah. Hi, Mom. I'm not going to make it for dinner today."

She paused for effect. "And why not?"

"I—I have some important stuff to do."

"Why does it sound like you're not telling me the real reason, Noah?"

"That *is* the real reason!"

"Hmph. And this 'important stuff' is more important than your family? Including your brother's college graduation? He's only the first Fierro to graduate from a four-year college right out of high school."

Noah groaned. "I'm sorry, Mom. I'll try to come by later. If it makes you feel any better, it's about a girl."

"Which girl?"

"Huh? Kizzy. Who else would it be?"

"Fine. Well, come over when you get the chance. I want to hear more about this doctor girlfriend of yours." Then she brightened. "Or maybe you can bring her with you! I'd love to see her again."

He sighed. "I doubt she'll come."

Something wasn't going well there, but she wasn't about to get into it while everyone was within earshot. They said goodbye, and she finally returned to the table. "That was Noah. He'll be over later…and maybe he'll bring his new girlfriend. I don't know. He was very evasive."

Suddenly, Mallory began to shake uncontrollably.

"Babe?" Dante asked. He put an arm around her shoulders and murmured something into her ear.

The girl's bright-blue eyes were wide, as if she was afraid of something, and she quickly slipped under the table.

"I've got this," Dante said and held up one hand as if telling his family not to worry and leave everything to him. Then he slithered under the table too.

What the…

Gabriella's concern made her lean over and peek under the tablecloth. To her shock, a little monkey sat on the floor, hugging Dante's leg. Because the monkey was wearing Mallory's dress, it didn't take a genius to surmise that Mallory was a shape-shifter. And it appeared as if she didn't have terrific control over her shifts. Paranormals didn't just shift spontaneously in front of people they didn't know well.

Gabriella did a quick mental check of everyone. They were all aware of the paranormals living among them. Most were shape-shifters themselves. Misty was the newest member of the family, but she was comfortable with the "uniqueness" of the Fierro men—and in fact had her own unique abilities. Sandra was the only one who was a totally unadulterated human, but she'd been a part of this family for so long, she wouldn't bat an eyelash.

Gabriella smiled. "It's all right, Mallory. You can come out. We've all seen much weirder things."

Dante grinned at his mother. She resurfaced to see how the rest of the family was taking this. So far, everyone was being quiet and respectful.

Then Antonio peeked under the table and groaned. "Not another one…"

Gabriella gave him the stink eye. He winked at her, then stretched and yawned. "Yup. It's just another Sunday dinner at the Fierro house."

———

Kizzy had to admit she was missing Noah. He had been sweet and attentive and hadn't given up on her. He called her almost every night, and when he couldn't, he let her know why. He was the kind of dependable good guy she would have liked to have in her life—eventually.

She hated to defy her father, but it was her life. She was twenty-seven years old, for gods' and goddesses' sakes. She was still fighting with him over using a spell to cause temporary blindness in order to stay home, protecting the book. She understood that she would need an emergency leave, and certainly, a sudden loss of vision would preclude her from doing her job...but couldn't he come up with something better?

He wanted her to be safe, of course, but the idea of a seeing-eye wolf still rankled. Bostonians weren't likely to know the difference between a wolf and a dog, but what if she was visited by a colleague who hailed from Montana?

And what would she tell people when she got back? *Oh, it was hysterical blindness? It must have happened because I didn't want to see the news anymore? It's really depressing.* Or, *I poked myself in the eye really hard?* How could she explain something as dramatic as going blind?

So she became stubborn. Her father couldn't keep dictating what she should and shouldn't do. Especially who she should and shouldn't date. Wait a minute. *No, that couldn't have anything to do with it.*

Noah wasn't just gorgeous. He was interesting—in a geeky kind of way, but they had that in common. He told her about strolling around old bookstores, his interest in science, astronomy, as well as honing his skills as an EMT and firefighter. Plus she liked and respected him for all his charity work. Who wouldn't? She wanted to spend more time with him and get to know him better. At times, her mind wandered, and she fantasized about kissing him. Even that much got her panties damp.

One evening, during their nightly phone call, he asked her out to the firefighters' next charity event. It was really hard to say no to charity. And this was something a little goofy, but it sounded like fun. He was participating in the hot dog eating contest. He even mentioned that it might be handy to have a doctor close by in case of choking. How could she say no? Sure, all the firefighters were EMTs, but she was an ER doctor, and her presence might make them feel even safer—and for a good cause.

She agreed to go. Now she just had to come up with a story to tell her father, something that couldn't be a lie but wouldn't include the whole truth. She'd tell him she was going to volunteer her time at a charity event. The charity was raising money to benefit widows and orphans. The firemen's fund did benefit the kids, widows, and widowers of fallen firefighters. *That should do it.*

The day of the hot dog eating contest arrived, and Kizzy had her sister pick her up. The two of them were going together, and Daddy would stay home, guarding the book.

When Kizzy spotted Noah, she wanted to run to him and throw her arms around him. Instead, she decided to control herself and sneak up behind him, snaking her arms around his waist. No need to look like a teenager.

He stiffened and swiveled enough to see who it was. A grin split his face when he saw her. He turned around and lifted her off the ground as they shared a warm hug. It didn't seem like the right time and place for kissing him, but she wanted to. He greeted Ruth as if she were an old friend, giving her a quick hug too.

Long tables had been set up on a makeshift stage. The smell of hot dogs cooking filled the air. It wasn't the most pleasant odor, especially knowing how many disgusting things went into hot dogs. She didn't have to eat them, however, and Noah would be downing them for charity. She could always pump his stomach later.

Someone blew a whistle.

"I wish I had more time to talk with you, but they need me on stage."

"I understand. We'll talk later."

He swooped in for a quick kiss and jogged up the stairs of the platform. All the contestants found their seats, and piles of hot dogs were placed in front of them.

"Shouldn't they have buckets up there too?" Ruth asked, smirking.

Kizzy rolled her eyes. "I think they're disqualified if they vomit."

"I can't believe you agreed to watch this disgusting display. You must really like him."

She laughed. "Yeah, I guess I must."

When everyone was ready to go, the MC reiterated that one hundred percent of the money raised would go to the charity. It was for the families of fallen firefighters. The thought of Noah ever being one of those lost frightened her.

When the MC blew the whistle, all the contestants started wolfing down hot dog after hot dog.

Just watching Noah shoving more food into his mouth than was healthy, barely chewing, and swallowing down the mashed mess made her feel like turning green. The whole look was extremely unattractive.

Just then, one of the participants threw up. All.

Over. The crowd made the grossed-out sounds she'd be making if she weren't trying to be professional. But did she really want to watch this gluttony? Short answer, no. Longer answer, "Mother-hummer and her five sisters... get me outta here!"

"Really? You want to leave? I thought you were supposed to be on hand in case anyone chokes."

"If any more of them vomit, I'm going to too. Can you watch the fracas for me and tell me if anyone is in trouble? I'll pretend to look at my phone."

Ruth burst out laughing. "I'm pregnant and less nauseous than you are?" She gasped. "Unless you—"

"Whoa. Not even possible. Get that thought out of your head."

Ruth planted her hand on her hip. "Kizzy, you're a doctor. You've seen way worse things than this."

"I'd rather hold blood and guts in my bare hands. The minute this thing is over, I want to go for a walk."

"Not go out to lunch?" Ruth teased.

"Not right away, no."

Her sister, still giggling, watched the contest as Kizzy pretended to look at her phone.

"Oh shit. I've got to go."

"Why?"

"Massive trauma. They're calling me in."

"On your day off?"

"Yeah, it must be really serious."

"Let's go."

When the contest ended and Noah came in second, he looked around for Kizzy. She was nowhere to be found.

He'd had her in the corner of his eye at the beginning of the contest, then he was hunched over for the rest of it.

Glancing down at his mustard- and ketchup-stained shirt, he realized he should change his clothes before he saw her anyway. The guys were given a few temporary lockers inside the fitness center. He washed up and dressed, fearing the worst. What if she hadn't wanted to see him afterward? Did he disgust her now? Maybe he shouldn't have even told her about this stupid contest.

When he was finally dressed and clean, he went back out to the platform the sponsors were breaking down. The crowd had thinned out, and he still didn't see her. There was something glinting on the ground where she had been standing. He jogged over to it and noticed it was a phone with a sparkly gold sleeve. Kizzy's phone!

Suddenly, the ideas of an assailant and a threat became very real. *Oh shit! What happened?* Did somebody grab Kizzy and Ruth? Or did Kizzy just drop her phone without realizing it? He would've thought there would be a ruckus of some kind if the girls had been taken against their will. Or maybe his smart girl managed to hide herself somewhere else. Realizing that, he tamped down his temporary wave of panic and tried to think rationally.

Noah scanned the area, tapping into his paranormal senses, where he could smell and see farther and clearer than most humans. There was no sweet scent or anyone that resembled Kizzy or Ruth as far as he could see.

What the heck could he do now? He had her phone, but he didn't know the password. He had his own phone, but he didn't know Ruth's phone number or even her last name. Wait. Her last name would be Samuels if she wasn't married yet. Right? Maybe?

He quickly connected to the internet and looked up Ruth Samuels in the Boston white pages. If she had a landline, he could probably leave a voicemail. *No listings*. He could go town by town, hoping he'd happen upon some names to call and one of them was her. That would take way too long and was far too inefficient.

He was fighting with himself over the idea of going to her father's home. It would likely be an unwelcome visit, especially since the elder Dr. Samuels had already told her to break up with him. But if something had happened to his kids, he'd want to know immediately.

It was an easy walk to the nearest subway station, but before alarming their dad, he should at least fly overhead and see if he could catch sight of the telltale white van used for kidnapping victims, or, more likely, Ruth's Prius. He jogged toward a parking lot that seemed deserted. Behind a car covered with dust, he was able to shed his clothes, shift, roll around in the dirt to hide his red and yellow tail feathers, then take to the sky.

He scanned the entire area, gliding on the wind, until he saw a couple of dark-haired girls walking. He flew over the two young women, landing in a tree before them as they were walking toward it. Nope. They weren't Kizzy and Ruth. He'd know their similar sweet faces anywhere.

Flying again, he fanned out in gradually widening circles. He began looking at cars and pedestrians who might be the troublesome men he'd seen at the Samuels residence. There were plenty of white sedans but nothing that looked exactly like the vehicle he'd seen in Brookline.

He tried to remember any identifying details about

the men and their car. The men were different ages. One was in his late forties or fifties with dirty-blond hair edged with gray temples, and the other was maybe in his twenties. His hair was a light brown. He never saw their eyes up close, but he thought they might be light-colored, like blue or green rather than brown. The car didn't have any identifying marks or bumper stickers. It was probably a rental.

Flying around and racking his brain for some kind of clearer identifying information was just wasting time. He needed to get to their father, who knew more about the women than he did. Together, they might figure out where the girls were. He'd feel completely stupid if he showed up at her dad's house and found out she was having coffee with her sister and had just dropped her phone. But if something was wrong…

He headed back to the parking lot where he'd left his clothing. Thankfully, the car hiding his stuff hadn't moved. Shifting again, he quickly dressed. He was relieved to see both his and Kizzy's phones were still there under the pile of clothes. He tucked them into his pants pockets, then he raced for the subway.

About forty minutes later, he was walking up to the Samuels' stately home in Brookline. He rang the doorbell and waited. And waited. And waited…

At last, a stout woman with gray hair opened the door. "May I help you?"

"I'm Noah Fierro, a friend of Kizzy's. Is her father here?"

"Yes, I'll go get him. Would you like to come in and wait in the parlor?"

Noah wasn't sure how much the patriarch would

appreciate his coming into his home, but he certainly didn't want to refuse hospitality, so he stepped inside.

The woman ushered him into a separate formal living room and told him to have a seat. He was too antsy to sit still, so he wandered around the room, scanning the built-in floor-to-ceiling bookshelves. It looked like their taste in literature was eclectic. There was everything from how-to books, to biographies, to World War II stories, to—*Fifty Shades*? Oh wow. He wondered who was reading that…and what they thought of it. Something to file away for another day.

When Dr. Samuels entered the room, Noah put on a pleasant expression and stuck out his hand. "Hello, Dr. Samuels. You're Kizzy's father, right?"

The gentleman shook his hand. "Yes, and you are?"

"I'm Noah Fierro. A friend of Kizzy's."

"I don't remember hearing your name. What can I do for you?"

"Forgive me. I don't want to alarm you, but I found Kizzy's phone on the ground outside Government Center." Noah produced Kizzy's phone, handing it to her father. "I was participating in a charity event, and I saw her there before it started. After it was over, all I found was her phone."

"And where is my daughter?"

"Last time I saw her, she was with her sister. I don't know her sister's phone number, or I would've called her."

Dr. Samuels took his own phone out of his pocket, touched the screen a couple of times, and waited. After several rings, he was listening to a message. "Ruth, this is Dad. Call me back. Right away. And if Kizzy is there with you, tell her I have her phone." He touched the screen once more to end the call. "Thank you for bring-ing this to me." He laid the phones on an entry table. Stroking his beard, he said, "I guess Kizzy must've told you where she lived. She doesn't usually do that. You must be a good friend."

Something like that. "If I may, sir, I overheard her and Ruth saying something about a possible threat. I don't know any of the details, but if you can tell me anything, I'll do whatever I can to protect her. I only want to help."

Dr. Samuels didn't speak for several moments. When he finally did, Noah could see the man struggling to make up something plausible, since he spoke slowly and deliberately.

"It's probably nothing. Just a rumor. And although I appreciate the offer, I don't expect there's much you can do. Unless you see her and then tell her to come home immediately. Please."

"Of course. You must be worried. I know I am."

Dr. Samuels walked him to the door, clasping his shoulder. "You're a good man, Noah Fierro. I appreciate your looking out for my daughter."

Noah knew when he was being dismissed. If only he could tell the guy he was a phoenix shifter. But how would he explain that he knew the guy believed in shift-ers? Nobody believed in shifters...unless they had some paranormal abilities themselves. *Whoa. Could the good doctor be some kind of paranormal? Maybe a vampire? The patriarch opened the door and didn't burst into flames, so no. Not a vampire. Maybe some kind of male witch or wizard?*

There was really no polite way to ask. He shook the

man's hand and strode down the flagstone walkway to the street. He wished he didn't have to work that night. He'd be worried about Kizzy the entire time—unless she called.

Noah pivoted and bounded back up to the front door. Before he reached it, Dr. Samuels opened it again.

"Did you forget something?"

"Yes. I forgot to ask you to have Kizzy call me as soon as you hear from her. I have to work a seventy-two-hour shift, and I'll be unfit for duty if I can't sleep."

"Ah. You're the firefighter."

"Yes, sir."

To Noah's surprise, the older gentleman smiled. "I'll be sure to give her the message."

Chapter 9

DANTE HADN'T SEEN HIS TROUBLESOME BROTHER FOR several days. Of course, they'd had seventy-two-hour shifts, and after that, he'd spent a lot of time with Mallory. That's what happened when people fell in love. They spent every spare minute together. He'd even been sleeping at her town house when he wasn't at the station.

To her excitement and horror, the gallery owner had loved her work when she'd stopped by to show it to her. Now her big gallery show was coming up, and she was terrified. Despite assurances to the contrary, Dante was terrified for her, knowing she could turn into a monkey at any moment. It seemed to be her way of escaping stressful situations.

In her basement studio, Mallory lifted a heavy canvas and walked to the stairs. Before she carried it up and out to her car, she stopped. "Dante, I'm not sure I can go through with this."

Dante set down the two canvases he was carrying and leaned them carefully against a concrete post. He walked over to her, took the canvas out of her hands, and placed it next to the others, then he braced her with his hands on her arms and looked her straight in the eyes.

"I know you're scared. You don't need to be. I'll be right there with you, and I won't leave your side. No matter what."

She sagged. "I know. If it weren't for you, I wouldn't

even consider this. Who wants a monkey bouncing around their gallery?"

Dante enfolded her in his arms. "If I had a gallery, and you were the monkey, I'd want exactly that. What better way to attract attention?"

She laughed. "You're nuts."

"Maybe. But I'm only telling the truth when I say you can handle it. You've got this, honey."

They shared a reassuring kiss and returned to the task at hand.

Mallory lifted her canvas again and shuffled. "I think I can, I think I can, I think I can..." She made the *chugga-chugga-choo-choo* sound of a train.

"Now who's a nut?" Dante chuckled.

Mallory looked over her shoulder and grinned as she preceded him up the stairs.

The large canvases wouldn't fit in Dante's car, so he'd borrowed a van from one of his firefighter buddies. He'd actually trusted the guy to take care of Joanna while they traded vehicles.

As soon as they had the paintings draped in clean sheets and stabilized in the back of the van, they went back for more. They repeated the procedure three times, loading the van with nine paintings total. When everything was ready to go, Mallory stood before the open van doors, closed her eyes, and clasped her hands in prayer. Dante sensed the need for some respectful silence, so he simply waited beside her.

When she opened her eyes, he saw a sparkle in them. She seemed happy—not that she hadn't been—but he could tell there was a sense of accomplishment just by making it this far.

"I'm proud of you, Mal."

She smiled. "I'm kinda proud of me too."

"Ready to go?" he asked.

"As ready as I'll ever be. I guess. No. No, I mean yes! I'm ready!"

"That's my girl." He closed the van doors and strode to the driver's side while Mallory made her way to the passenger side. They both hopped in, and she slid right across the bench seat. Sitting right next to him, she laid her head on his shoulder.

"Do you mind if I'm this close while you drive?"

"Not at all. I'll have to keep both hands on the wheel, despite my wanting to put one of them somewhere else." He glanced at her crotch.

She laughed. "Stop it. You wouldn't do that, and you know it."

Had he said that to any woman before they'd become so intimate, he'd probably have had his face slapped. As it was, her face turned pink, but she was grinning from ear to ear. She kissed his cheek. "Let's go, handsome."

Dante pulled away from the curb, and as soon as he was on a straightaway, he rested his hand on her bare knee. She had taken to wearing short dresses or tunics rather than skirts with blouses…just in case she wound up exposed after shifting back. The dress she wore today was adorable. It was sleeveless with some kind of artsy splashes of color that were vaguely reminiscent of flowers. She had sweated over what she was going to wear for days.

As if she'd read his mind, she glanced down at her dress. "Did I wear the right thing? It's not very sophisticated."

"I was just thinking about how adorable you look."

"Oh no! I don't want to look adorable. I want to look sophisticated."

"That's what I meant. Adorably sophisticated. Or sophisticatedly adorable. Whichever one will get you to stop worrying."

She laughed. "I guess it's too late to second-guess my ensemble. If I become a famous artist, I'll have money to buy a whole new wardrobe."

Dante enjoyed her flights of fancy, even though he knew the chances of her becoming rich and famous were slim to none. He wasn't about to burst her bubble — especially after having watched her recover from the despair of being fired from her job at the mall.

"Did you invite anyone?" he asked.

"To the gallery show?"

He was tempted to say something silly, like "No, to Sydney Opera House," but he didn't want to come off sounding like a jerk. He just nodded and waited for her reply.

"You know, I thought about it. I just didn't know who would be interested. I've lost touch with most of my fellow Mass Art students. I wasn't close to any of my professors. And the other friends I've had since high school don't really care about art.

"Actually, as I think I mentioned, my real friends are far away. I only have acquaintances left here in Boston. I wouldn't want anyone to think they should buy something just to support me. I don't know what the gallery owner is going to charge for my work, but I know my fellow struggling artists can't afford it."

"They couldn't just show up, eat the cheese and crackers, and look like they're enjoying the show?"

She laughed. "I don't think they'd be comfortable snacking on someone else's food with no intention of buying art, knowing they could be mistaken for homeless people."

"Well, I have a giant family I can invite. Actually, I hope you don't mind, but I kind of already did."

She straightened her spine. "What? Who did you invite? And what does 'kind of' mean?"

"It means I told my mother when she called me at work to ask how I was doing. I said you had a show at a gallery on Newbury Street this Friday. She said she would like to come and asked exactly where and when it would be held."

"And you told her?"

He faced her for a moment. She looked nervous. "I did. Was that wrong? Do you not want her to come?"

"Oh, I didn't mean that. I like her a lot. I like all of your family. It's just that…"

He glanced at her again. "What?"

"Well, I'm not sure it's fair to them either. I doubt they want to buy any artwork."

"Who says? I remember Misty saying Gabe was living a spartan life before she moved in. No artwork on the walls. He didn't even have wineglasses. He gave her a glass of wine in a Solo cup. But he had plenty of money he could have spent on art or glassware. He just didn't think of it, apparently."

Mallory chuckled. "Yeah, that sounds like a typical bachelor's apartment."

"Maybe there will be some rich bachelors coming to the show with their girlfriends. Or rich women with their boyfriends. You never know." Dante wondered who his mother might have mentioned the show to. His dad, of course. She had already said they would be there with bells on.

Going through the rest of his brothers, he knew Ryan wouldn't dare come back to Boston and risk being seen in public. As far as the city of Boston was concerned, he was supposedly a dead and buried firefighter. His wife, Chloe, might come back from Ireland for it. She had an entire castle to furnish.

Jayce and Kristine lived in a one-bedroom condo and both had good salaries. His brother didn't have much artwork before Kristine moved in. Dante hadn't seen the place recently. It was possible they might want a large piece over their bed or something.

Miguel and Sandra had been living in their second-floor apartment in Brighton for years. They had artwork, but that didn't mean they might not change it out for something special.

If Misty hadn't already bought some, he knew Gabe would probably hand her a blank check and tell her to pick out anything she wanted.

All the brothers below Gabe were still young bachelors—Luca didn't even have his own apartment yet. But it sounded like his mother might have invited the others, hoping to help her make a few sales.

"What kind of advertising did they do for you?" Dante asked.

"I don't know. She said something about a notice in the *Boston Phoenix*, in their online list of things to do, and a notice in some trade journal or magazine. I can't remember which one. I was half frozen in fear as she was talking about it. I just realized something. You're a Boston Phoenix, just like the newspaper!"

Dante laughed. "I wish we could say we owned it, but we have nothing to do with the newspaper...unless we wind up in a cage and somebody puts a few pages in there for us to poop on."

She gasped. "Has that ever happened? Have any of you wound up in a cage?"

Dante realized this might not be the best time to talk about how his family handled death and reincarnation. That was a pretty involved subject, and they were two blocks from the gallery.

"Let's table that discussion for another day. I'll tell you anything you want to know, but we're almost there."

"Okay." She folded her hands in her lap and took a few deep breaths.

He glanced over at her. "Are you all right?"

She opened her eyes. "Yeah. I'm fine. I think."

"I think you can, I think you can, I think you can."

She smiled. "Choo-choo!"

———

Noah couldn't stand waiting for Kizzy to call and tried her phone number. Perhaps her father had forgotten to give her the message. *Yeah, right.* He'd thought he'd made a good impression. Maybe the guy was just *grin-fucking* him.

After an inordinate number of rings, Kizzy finally picked up. "Hello?"

"Kizzy! It's Noah. Are you all right?"

An audible sigh met his ears. "Yes and no."

Noah hesitated, but she didn't elaborate. Finally, he asked, "What's wrong?"

"Um...it's...complicated."

"Why are you being evasive? If something is wrong, you can tell me. I won't tell anyone else."

"I'm sorry, Noah. It's my father. He really... I shouldn't share the details. That family situation I told you about? It's getting worse. I really can't see you right now."

"Are you sure? I want to help."

"You can't." Her voice wobbled a bit.

Noah wished he could tell her "Yes, I can." But how could he reveal his supernatural identity without compromising their relationship? It already seemed tenuous, at best.

"Kizzy, whatever it is, I'm here for you. I really wish you'd let me in."

"I wish I could. You'll just have to trust me. It's the timing. It's not you."

Without meaning to, Noah let out a resigned sigh. "Okay. Is it all right if I call once in a while and check on you?"

"Yeah. That would probably be all right. But if I don't pick up, don't worry. It's just..."

"I know. Not a good time."

"Exactly."

"Just tell me one thing. Did your father tell you I returned your phone?"

"Huh? No. He didn't. I found my phone here in his kitchen and thought it was weird. I texted you to say I had an emergency and had to go. I must have dropped it when I thought I hit the send button. I couldn't find it while Ruth and I were on our way to the hospital."

"You went to the hospital? Are you all right? Is Ruth okay?"

"Yeah, we're fine. There was a major car wreck, and they needed me."

"Shit. I didn't hear about that."

"It was on the news."

"I don't like to watch the news these days."

So her father hadn't mentioned him at all. What the hell was going on? Why would he feel he needed to lie about that—even if it was lying by omission? Maybe this relationship really wasn't a good idea. His heart broke a little bit as he thought about never seeing her again.

"All right. If things settle down, let me know. Meanwhile, I'll leave you be."

"I'm sorry, Noah. I wish things were different. Just know that."

"Fine. Take care."

"You too."

After he hung up, Noah laid his phone down on his kitchen table. He seemed to be on the outs with everyone. He wished he could talk to Dante, but he was busy helping Mallory today. Her gallery show was this evening.

Gabriella had called and invited him to the show—more like twisted his arm. At the time, he'd said he didn't know if he would be able to make it. Now, he really felt like going. He needed his family. More accurately, he needed to be surrounded by his family's unconditional love and acceptance. The sting of rejection was weighing heavily on him.

Maybe it was time to accept Dante's choice of Mallory. He really had no business telling his brother who to date. Someday, she might become his sister-in-law, and he didn't want any awkward history following them throughout their lifetimes. His and

Dante's lifetimes would be a heck of a lot longer than Mallory's.

That helped him put things in perspective. His father and some of his brothers would deal with the loss of a spouse long before they took their final flight. A human spouse would face mortality long before a phoenix. If he ever found his soulmate, chances are he would have to deal with the loss too. Two of his brothers were lucky in that respect. They married dragons and would probably be outlived by their wives. However, the rest of the phoenix family would need one another for support when the time came.

Kizzy might be a doctor and know how to take care of her physical health as she aged, but she couldn't escape death. It might be best to forget her—while he still could.

He would set up the rest of the lab, then clean up, put on a suit, and go to the gallery for the show. Chances are he wouldn't buy anything, but he could at least lend emotional support to Dante and his girlfriend. He owed them that.

Helen Smythe, the gallery owner, sat down with Mallory about an hour before the show opening. Mallory had confessed how nervous she was, and the woman seemed to understand. The funny thing was, she'd said Mallory appeared better adjusted than some artists she'd worked with. Mallory almost burst out laughing at that. Instead, she just said, "Oh dear."

Now, the day had arrived and they were actually doing this. Dante leaned against the doorjamb, listening quietly.

"How are you feeling?"

"Scared. Unprepared. Like an imposter."

Helen laughed. "At least you're honest. That's why I asked you to come early. A lot of artists blunder or bluster their way through a gallery show—even those who've had several. Because this is your first, I thought I'd prepare you a bit in advance if you're open to it."

Mallory sat up straighter. "Yes, please! I want to know what to expect and anything else you want to tell me."

"Good. Every art show or exhibition opening marks a milestone in your career as an artist. This is your premier and a critical window of opportunity. It may only last a few hours, but think of it as taking a shot at changing your destiny. Why? Because anything can happen—and it often does—which means you've got to be 'on' and be ready."

"Oh crap."

Helen laughed again. "Don't worry. You look gorgeous, and your art is fantastic. Of course, it's my job to make sure it shows as well as it possibly can at your opening."

"And thank you for that! It doesn't show nearly as nicely in my unfinished basement." She cracked a smile, and Helen seemed to know she was joking—sort of.

"Well, there's a reason that we make it look pristine and perfect. Everyone wants favorable reactions, healthy sales, and great reviews. But the most important ingredient is you, and the more aware you are of the art lovers, the better the chances to upwardly alter the course of your success."

"I was nervous before. Now, I'm terrified."

She patted Mallory's hand. "You'll be fine. Do you

want to know how I know that? Because you care. I'm amazed at the number of artists who have cavalier attitudes toward their openings or, worse yet, see them as inconveniences or distractions they'd rather not bother with. This makes no sense. They spend weeks, months, or years creating the art but not ten minutes reflecting on how they'll present themselves at its public debut. They show up, stand around, smile, chitchat, schmooze with friends, sip wine, shake hands, endure the imposition, go home, and forget about it. You can do better than that."

"But how? That's all I was planning to do. Smile and chitchat."

"Oh, there's plenty of that. Plus I'll introduce you to some influential people. It's tempting to hang back in the shadows or fall back on your friends and people you know. But it's important to push yourself out of your comfort zone."

"Oh no. I'm not good at that."

"Relax. You've already accomplished your two most important jobs for the night."

"Really? Like what?"

"You got the artwork done and delivered on time. That's number one. And second, you're here, you're presentable, and you're prepared to stay the entire time." She narrowed her eyes. "Wait… You *are* prepared to stay the entire time, aren't you?"

Shit. Her deer in the headlights look must have given her away. "Of course! I wouldn't leave unless…well, unless there's an emergency." *Like a monkey crashing the show*.

"If for any reason you need to leave, even for a bathroom break and a cigarette, find me first and let me know how long you'll be. That way, if someone wants to speak to the artist, I can tell them when you'll be back. Giving a vague answer is inconsiderate of their time. And remember, anyone can show up at any time with any agenda. Your duty is to be available or accounted for the entire time. Remember, this is a commitment. And it only lasts hours, not days or weeks."

"It sounds like you're thinking I could be discovered and become the next Peter Max or somebody famous."

She shrugged. "Things like that can happen. That's why you *must* make yourself available to the people you don't know. You can see your friends anytime. And if some old gasbag wants to monopolize you, be discreet, but excuse yourself and mingle."

She giggled. "How do I do that?"

"Just say something like, 'Oh, I must say hello to a friend I haven't seen in a while.' You may have seen her yesterday, but saying 'a while' is truthful enough to sound convincing."

Mallory nodded but still felt like she had no business being here. Suddenly, another horrible thought occurred to her. What if she was talking to someone she didn't know and then was discovered talking to herself! It hadn't happened lately, but what if it did? *Oh God*. She wanted to drop her head in her hands and cry.

"Basically," Helen continued, "keep the traffic moving, keep conversations basic and answers short. That way, you maximize introductory opportunities as well as the potential to add to your fan base. Always speak in everyday language anyone can understand, especially when you're talking to someone you've never talked to before. Don't try to sound highbrow."

Mallory laughed. "There's little chance of that. I'm your garden-variety average American girl who happens to have a bachelor's degree in fine art."

Helen smiled. "You're perfect. Very relatable. People will love you, and that's exactly what we want. Oftentimes, people buy art because they like the artist, not because they're wild about the art. Resist the urge to tell people more than they want to hear, and avoid answering questions with insider art jargon that only MFAs can understand. The best idea is to answer all questions in thirty seconds or less. The longer your answers, the fewer people you'll have time to talk to. If someone wants to hear your life story, tell them you'll be happy to get into it later, after the opening, and hand them your card."

"My…card?"

"Oh dear. You don't have any with you?"

"Uh, no. I didn't know I needed any."

Helen reached into her drawer and extracted some business cards. "Here. You can give any interested parties one of mine, and I'll get in touch with you."

Mallory took the cards and tucked them in her dress pocket. "Thank you." She'd thought the pockets were a great idea in case she needed something to do with her hands. Now, it seemed like stuffing her hands in her pockets and standing around would be a mistake. Jeez, this whole thing seemed like a mistake.

"Oh, I almost forgot…" Helen said. "Most importantly, avoid the tendency to be argumentative or to correct anyone who misinterprets your art or sees it differently than you do. Everyone is entitled to their opinions, especially around art."

"Got it."

"Any questions?"

"I feel like I have a million, but I don't know what they are."

Helen laughed. She patted Mallory's hand as she rose from her desk. "You'll be fine. Just don't drink too much. Stay sober for the show, and party your brains out later."

It was Mallory's turn to laugh. It was bad enough picturing her monkey running around, but a drunken monkey? Not. Happening.

"Well, I need to go check on some things," Helen said. "If you'd like to relax with your young man for a while, you're welcome to stay here in my office. Or go for a stroll. It's a nice evening. Just be back at least five minutes early. Not one minute after that."

"I guess I'd better stay right here. I don't want to blow it by being late."

"No," Helen said seriously. "You don't." She left the office without a backward glance.

Mallory was terrified. Her first, and possibly last, gallery show was about to begin. At least no ghosts had shown up since they'd seen Kurt. Maybe the wizard was able to break one of her two curses. She just hoped her crazy little monkey didn't make an appearance.

She had been practicing the self-hypnosis techniques she had learned from the hypnotherapist. She just needed to remember to use them when she started to panic. *Before* she started to panic, if possible. Once the panic took hold and the shaking started... *Pop goes the monkey*.

Mallory glanced at the clock on the wall. *Oh God*.

Half an hour. She closed her eyes and took several deep breaths. Picturing herself in the woods, walking beside a stream, she listened to the babbling brook. She did as the hypnotist had suggested and immersed herself in the pleasant setting completely. Smelling the fresh pine-scented air, she felt the sun on her shoulders and the top of her head, then she let the warmth flow through her whole body. After that, she lost track of time and her immediate surroundings. Time was irrelevant. Gallery shows were…not irrelevant, but not the end of the world either.

"Am I interrupting?" Dante's whisper brought her back.

She let her eyes flutter open and took one last deep breath, letting any remaining stress slip away on exhalation. Dante was sitting next to her. When had he moved?

"No, it's fine. What time is it?"

"It's almost time for the show to start. I just wondered if you'd like me to get you a glass of wine."

She chuckled. "For courage?"

Dante rose, stood behind her, leaned over, and massaged her shoulders. "I don't think you need courage. I just thought it might help to relax you."

"I'm actually pretty relaxed already. That self-hypnosis thing actually works."

"Yeah, I've used the relaxation technique he taught us at the station when I have trouble going to sleep sometimes. I'm glad you gave it a try—but I was afraid you were falling asleep just now."

"Ha! Not much chance of that happening." Mallory rose and turned to face him. She draped her arms around his neck. "How about a kiss for luck?"

"You got it."

He leaned down until their lips met. His kiss was always perfect. Soft but firm. She felt safe, secure, and loved in his arms. When they finally broke apart, she smiled. "I'm ready now."

"Glad to hear it. Go get 'em." Dante led the way but didn't hold her hand or make her feel like she needed to lean on him—or anyone.

Since she had been seeing him, she'd changed and hoped the changes would continue. Her self-confidence had grown. She felt less vulnerable and less defensive. She had heard that love brought out the best in people and figured that must have something to do with it. She always smiled when she thought about how much she loved Dante. How lucky she was that he was there for her that day. Things could have turned out much differently.

Walking out onto the gallery floor, she stopped in her tracks. The gallery was full. She had never expected a turnout like this. She recognized several of the Fierros, but they weren't the only ones there. For some reason, she'd thought they would be. *Okay, so I still have a ways to go with that self-esteem thing.*

Gabriella came up to her and gave her a kiss on both cheeks. "Don't you look lovely!"

"Thank you." She didn't know what to say after that. She didn't know what to say to anyone. She felt her panic begin to rise, but it wasn't spiking like it ordinarily would. She took a breath and made herself go back to her relaxed state from a few moments ago. It had to last longer than a minute, right?

A pretty young woman with strawberry-blonde hair

came over to her. She stuck out her hand and said, "Hi, I'm Kristine. We didn't get to meet the other day."

"Oh, that's right. How is your mother and the new baby?"

Kristine grinned. "They're great. I love having a little sister I can cuddle and spoil."

Mallory liked Kristine immediately.

"Hey, I saw this painting I thought would be perfect for Jayce's and my living room. Can I ask you about it?"

"Sure." She followed Kristine over to one of her recent pieces, which Jayce was currently admiring.

"I love the colors and long, gentle brushstrokes. It reminds me of sunset over the ocean. That's one of our favorite times to go sailing."

"You got it in one. I like to take walks along the beach at that time of day."

"So it's inspired by a calm evening on the sea?" Jayce asked.

"Essentially. I think my mood was pretty relaxed that day. Usually, I just paint what's inside me at the moment."

"Were you having a bad day when you painted that one?" Luca asked. She hadn't even seen him listening behind her. She followed his pointing finger but had already guessed which painting he was referring to. She glanced over at the gray-and-black painting. The strokes were bold and sharp on one side, but on the other side, a face was emerging out of fog. She remembered that day vividly—the day she was fired from her job. Maybe it was the best thing that could have happened to her. She wouldn't be here now if the photo shoot had gone smoothly.

"Yeah. I was struggling with some confusing feelings that day. Painting them out was therapeutic."

Luca crossed his arms and stared at it. "Yeah? Well, I kinda like it."

The gallery owner picked up on their conversation and moved closer. "Quite often, that's what art does for us. It brings out emotions we can identify with. The artist expresses what we all feel from time to time."

"So what's got you upset, Luca?" Dante asked.

Luca shrugged. "I don't know. Stuff? The world?"

Gabriella put her arm around his waist. "This is my son, who's in the police academy," she said, as if that answered the question.

Helen nodded. "I imagine that job brings up all kinds of feelings. I know a couple of cops who are artists, and they talk about trying to counteract some of the aggravation they're stuck with at the end of the day. Do you have any creative outlets?"

Luca laughed. "Not really. I've been in school for the past four years, and now I'm going through even more training. Maybe someday, I'll have the time."

Mallory didn't know why she was surprised the sophisticated woman might know some cops well enough to be acquainted with their personal feelings. She just pictured this woman only socializing with the rich and famous. She was glad to have that stereotype busted and progressively felt more comfortable.

Then Helen excused herself. Just like she'd told Mallory to do. Quick conversations, then go on to the next. She did a nice job of modeling what that looked like.

Dante was striding toward the front door. "Hey, man! I'm glad you could make it."

Mallory followed him with her gaze. *Noah?* She hadn't expected him. Last she'd heard, the two were on the outs. She was almost as happy to see him as Dante was. The last thing she wanted to do was create a rift between brothers.

Behind Noah, a vaguely familiar young woman stepped through the door.

Oh my God. It's the woman who got me fired! Mallory took a calming breath and remembered that the same woman put her in touch with Helen. She was wondering whether she should say hello when the woman made a beeline for Helen.

Yeah, that made sense. If they were buddies, she'd want to greet her friend and at the same time check out the work of the crazy artist she had referred. Mallory stayed in the background while the two women embraced and said their hellos.

Noah strode over to her. "Hi, Mallory. It looks like a great turnout! You must be excited."

She grimaced. "More like terrified, but thank you for coming. A familiar face is always welcome."

"Even mine?"

"Of course! Why would you think otherwise?"

Noah kicked at the floor. "I don't know. Maybe because I haven't been the most supportive brother on the planet recently. In fact, I've been kind of an ass."

Since Dante was talking to Luca, he wasn't there to elaborate.

"I'm not sure what you're talking about, but I wouldn't worry. Dante seems like the understanding type."

"Yeah. He is. I just thought… Never mind. I should check out your artwork!"

"Please do. And grab a glass of champagne."

He glanced at the waiter pouring some into fluted glasses. "Oh, the good stuff. Nice."

Noah wandered off, and she found herself alone for the first time since she'd walked onto the gallery floor. She took the opportunity to do some deep breathing again.

Just remembering that little trick kept her relaxed. She spotted a man alone, admiring one of her ribbon paintings. She'd noticed multicolored ribbons tied to a fence, blowing in the breeze one day, and snapped a picture. Later at home, she had tried to capture the feeling they evoked on canvas.

She approached the gentleman. "Uh, hi. I'm Mallory Summers." She offered her hand, and he shook it, smiling broadly.

"I really like this. So many artists paint gritty pictures of the city, but this looks like a chain-link fence with a twist. And it's a pleasant surprise."

"Thank you. That's exactly what I was going for."

Just then, above the murmurs, she heard, "What the... Helen!"

Oh no.

The woman from the photo shoot was staring at her dead husband. His ghost face looked like it was coming out of the fog in the dark painting.

"Sh—shoot," Mallory muttered. Suddenly, the tremors overtook her. *Oh no, oh no, oh no...* "Please excuse me," she said to the male patron. She sprinted in the direction of Helen's office, latching onto Dante's sleeve as she passed him.

He seemed to understand what she was doing and followed close on her heels. As soon as she entered the room, she dove behind the desk and felt her body change. She heard the door shut and a lock snick into place.

"Honey? Are you all right?"

All Mallory could say was "Eep!" One glance at her thin, hairy arms confirmed she'd taken on her monkey form. She flopped onto her back and tried her relaxation techniques, even though she was a little late.

Sounds of someone pounding on the door prevented her from relaxing.

Dante tried yelling through the door, "It's okay. Just give her a moment."

The muffled comment from the other side of the door was Helen demanding to know what was wrong with her artist.

"Uh... She's having a seizure."

"I'll call an ambulance," she heard Helen say clearly, even though it was coming from the other side of the closed door. Her senses sharpened...maybe because animals could hear better than most humans. Right now, she didn't care about the benefits. She wanted her human body back.

"No! No ambulance," Dante called out. "I'm an EMT. And...and she would be embarrassed. She'll be fine, I promise."

She heard a few other voices out there, notably Antonio Fierro calmly stating there were five EMTs in the gallery, including his son who was with her right now. A seizure just had to run its course. The only danger would be if she were to fall or hit something sharp, and his son was with her to prevent that.

He seemed to be calming Helen down. There were several distant murmurs, but she couldn't pick up many exact conversations. She heard the word *seizure* repeated more than once.

That was sort of brilliant on Dante's part, she thought. For one, she was probably shaking as she entered the office. For another thing, a seizure wasn't life-threatening, and she wouldn't look any different once she recovered. At least she didn't think so.

Dante came around the desk and found her lying on the floor, her dress twisted about her. Straightening it beneath her little legs, he murmured, "You're safe. I'm here." He stroked her forehead, as if she were a frightened pet.

How could this keep happening? Why didn't the wizard's hex-breaking spell work? She hadn't seen ghosts since that day, so maybe some of it worked. Maybe seeing ghosts was the hex part, and this was something else completely.

Now that she had a few moments to breathe and with Dante stroking her forehead, she regrouped. She concentrated on her human form and felt her torso, arms, and legs expand. Dante shuffled back a foot or so, then helped her up.

"Are you okay?"

She nodded. When she tried her voice, she sounded like a scared little girl. "I'm fine." She cleared her throat and tried again, this time with more conviction. "I'm fine. Really. Thank you."

"Okay. Shall we go back out there? I'm sure a lot of people want to see that you're okay."

"Yes. I should show everyone I'm all right."

As she walked toward the door, Dante splashed the back of her skirt with his champagne.

She whirled on him. "Why did you do that?"

"Because when someone has a seizure, they lose control of their *whole* body. You don't want people to think you faked it, do you?"

"I don't want people to think I peed myself either!"

"Well, I'm sorry. That's the embarrassing part."

She hung her head. "Great. Just great."

Chapter 10

KIZZY HAD TO GIVE IN AND ADMIT THE THREAT WAS VERY real. She trusted Ruth's intuition, and her psychic alarms were going off big-time.

Even though her father's idea seemed ridiculous, she hadn't been able to come up with anything better to require an emergency leave of absence while staying home. So here she sat, blind and interviewing a werewolf, who planned to protect her by posing as her seeing-eye dog.

She didn't like it, but she insisted on putting the spell on herself. If anyone had done it for her, she might not know how to reverse the blindness properly. She would only feel okay with this crazy idea if she had total control over how and when she could see again. Still, the whole thing rankled. "This is stupid. Why can't I just pretend to be blind?"

Kizzy's father sighed loudly.

"Have you met you?" Ruth asked. "You're not the best actress."

"And blindness is a very difficult thing to fake," her father added.

"I know."

The werewolf spoke up. "It's very normal to distrust someone you've just met. Putting your faith in me to keep you safe while you're completely blind is asking a lot."

He had been introduced to her before she went blind, and the six-foot-three blond hulk could probably protect her very well. But when he became a wolf, would she need protection from *him*?

"I don't doubt that you can keep me safe. But what about the full moon?"

"You will stay inside with me on the full moon," her father said.

"And Mr. Wolfensen?"

"I'll be with my pack."

That was not reassuring. She didn't know where his pack went on those nights, and thinking about it made her a little nervous. What if she accidentally wound up there some evening?

"Where is your pack?" she asked.

"They run a private school out in the suburbs."

That wasn't the answer she'd expected. Werewolves running a private school? Unless...there were little werewolves who needed an education. *Oh dear*. She was feeling more and more vulnerable. As a witch, she realized the supernatural world was real, but every time she learned the truth about some paranormal legends, it blew her mind anyway.

"Keep in mind that I'm trusting you too. A witch could do some damage if she wanted to."

Kizzy snorted. "It's not like I'm going to point my wand in the wrong direction and accidentally zap you with it."

"I don't know many witches. The ones I know are sweet as can be, *most of the time*. But like anyone else, they have their moments."

"Have any of them tried to harm you?"

"No. Not at all. In fact, the only one I know well told me there was some kind of rule against it. Something called the rule of three, I think."

Kizzy nodded. "Yes. That's one karmic kick in the acorns. Most witches have to worry about the type of magic they do. If at any point they attempt black magic, it will backfire on them three times."

"Ouch," he said. "That seems excessive."

"Tell me about it."

"You said most witches? Does that mean you're not affected?"

"I've never tested the theory, and I don't intend to." Kizzy stated a fact, but it may have come out sounding a little intense.

"Good. I feel safer already." Mr. Wolfensen chuckled.

"Protection and healing spells are my specialty," Kizzy said. "My sister's talents lie in the psychic and female empowerment areas."

"So who takes care of male empowerment?" he asked.

"I do," Dr. Samuels said. "I pay you, don't I?"

She sensed a smile in his voice, so she knew he was kidding. At least she hoped he was. Her father wasn't usually that arrogant.

"How long do you think this will go on?" Kizzy asked. "I reinforced all the wards around the book."

"I don't know. I wish I did." That was Ruth speaking.

Thank goodness everyone's voice was distinctive. In a crowded room with strangers, she wouldn't know who was speaking or to whom. Yup. The ER was definitely a no-go.

"Have you been able to find out anything new or specific about this threat, Ruthie?" her father asked.

"I tried some divination. I saw two men in my black mirror. I didn't know either of them, but I would recognize them if I saw them standing in front of me."

"I'd ask you to describe them, but you'd be wasting your breath on me," Kizzy said.

"I don't think you've told Mr. Wolfensen yet."

"You're right. I should. After all, if you answer the door instead of our housekeeper, you need to know who to bite."

"Bite? You're expecting me to answer the door in wolf form?"

Ruth giggled. "I don't know what you can or can't do in your other form."

"Well, I won't have opposable thumbs, so turning a doorknob is tricky."

This whole conversation was getting too weird for Kizzy. "I think I'll go try to find the bathroom." She used her cane to tap her way around the coffee table and check the path in front of her as she navigated her way to the stairs.

Once she had hold of the handrail, she was fine. Walking upstairs, she realized she didn't know how many stairs there were. She should've counted them. When she got to the top, she took an extra step and felt like she was about to topple over when her foot came down and didn't land on anything but air.

She sighed. *I can do this. I* have *to do this. Look for the silver lining, Kizzy.* The only silver lining, besides a long overdue vacation, was the possibility of learning what her newly blinded patients were going through.

Noah and Dante sat at their kitchen table, each deep in thought. Noah hadn't told Dante about breaking up with Kizzy yet, and he wasn't sure he wanted to. The whole situation really sucked. He knew she was in some kind of danger, but she clearly didn't want him involved.

At last, Dante broke the silence.

"Thanks for coming to Mallory's show, man. I know she appreciated it."

"How's she doing, by the way?"

Dante shrugged. "Well, the gallery owner suggested an alternative to the whole fine art, gallery-showing scene. It made a lot of sense. I was surprised Mallory was open to it, but I guess she took the advice in the spirit it was intended."

"What's that?"

"Art therapy. Helen said it was because she was so good at putting her emotions on canvas, but Mal suspected it was to get a little free therapy of her own."

"Mal? You're calling her Mal now? That's a guy's name."

Dante smirked. "No, to her face, I call her honey, babe, and sweetheart."

Noah smiled wistfully. "So, things are going well for you two." He couldn't help being a little envious, but at least one of them was happy.

"Yeah. Really well. We've talked about me moving in with her at some point."

"Wow!" Noah chewed his lip as he thought about what to say. "I—I know we've had our differences, but don't move out because of me. I really feel bad about giving you a hard time. I've come around. You two make a good couple."

Dante smiled. "Thanks, Bro. I appreciate that. I'm not going to do anything rash. It's just something to think about."

"Okay. Good. I'm not going anywhere, so there's no need to rush into anything."

"So…uh…we were thinking that maybe Kizzy could give Mallory a few leads on art therapy jobs. Apparently, these jobs are hard to come by, and she might have some connections."

Oh crap. "I…uh…I'm not seeing Kizzy anymore."

Dante's spine straightened. "What? I thought you really liked her."

"I did. I mean, I do. She's just going through some family shit right now. It's not a good time for a relationship."

"Okay, so don't be in a relationship. Try just being her friend. It sounds like she might need one."

"I—I don't think she wants me involved."

"So don't get involved. Just keep the lines of communication open. When stuff settles, and I'm sure it will, you'll still have a friendship. At least call her and ask how she's doing. Where would Mallory and I be if I just dropped her like a rock?"

Noah leaned back and crossed his arms. Her brush-off seemed pretty firm, but he really would like to stay in touch with Kizzy, more than just hitting the like button on a Facebook post—although she hadn't posted anything there for a while. "You know, maybe asking her about a job for Mallory would be a good excuse to at least call her." *And figure out if she's done with me for now or forever.*

"Now you're talking," Dante said.

Noah got up and disconnected his cell phone from its charger. "Here goes nuthin'..."

Fortunately, Kizzy did have her phone, thanks to him. After a few rings, he heard her voice, sounding harried as she puffed, "Hello."

"Hi, Kizz. Did you have to run for the phone?"

"Uh, yeah. Sort of. Hi, Noah. What's up?"

"I'm actually calling for a favor. I mean, if you can handle it right now. I want to help out my brother's girlfriend. She's looking for a job as an art therapist. We thought you might know someone who could use an apprentice."

"Oh. I...uh...I don't know if I can do much for her right now. I mean, I wouldn't be able to write a letter of recommendation..."

"Yeah. No, I'm not asking for anything like that. Just a lead, if you have one. Someone she can call."

"Okay. The psych ward at the hospital might have some suggestions. They refer people to day care programs all the time."

"Day care? We're talking about adults, right?"

She laughed. "Yes. That's a terrible name for it. Outpatient care or aftercare might be better."

"Okay. So she should ask the psych department about outpatient care. That's a great idea. Who should she ask for?"

"Um, I don't get up there very often. And actually, I'm not working right now anyway. You'd be best just asking for the social work supervisor."

"You're not working? Why? I mean, if it's not too personal a question. I'm just asking as a friend. I won't tell anyone."

She sighed. "I know, and in a way, I'd like to talk about it. It's really weird."

"Weird is my specialty."

Her soft chuckle reassured him—somewhat.

"Okay, you can't share this with anyone. Not even Dante. Swear."

He didn't dare hesitate, even though he knew his brother, with his paranormal senses, could hear every word. "I swear I won't repeat anything you tell me."

"Good. Here's the weird part. I'm blind, and medical science can't fix it."

Noah was stunned. "Blind? As in, you can't see *anything*?"

"Yeah. A real pain-in-the-asphalt for an ER doc."

He loved how she reworded bad language to keep it PG. She must have learned that from working in a very public setting.

"I'm sorry. That's got to be—disturbing!"

"You got that right."

"Do you think it could be temporary?"

"I hope so."

"Is there anything I can do? You know, as a friend. Can I shop for you or anything?"

"That's sweet, but the housekeeper does the shopping."

"Oh." What could he say? Her father obviously didn't like him, so a visit was out. "Can I call you once in a while? Just so you can talk to someone, if you need to?"

She hesitated but at last relented. "Sure. Not too often though. I had a heck of a time finding my phone before it went to voicemail, and I bumped my shin in the process."

"Ouch. That's why you were breathing funny."

"Yeah, I was trying not to yell or curse under my breath."

He chuckled. "You can curse to me anytime."

"Well, I don't want to get into the habit. I may go back to work eventually."

"I hope so."

"You and me both."

A few days later, Kizzy was going stir-crazy, just sitting around the house with nothing to do—or see. Her father was at work. She envied his power of invisibility. He rarely used it, but he felt it gave him enough of an advantage so he didn't need to worry about being followed by whomever was after the book.

Her sister didn't seem to mind staying home. Her fiancé liked it too. He said the house was cleaner. She could almost hear Ruth's eyes roll.

She could clean the house too—if she could see it! At least her sister had found a case for her phone that had a wrist strap. She could keep it with her more easily that way. But she couldn't call and bother Ruth again. They had just talked for an hour.

Nick Wolfensen had gone home to have lunch with his wife and daughter. He seemed to go back and forth in a jiffy. She'd heard he lived on Beacon Hill but couldn't figure out how he got there and back to Brookline so fast. Maybe he had more than one paranormal secret?

Fortunately, someone picked that moment to call. "Hello?"

"Hi, Kizzy. It's Noah. How are you?"

"Oh, you know. Blind. But in some ways, I see a lot more."

"Yeah? Like what?"

"Like what a good friend you are. Nobody from the hospital has called to see how I am."

"Nobody?"

"Nope. Not a nurse. Not a secretary. Not a janitor. No one."

"Jeez, that's not right. You'd probably have thought to call them if one of your coworkers suddenly went blind."

"Uh, no. That's one of the things I actually saw. How much I let life interfere with important things like friendships or just plain courtesy."

"I guess I know what you mean. I should call my brother. I don't see him much anymore. If something happened to him, I wouldn't know about it."

"But I thought you two were roommates and on the same schedule."

"He's spending a lot of time at Mallory's house. He's even thinking of moving in with her."

"Oh! That's...nice?"

Noah chuckled. "Yeah. That was my initial reaction. It's fast, but they seem to be crazy about each other, so I guess it's a good thing."

After a brief hesitation, Kizzy asked, "Where are you?"

"At home. Why?"

"Are you busy?"

"Nah. I'm just puttering around the lab."

"The lab?"

"Yeah. I'm building a chem lab in our spare bedroom. I know, I know. That makes me sound like a total geek."

"No, it sounds interesting. *Really* interesting!" After a brief hesitation, she said, "I'm going stir-crazy. I wish I could come over."

"You can. Of course. I'll come and get you. Dante has the car, but I can call an Uber and be there in half an hour or so."

"No, I can do the same thing. I just need your address and directions."

"But you're blind! It's no problem, honest. I can come and get you. Or visit there. We can play it by ear. Maybe you just need a distraction."

"Okay."

He was a good friend and would probably understand if she said she wasn't really blind but had to come up with an excuse to suddenly stay at home. But how would she explain *why* she needed to stay at home. She couldn't very well say, "Well, we have this book to protect, and I needed an immediate leave of absence without being able to say when I would be back—so I spelled myself."

She was sick of the whole thing. The book was fine. It was behind so many reinforced wards, nobody outside her family would be able to take it. Even Mr. Wolfensen—who would be back any minute—couldn't touch it unless a family member handed it to him. She wished he didn't have to hang around while she visited with Noah. He hadn't asked about her love life at all, but the guy was working for her father, not her. And her father didn't approve.

Maybe she could send him on an errand. She wanted to be alone with the handsome firefighter. The admission surprised her. There was probably something wrong with this plan, but she had nothing else. She said good-bye to Noah, relieved that their friendship had survived.

———~~~———

Strolling hand in hand through the South End, Mallory listened as Dante tried again to talk her into calling her parents.

"I can't. Seriously. They're on a construction site."

"Don't they have cell phones?"

"Yeah, but they don't work well in the middle of the Amazon rain forest."

Dante shook his head. "Don't you miss them? I mean, I'd miss my parents if I hadn't seen or heard from them for a couple of months."

"It's okay. I knew it would be like this before they left. I had to assure them about a billion times that I would be perfectly all right. Even if I did find a way to get in contact, my mother would assume something was wrong, and she'd insist they come home. Then my dad would disown me for jeopardizing his multimillion-dollar deal."

"He would not."

"I wouldn't put it past him. He's a driven, type A kind of guy. If something gets in his way, he steamrolls right over it."

"Well, then my parents would just have to adopt you."

She laughed. "Are you sure about that? Wouldn't that make us brother and sister?"

"Oh yeah. Ewww."

"Not only that, but don't they have enough kids already?" As they were walking up the steps to the Fierros' brownstone, she hoped Dante's parents didn't hold what happened at the gallery against her. Dante assured her his mother would be delighted to see her again.

She had only taken a couple of steps inside when Gabriella hurried to the door and gave them each a tight hug.

"Come in, come in." Gabriella grabbed Mallory's hand and pulled her toward the kitchen. She glanced over her shoulder at Dante, who just grinned, following behind with his hands in his pockets.

Gabriella seemed anxious to see them. But why? Maybe she wanted to talk her out of seeing her son. *No, Mallory. Stop talking to yourself that way!* She had been trying to catch her inner negative Nellie whenever she showed up uninvited.

"I'm so excited to see you," Gabriella said.

"Why?" Mallory asked.

Gabriella's brows tented. "Why? Because I want to get to know you better. I'm happy that you're in my son's life. You seem to make him happy."

She glanced at her boyfriend, who was rolling his eyes. "Dante's always happy."

"It would seem that way, because he has been ever since he met you."

Mallory worried her lip. "I didn't think you'd want him to see me anymore, especially not after the whole, you know…gallery thing."

Gabriella smiled. "Oh, honey. I'm so sorry that happened to you, but it's not a big deal. Not around here. I mean, who doesn't freak out and turn into a monkey once in a while?" She gave her a sly grin, and the three of them laughed.

"Dante, you never told me your mother was so funny."

Dante shrugged. "She has her moments."

"I was just about to make my husband's favorite bread. Would you like to help me?" Gabriella asked.

"Sure!" At that moment, Mallory's phone rang. "Give me a second." She walked off toward the back of the house and wound up in a laundry and mudroom while Dante stayed in the kitchen with his mother.

"Mallory?"

It sounded like the gallery owner's voice. "Yes?"

"It's Helen. I have some interesting news for you."

"Oh, hi, Helen. It's nice to talk to you again." She could fake confidence over the phone much better than in person. "News? What news?"

"Yes. Apparently, someone at the show liked what he saw and wanted to get in touch with you."

"Really? What was his name?"

"Maurice Winston. Do you remember speaking with him?"

"Um, no?"

"He's a textile designer. He liked the color and movement and how you evoked emotion in your work. He was inspired and thought the patterns would be unique and beautiful in clothing. I have to say I agree with him."

"You mean he wants to print my paintings on rolls of fabric? Then sell the fabric to make dresses, that sort of thing?"

"Exactly. Well, it's done on computers these days. I was picturing it in my mind, and I think it's a great idea. I'd love a dress made with one of your paintings as the fabric."

"Wow. I had never thought of using them that way. I'll gladly make sure you get one, especially since you were so nice to me, considering…"

"Oh, don't worry about that. I'm just happy to help. I think it might be a good job for you. You can probably even work from home if you'd like. I'll send you his office phone number along with your check, and you can get in touch."

"Fantastic! Honestly, I can't thank you enough. The money will definitely help."

"Great. I hope one of you will call and tell me how things are working out."

"Thanks, Helen. I'll do that. By the way, how is your friend? The one who told you about me?"

"Ah, yes. She's just fine. Seeing Mike's face was a shock, but after her initial reaction, she was happy to have another picture of her beloved husband."

"Have? You mean she bought it?"

"Yes. That's only one of several paintings you sold."

"Please refund her money. I'd like to give it to her as a gift."

Helen chuckled. "You won't make a living that way. Seriously. As a professional, you have to learn to place value on your art. They're paying for your time, your talent, your supplies, everything. Could they own that piece without all you did?"

"I guess not."

"That's right. She knows that. She paid for it because she wanted your interpretation of the subject matter. No one forced her to buy it."

"Maybe she just didn't want anyone else to have it."

"You'll never know why anyone buys or doesn't buy your work. And to be honest, that's none of your business. Your job is to provide it. That's all."

They said goodbye, and Mallory tucked her phone back into her purse. She rejoined the other two people in the kitchen. Dante was sitting at a stool, sifting flour into a bowl.

"Guess what?" she said brightly.

"What?" Dante asked without looking up. He wore a lopsided smile, as if he knew exactly what was up.

"I may have a job designing fabric!"

He set the sifter down and caught her in his arms, giving her a strong, reassuring hug. "I knew it! I knew that gallery show was just the start."

She tipped her head and studied him. "How did you know?"

"That someone would snap you up if they saw your work? I didn't know for a fact, but I believed it would happen. I believe in you."

After sharing a quick kiss, he whispered, "The question is, do you believe in yourself yet?"

She smiled, realizing that she did. "I could do it."

"Do you want to?"

"Of course I want to. I think it sounds like fun. And how exciting would it be to see my paintings on someone's dress or purse or shoes?"

"Or butt," said Antonio as he entered the kitchen from the man cave downstairs.

Mallory giggled.

"Hey, Dad. I didn't know you were home." Dante rounded the counter and gave his dad a hug and a slap on the back.

"Oh, I'm here pretty much all the time."

"I thought you still went down to the station, just to hang out and shoot the breeze with the guys."

"Yeah, well, most of my contemporaries have retired. I don't know the new guys very well."

"Don't you have a son in almost every fire station?" Mallory asked.

Antonio chuckled. "You have a live one, Son. You know I like to tease, and when someone can dish it back, I like it even better." He winked at her. "Congratulations, by the way."

"So you heard the whole conversation?" Mallory asked.

"Yes. Probably the only one who didn't was Gabriella. She's completely human, but we won't hold that against her."

"Gee, thanks." Gabriella sidled up next to him and slipped her arm around his waist, giving him a squeeze. He kissed the top of her head.

"How does that work?" Mallory asked.

Gabriella gave her husband another side squeeze.

"If you're the only human among a whole family of shape-shifters, it must be kind of strange," Mallory prompted.

"I've had a few years to get used to it."

"Mallory? I...uh...I was hoping to talk to my dad for a few minutes," Dante said.

She nodded, then bit her lip. He hadn't said anything about talking to his father before now. Had he avoided telling her so she wouldn't ask why? *Stop it, Mallory. It's not always about you.*

"Why don't you take over for Dante, so he and his

dad can talk downstairs? I have some stories I can tell you." Gabriella smiled evilly at her son.

"Oh no, you don't. At least don't take out the baby pictures, Mom."

"Only the one of three boys in the bathtub."

"No, not that one!"

"Rub-a-dub-dub," Antonio said and winked. Then the men disappeared downstairs.

———

"So, what did you want to talk to me about, Son?"

Dante leaned forward and clasped his hands. "I don't want you to get the wrong idea. I'm not asking your permission as head of the family. I just want your wisdom. Okay? I'm thinking of moving in with Mallory."

His father leaned back on the couch and studied him for a moment. "Haven't you only known her for a little while?"

"Yes and no. I've known her since high school, but back then, I was only an admirer. I've gotten to know her well over the past couple of months or so."

"And you're ready to move in with her already?"

"I don't know. It feels right, but I don't want to leave Noah in the lurch."

"Have you talked to Noah yet?"

"I mentioned it. We haven't really gotten around to the details yet."

"I can tell you're in love with her. But is it the kind of love that will last?"

Dante mulled that over. Yeah, he loved her. No question. And yes, he was probably a little starry-eyed at the moment. Colors were brighter. His step was lighter.

Whenever they were apart, he couldn't stop thinking about her. "How do you know—how does *anyone* know if it will last?"

His father shrugged. "You feel like you can trust them completely, and you would forgive anything they could ever do."

Dante thought about that. Did he trust Mallory totally and unreservedly? Could he forgive her for any mistake she might ever make?

"Probably. Maybe I should wait before making it permanent. Just test the waters by living together. In fact, that might help answer my questions."

"What questions?"

"Huh? Oh, just the same ones you had a minute ago. Will it last? Also, will we drive each other crazy—or will none of the little things matter when you love someone so much?"

"I probably shouldn't say this, since I'm supposed to be a fuddy-duddy father, but it seems like the living together thing has its advantages."

"I'm glad you feel that way. It seems the safer route to go instead of getting married too soon."

"See? I knew some of my wisdom rubbed off on you," Antonio said.

"I feel bad about leaving Noah, though."

"He'll find another roommate or move to a smaller place he can afford by himself. You shouldn't base your decision on guilt for leaving your brother. Don't you think that someday he'll find his soulmate?"

"Of course he will."

"And if you're still roommates at that time, he'd probably leave you in a heartbeat."

Dante half smiled. "I would hope so."

"That's how you know you love someone, Son. When you want their happiness as much as or more than your own."

Dante nodded thoughtfully.

"Is that how you feel about Mallory?"

"Yeah, but I don't need you to tell me I'm in love. I know that."

His father slapped him on the knee and rose. "Good. One of your knucklehead older brothers needed to have it pointed out to him."

Dante chuckled. "Let me guess. Gabe?"

"That's father-son privilege."

"Does that mean you'll keep our conversation in confidence?"

"Except for your mother, of course. She's half of me. I can't keep secrets from my other half. If you're smart, you'll avoid keeping secrets from Mallory unless it's for her sake."

"Good to know."

"Now let's go upstairs and watch your mother teaching your future wife to cook."

Dante laughed. "I don't know who will be doing the cooking. I'm a pretty good cook, you know."

"Yeah, I've seen your kitchen. You cook a mean TV dinner."

Chapter 11

SOMEONE KNOCKED ON KIZZY'S DOOR.

She tap-tap-tapped her way across the floor to answer it. Hopefully, it was Noah. The PI wasn't back yet. She opened the door, realizing there was no way to know unless they spoke. Why did her father think this was a good idea? Oh yeah…because she was a witch and could break the spell—or someone's neck—in an emergency.

"Kizzy…" Noah's voice was full of kindness and concern, and all he had said was her name.

"Hi, Noah. Come in."

As soon as he stepped over the threshold, he engulfed her in a warm hug. She returned it, gratefully. Here was this wonderful man, just offering his friendship…and he was there for her. She did wish she could see his handsome face, but she remembered it quite well.

"Close the door, please. I need to lock the dead bolt."

"I'll get it."

She heard the door shut and the lock snick in place.

"Is there anything else I can do for you?"

Kizzy sighed. "Please don't treat me like I'm made of glass. I'm okay. It's good for me to get used to finding my way around without someone waiting on me hand and foot. Speaking of which, why don't we go to the kitchen? Can I offer you something to drink? Maybe iced tea or a beer or something?"

"Sure. Iced tea would be fine."

She tapped her way to the kitchen, with Noah's soft footsteps following.

"Have a seat," she said when they got there. She heard a chair slide across the floor, and she was pretty sure it was the one on the left of the small round table.

She wanted to impress him with how well she could function with her other senses alone. She retrieved two glasses from the cupboard and placed them on the counter next to the fridge. Then, holding each glass in turn, she poured two glasses of sun tea that she had made that morning.

She found her way around the center island without her cane and placed a glass in front of him. The other one she set at her spot across from him.

As soon as she sat down, she took a sip and spat it out. "Gaaaah! That wasn't iced tea. That was iced coffee, without cream or sugar. Definitely not the way I take my coffee."

Noah started to laugh, then stopped suddenly. "I didn't know if it was some kind of dark tea or if you changed your mind... I would have warned you."

Kizzy laughed at herself. What else could she do? "So, do you like iced coffee? And if so, how do you take it?"

"I see there's some sugar on the table, and I can get my own cream, if you'll allow me in your refrigerator."

"Sure. I try to keep it fairly tidy so I can find things, but someone must have reversed the order of the pitchers." She sighed. "So much for that."

Noah's chair scraped across the floor again. A couple moments later, she had her iced coffee with cream and sugar, and he even added a kiss on the top of her head.

That made her smile inside, but she didn't dare encourage him. Not yet. When this nonsense was over, she'd tell her father where to go and hope Noah was still interested in her as a woman, not just a friend.

When he was reseated, he asked the inevitable question. "So, how do you think this happened?"

"I assume you mean the blindness, not the coffee mix-up."

"Definitely. I'm pretty sure the second problem was caused by the first."

"I don't know what to tell you." *There. An answer that's short and true.*

"I did a little reading on the internet…"

Kizzy groaned.

"I know, I know. Not the best source for good information, but I didn't want to ask any doctors just in case they—" Suddenly, a loud crash stopped their conversation.

"Stay here, Kizzy!" Noah's chair scraped back so hard, it tipped over.

"What the…" If something was very wrong, she'd rather *not* be blind. Breaking the spell meant they'd have to go through the whole ritual again, but screw it. She held her hands over her eyes and whispered, "Goddess, break the spell and restore my sight." She took her hands away from her eyes and blinked when her vision returned, accompanied by stabbing bright light. After a few blinks, her eyes adjusted. Ah… It felt so good to see again. Her vision seemed okay despite the spell. She had missed colors most of all…and knowing where furniture was placed, of course.

"Where's your fire extinguisher?" Noah called out.

"I don't think we have one. What's going on?" She rushed to the living room. Flames leapt from the curtains and sofa, which was covered in shattered glass. It looked as if someone had lobbed a Molotov cocktail through the window.

"Stay back." Noah grabbed an afghan from the back of a chair and beat the flames. Clearly, that wasn't going to do enough. Whatever had been thrown through the window contained a great deal of gasoline, if Kizzy's nose wasn't mistaken.

She had to get to the book. Maybe whoever wanted it started the fire, but she couldn't let it burn.

She ran toward the study, but Noah grabbed her. "Kizzy, no! The other way!"

She fought him off. "I have to get something important."

"Nothing is worth your— Ow!"

She hit the back of his calves with the cane. When he let go, she ran to the study and, thank goodness, got there before the fire did. She yanked a book, which acted as a lever to open the hidden cabinet behind.

Grasping the precious spell book to her bosom, she rushed back the way she came but stopped before entering the living room. "Come on, Noah. Let's get out of here through the kitchen. I have my phone, and we can call the fire department from outside."

"Yeah. I thought I could get it under control, but it's too late for that."

He looked at her strangely when she glanced up at him, but he didn't say anything until they were safely out of the house.

It was more important to get the fire department there

immediately than to hold up the pretense of blindness. She tucked the book under one arm and dialed 911 to report the fire.

As soon as she hung up, she noticed Noah staring at the book. Then he looked up and stared at her eyes. "You can see…"

"I—I must have recovered."

He looked at her skeptically, then pointed to the book. "Where did you get that? I have one just like it."

She gasped. "You have the other one?"

"There are two of them?"

"Three, actually. And we can't let them fall into anyone else's hands."

Two men came around the back corner of the house, both pointing guns at them.

Oh no! The entity found us.

"Give the book to me," the older one said.

Kizzy clasped it to her chest hard and backed up. "No."

Noah stepped in front of her. "Leave. Now."

The younger blond man looked at his partner and smirked. "Oh, he asked us to leave. I guess we should just go then."

The older man raked the salt-and-pepper hair out of his ice-blue eyes and chuckled. "We're not going anywhere without that book. Hand it over."

Kizzy glanced between Noah and the two advancing men. She couldn't let anything happen to him. "Noah, step aside."

"Yeah. Get out of the way, boy," the older man said.

"I'm not leaving." Sirens interrupted the tense conversation. "The cops and fire department will be here any second."

"Then there's no time to waste." The younger one raised his pistol and aimed it right at Noah's head.

"No!" Kizzy swept the air and pushed Noah aside without touching him. Then she punched the air in front of her, and the two stunned criminals flew backward, landing on their butts. Their weapons flew out of their hands and landed a few feet away. They staggered to their feet, and as soon as they regained their equilibrium, the older man scrambled for his gun.

Kizzy tossed the book to Noah, then held out her hands, and the guns jumped into them. Now she was armed, and her assailants were on the defensive.

"Let's get out of here," the younger of the two men cried.

"Not until we have that book!"

As the first fire truck pulled up out front, so did the cops.

Kizzy drew a circle in the air, enclosing Noah and the book in a translucent bubble.

"Shit. We can't afford to get arrested. Run!" The two perpetrators rushed through the hedges toward the next street.

Kizzy drew the circle the opposite way, and the bubble dissipated.

Noah put his hand on her shoulder. "Are you okay?"

What could she say? She was definitely not okay. She had just used her powers in front of three people. All humans. She had broken one of the strictest rules of the paranormal world.

In his best Ricky Ricardo accent, Noah said, "Lucy, you got some 'splainin' to do, but it can wait. Let's meet the firefighters and tell them what we know."

Her startled gaze snapped to his face.

"About where the fire started and how. I have the feeling there's a lot more to know than what you've told me, but I'll let you take the lead on that."

"Please don't say anything about me and what I can do."

"Don't worry, babe. I have secrets too. At some point, we'll share them. I trust you."

She smiled. "I trust you too."

———

Kizzy was on the phone with her father. Or she would be if he hadn't placed her on hold. The fire department was just finishing up, and they'd managed to save most of the home. The police had taken statements from both Noah and Kizzy. Nick Wolfensen had been delayed at home, and when he finally arrived, he said he felt terrible about leaving her alone for so long.

That's when Noah spoke up. "She wasn't alone. I was here."

Kizzy slipped her arm around his waist. "I don't know what I would have done without Noah. He really did save me—and more of the house than I could or would have by myself."

Kizzy's father came on the line. "What happened?"

"The house caught fire. Somebody threw something like a Molotov cocktail through the window."

"My God! Are you all right?"

"Yes. Umm…my vision even came back."

Dr. Samuels said, "Put Nick Wolfensen on the phone."

If Noah didn't have paranormal hearing, he wouldn't have been able to follow the conversation. Nick grabbed the phone and moved a few paces away.

"Where were you, Wolfensen? Is Kizzy really okay?"

"Yes. Kizzy must have had to lift the blindness spell to get out. I'm sorry, Dr. Samuels. Truly, I am. My wife needed my help with something, and I thought Kizzy would be okay for a few minutes. Fortunately, the young man, Noah, was with her. He's a firefighter and did contain the fire to a smaller area while Kizzy got out and called 911."

Nick glanced over at them. With one hand around Kizzy's waist and the other in his pocket, Noah tried to look casual and supportive. Not possessive.

"Why were they alone together? You were supposed to make sure they stayed apart."

Wolfensen turned away and growled into the phone. "She's a grown-ass woman. If she wants to see him, there's nothing you or I can do about it. I wouldn't want to stop her from having a friend."

"Sure, having him as a friend and talking on the phone is fine. But now he's saved her life, and she'll probably think of him as some kind of hero. I had hoped by her being blind, she'd *not* be under the influence of the handsome firefighter's looks. If she'd actually get to know the guy, who is probably just an average Joe Schmoe, she'd realize she can do better. I thought by letting her discover that on her own, she'd make the right decision."

Noah tried not to show his irritation. How dare this guy assume he was some kind of moron? He became a firefighter because he wanted to. He could've gone to college, but why? His destiny was to protect the city just as his father and his grandfather had, and he was the sixth brother to follow that path. He was proud to be one of the legendary Fierro firefighters.

"Now she'll be gazing up at him with adoration," Dr. Samuels said, sounding dismayed.

"Maybe she genuinely cares for him. He seems like a good guy," Nick was saying. "Won't you even give him a chance?"

After a brief silence, the elder Samuels said, "I hadn't realized I'd hired a relationships expert. I thought I'd hired a PI and bodyguard for my daughter."

Nick shrugged absently. "You did. And if that's all you want, that's all you'll get."

Noah had hoped to invite Kizzy to his place, but he didn't know what kind of luck he'd have now. She had already snuck in the back door and put the book back in its hiding place. It was probably time to find out where her loyalties lay.

He bent and whispered in her ear. "Why don't we go to my place? There's nothing you can do here now, and I can show you the other book."

Her gaze snapped to his face. "You would do that? Show me the other book?"

"Absolutely. It's important to compare them, but it seems as if they'd be safer apart...for now."

"You're right. Let me just speak to my father for a minute."

Noah nodded and removed his arm. He watched as she strolled over to Nick's side and waited her turn.

"I think your daughter wants to speak to you."

"Put her on."

"Dad, I'm going to Noah's apartment for a little while. I need to tell you something but not here with all these people around."

"Can you stay there until I get home?"

"The place is a mess, and I don't even know if we can live in it."

At last, her father sighed. "Wait until I get there. Then I want you back home as soon as things settle down. I can wait for the insurance inspector and the fire inspector, but the minute they deem the place safe to go in, we'll grab some important things and relocate. I also want to ask you some specific questions about how close they came to the you-know-what."

"Very, but with Noah's help, they didn't get it."

"How did he help?"

"I tossed him the book so I could have both hands free. He held it so I could use my powers to force the entity to retreat."

Dr. Samuels's voice raised. "Did he see what you did?"

"Yes. There was no way to avoid it. And he didn't freak out. We haven't had a chance to talk about it, but I think we need to do that and soon. There's something else I want to check out at his place. Something he just told me about."

"What is it?"

"I'll tell you after I see it. It might be something important or nothing at all. I won't know until I see for myself."

"Fine. Just don't leave yet. Let me get there first. Can you hand the phone to the police? I'd like to talk to whomever is in charge."

Kizzy returned to Noah while her father spoke to the police and the fire chief. He must have asked to speak to Noah, because the chief walked over to the two of them and handed Noah the phone.

"Hello, sir."

"I understand Kizzy wants to go to your apartment. For how long?"

Noah looked at Kizzy. "I wasn't planning on an overnight guest. I just thought…"

"Yeah, I don't need to stay overnight," Kizzy said quickly. "I'm sure we'll all go to a hotel, won't we, Dad? I just wanted to get out of this place and…"

"I understand," he said. "Why don't you both come out to dinner with me?"

"No, Dad. I really need to see something at his place. I can meet you at a restaurant later."

"That's fine. Can you come to Elephant Walk at seven?"

"I should be able to be there by sevenish. I'll call if I'm going to be late."

"Good. And, honey?"

"Yes?"

"Forget what I said about Noah. If he kept you safe, he's all right with me."

Kizzy couldn't wait to see the book, but she wasn't going to rudely interrupt Noah as he showed her around his makeshift chemistry lab. She was right. He was kind of geeky, but in a sexy way. Whenever he walked by her, he touched her in some gentle way, like running his warm hand across her back. His touch made her shiver.

"So you thought the book was about alchemy?"

"Yeah. I still do unless…"

"Unless?"

"Unless you see something in there that changes the interpretation. You know your book. Maybe we can figure out how it fits with mine."

"I won't be able to draw any parallels...if I don't see the book."

Noah laughed. "Yeah, I guess I should show it to you." He opened the closet and took the leather-bound book off the top shelf.

Once she had it in her hands, Kizzy knew this was indeed one of the companion books. She opened it and hoped it referred to certain pagan rituals. Then she might be able to piece together not only what this was, but also why the books were separated.

"Noah, this is a breakthrough. You have the ingredients of each spell, and we have the words."

"It's a spell book?"

"Yes. One of three."

"And you know this because...you're a witch?"

"Um, yeah."

Noah laughed. "I just realized something. You're a witch and a doctor. Does that make you a witch doctor?"

"Hardy-har." She had to get back to the book. There'd be time for teasing later—she hoped. "I don't know what the entity has, but most spells consist of certain props and particular words and steps that go with them. Maybe theirs is choreography, or a code breaker, or something."

"So, you're saying that my alchemy ingredients would probably never work without the wording that goes with it."

"That's what I'm guessing. Can I sit down and study this for a while?"

"Of course. Find a comfortable spot in the living room. Can I get you something to drink? About all we have is coffee and beer." He laughed. "Ice water if you don't like either of those."

"After the day I've had, I think I'd like a beer." Kizzy wandered back to the living room, gazing at the book the whole way. She found a comfortable chair, plopped down on it, and pored over the book in more detail.

What she saw was indeed some ingredients, but they were listed in an order she didn't understand. She and her sister had been instructed to study their book backward and forward. She couldn't make the ingredients go with the spells they had. For instance, the ingredients that would help turn lead to gold didn't match up with their words for increased wealth in a different section of the book. That's what made her think the third book might be an index. If she were creating this set of books, that's how she would do it. Let each one contain only part of the information needed, but use a third one to decode everything, in case they fell into the wrong hands.

When Noah returned with her glass of foamy ale, she sipped it gratefully.

Noah gave her an intense look. "I think it's time we had that talk about who we really are. Our hidden identities."

She set the beer glass on the table next to her and licked the foam off her top lip. "You're right. You know my secret. I'm a witch, if you want to put a label on it. And you said you had some secret too, but I have no idea what it is."

"Should I tell you or show you?"

"Oh, show and tell." She smiled. "You decide which to do first."

"Okay. Sit tight." He unbuttoned the top of his shirt.

Noah's body shrank and changed shape. Suddenly, a bird with colorful tail feathers flew out of his open collar. He made a couple of rounds of the large living room before he landed on the floor behind the coffee table. At last, he grew and changed back into his human form, in all its naked glory.

The coffee table hid his private bits. He raised one hand. "Toss me my jeans, will you?"

Kizzy plucked the pants off the floor, rolled them into a ball, and threw them to him. He snatched them out of the air and managed to get them on without exposing himself.

"You don't need to be shy around me. I've seen it all before." She gave him a teasing grin.

Noah smiled. "You've seen a phoenix before?"

Kizzy knew he was purposely misunderstanding her. "Is that what you are? A phoenix?"

"Yes. That's why we make good firefighters. If fatally injured in a fire, we'll reincarnate. We can take chances regular humans can't and shouldn't. At the same time, we have to be careful not to let anyone see our supernatural side. My brother Ryan died in a high-rise backdraft. There was a very public funeral for him."

"That's right! I remember now. I thought I had heard the name Fierro—and not just because of the type of Pontiac. So, he's actually alive? Just reincarnated?"

"Yup. He lives in a castle in Ireland. And then, my brother Jayce died when… Well, it's a long story. But he came back, and now he's a firehouse captain."

Kizzy could hardly believe what she was hearing, but she had seen it with her own eyes. Noah was a shape-shifter! She had heard of those, of course. Nick Wolfensen was a shape-shifter—a werewolf. But she had only heard of the phoenix as a legend…a myth.

"I'm a little stunned. I have to admit, you handled seeing my powers better than I'm handling yours."

"Really?" He rose and strolled over to her. Sitting on the ottoman in front of her, he took her hands in his and leaned forward. "Are you upset about it? I'm not dangerous. I'd never hurt you."

"Upset? Heck no. I'm thrilled. If anything happened to you…"

Noah smiled. "Can you finish that sentence?"

She took a deep breath. "I'll try. If you died in a fire, a piece of me would die with you. I'm falling in love with you, Noah."

He grinned, then lifted her hands to his lips and kissed each knuckle. When he had finished, he said, "I love you too," then pulled her closer and kissed her lips, deepening the kiss when she opened her mouth and sought his tongue.

The kiss grew hot. He scooped her under her buttocks and lifted her onto his lap easily. She was at the perfect height for them to devour each other's mouths.

When they finally broke apart, they were both panting. He cupped the back of her head and pulled her into a warm hug. She held him long and tight. When they finally pulled apart, they clasped hands.

Kizzy suddenly realized something. "I'm glad we were friends first. I was attracted to you immediately, but if I had acted on attraction alone, I would wonder whether this was love or lust."

"I guess I know what you mean. It was the same for me, but with one exception."

"What was that?"

"For me, it's love *and* lust. I want you, Kizzy, but I don't have a condom."

She rested her forehand against his and gazed down at their clasped hands. "I want you too. And I can create a magical condom."

Noah's brows shot up in surprise. He rose and pulled Kizzy up with him. He led her to his bedroom, closing the door behind her. They gazed at each other for a moment and then began unbuttoning and unzipping each other's clothing. Slowly and carefully, they removed each piece, folding and placing everything on top of the dresser.

Kizzy knew Noah was strong, but she hadn't expected such musculature all over. His powerful thigh muscles rippled under the skin as he walked. His pecs, abs, and arm muscles all worked together as he turned down the bed.

She was glad Noah wasn't one of those guys who wanted to maul her to show how macho he could be. He didn't rip off her clothes or throw them across the room. He held the covers up for her to slide under, and then he joined her.

He cupped her cheek and stared into her eyes. "Are you really ready for this? I know your father wouldn't approve."

"Well then, it's a good thing he's not here, because I want this very much."

Noah grinned, then laid her down and leaned over, kissing her soundly. Their tongues swirled together, and she tasted just a hint of beer along with Noah's unique flavor. They moved together as one. He dipped his head and kissed a path down her sternum then over to one breast, which he suckled thoroughly. Then he moved to the other one and gave that side equal attention. When he pinched the nipple he wasn't sucking, the electricity shot straight to her womb, making her hungry with need. The area between her thighs was growing damp.

When she reached down, she found him erect and hard as steel. She massaged his cock and then leaned over and took it in her mouth. He groaned but soon let out a breath of relief. She sucked harder and watched him respond. He lifted his back up off the bed when she tugged on his balls at the same time. She loved the moans and groans that said she was on the right track. She wanted to make him feel good. The way he made her feel.

"Good God." He placed a finger under her chin and tipped her face up until he could see her eyes. "Can I give you some of that action, beautiful?"

Kizzy smiled, knowing what awaited her and hoping nothing interrupted them. If Dante chose to come home at that moment, she might cry.

She scooted back up until her head rested on the pillow, and he moved down to take his place at the intersection of her thighs. He licked her labia, taking his time. The cool smooth action of his tongue woke up her neglected body. She'd had sex before, but not often, and it was never that big a deal. She'd never been in love, nor had anyone said they loved her. This man made her feel like she was important to him. He was certainly important to her…like breathing.

He flicked his tongue across her clit, and she raised her pelvis right off the bed. The amazing sensations that shot through her were nothing like she had experienced before. He returned to lavishing attention on her most sensitive bundle of nerves. She shivered and vibrated with repeated swipes of his talented tongue.

At last, the tension spiraled to a breaking point. She felt like she was leaping off a precipice, and then she was flying. She had never experienced an orgasm like this. She felt like she could escape the confines of her body. This magnificent experience was something she hoped to repeat often.

When her spirit had finally "landed" and achieved equilibrium, she calmly pulled Noah's face up to her own and kissed him thoroughly. "Thank you."

"It's not over yet. Unless you want it to be."

She laughed. "There's no way I want to stop now."

"Do you need protection?"

"I can take care of it with magic, if you trust me?"

He smiled and settled his belly over hers, with his legs between her legs. "I trust you." Gazing down at her, he kissed the end of her nose.

She closed her eyes for a few moments, then opened them and nodded. "Go ahead."

Pushing forward, Noah entered her waiting center. It felt perfect. When he was buried to the hilt, he began his rhythm. She lifted her legs and buttocks and met him thrust for thrust. Their mating sped up as the sensations they were creating deepened. After a few minutes, she could feel the spiral of sexual pleasure rising again. When she reached her climax, she cried out.

He encouraged her to let loose. "Go ahead. Let go. Scream it all out."

Kizzy allowed herself to be swept away completely. She screamed and quivered with the most powerful orgasm she could have imagined. It seemed to go on and on. At last, he followed her over the edge, jerking and grunting with his own release.

Eventually, he collapsed beside her, and they panted, inhaling and exhaling deeply.

"Wow," Kizzy said breathlessly.

"I second that." He gathered her in his arms and tucked her head under his chin tenderly. Still breathing deeply, they recovered until at last their inhalations returned to normal. Finally, Noah sat up. "Can I get you something to drink? Another cold beer or ice water?"

"I'm fine, thanks." Kizzy rolled up off the bed and looked for her clothes. Then she remembered they were on top of the dresser. "I'll just use your bathroom and get dressed…if it's safe to go out there like this."

"We're alone. Dante won't be back for another hour or so."

"Okay." Kizzy grabbed her clothes and peeked around the open door anyway. Then she ran across the hall to the bathroom, cleaned up, and dressed.

Smiling, she realized how satisfied she was. Completely sated. Completely relaxed. Noah was good for her. She hadn't felt this contented in weeks, months, maybe even years. Soon, she returned to find Noah in the kitchen. He handed her a glass of ice water—just the refreshment she needed.

"I want to see you more often, Kizzy."

"I think that can be arranged." She reached over and drew him in for another long kiss.

He sat on the kitchen chair and pulled her down on his lap. They sat there holding each other without words. None were needed.

At last, Noah broke their silent reverie. "I want you to meet my family."

"I already met your parents at the basketball game."

"Not just my parents. We all get together for Sunday dinner whenever our schedules allow. At least twice a month."

"Don't you have a big family? Are you sure there will be room for me?"

Noah laughed. "No, but we'll make room."

"So you want me to meet your *whole* family some Sunday?"

"Yeah. I want you to meet my big fat phoenix family, *this* Sunday. Please?"

The invitation was sweet and signaled a shift in their relationship. She realized it was a direction she wanted to follow. "Okay."

"Really?"

"Yeah. I'll meet your big fat phoenix family this Sunday."

Chapter 12

MALLORY RAN FOR THE PHONE RINGING IN THE NEXT room. "Hello?"

"Mallory, honey, are you all right?"

"Mom?"

"Yes. Dad is here too. We have you on speakerphone. So, are you okay?"

"Sure. Why wouldn't I be?"

"Oh, thank goodness."

"I knew it," her father grumbled.

"What's going on, Mom?"

"We just had a strange experience. One of the native tribesmen came to us with an interpreter. He said something about a group of men having put a curse on you. He wondered why we would abandon you when you needed us."

"Huh?" *I'll be damned. It was a curse!*

Her father's voice became gruff. "I knew it was all bullshit. I just didn't know why he would say something like that and walk away. He'll probably be back, asking us for money to remove it."

"But you're okay?" her mother asked again. "Nothing has happened?"

"Yeah. I mean, sort of."

"Well, which is it?" her father barked. "Are you okay or not?"

Mallory let out a sigh. "I'm fine...now. I went

through something upsetting, but everything's all right. I lost my job, but now I have a better one."

"You lost your job?" Her father sounded alarmed.

"It's okay, Dad. A customer at the mall kind of over-reacted and got me fired. But then she felt bad and introduced me to a gallery owner. I had a show, and from that, I got a better job."

"That's exciting. What kind of job did you get?" her mother asked.

"It's something in my field, actually. I'll be a textile designer—designing printed fabric on a computer. For clothes and stuff."

"I'm glad it all worked out, honey."

"You will be? In other words, you haven't started yet." Her father had a way of drawing conclusions and stating his suppositions as if they were facts.

"No, I've started. The fashion designer asked me to use three of my paintings as inspiration. He picked the ones he especially liked. Now I'm just learning to design straight on the computer."

"Well, that's great," he said. "I never thought that useless art degree of yours would come in handy."

She sighed.

Her mother huffed in the background. "Give me the phone, Albert."

"No. I'm talking to my daughter."

"So, how are you guys?" Mallory asked.

"We're fine, but we're coming home soon."

"Really? I thought you were going to be gone for a few months. Not a few weeks."

"There's been a lot of protesting, and your father has had a change of heart."

246246246246246246

That was something Mallory never thought she would hear. Her father was all about the bottom line. There must've been some reason it wasn't lucrative anymore.

"I'm sorry it didn't turn out the way you'd hoped. But it will be good to see you." Even though she had enjoyed her freedom, she was surprised to realize she really had missed them—her mother more, but hey, she'd like a hug from her dad too.

"You guys are okay, right? The protesters didn't hurt you? No one has threatened your life or anything, have they?"

"There have been no violent threats to us," her mother said. "We're all right."

"Except for that moron threatening *you*. Now that we know you're okay, we're fine."

"So, what were the protests like?"

Her father groaned. "It wasn't like at home, where people peacefully march and carry signs. The equipment has been sabotaged. People have managed to get through the gates and argue with the workers until they quit, but that chief coming to us and telling us there was a curse on you... Well, that was the last straw."

He cared. Her father actually cared about her. She wasn't surprised about his ability to power through equipment and employee problems. That's what he did. What he'd always done. But a threat to her safety stopped him. "So, are you going to take a break and go back later to finish?"

"No, honey. We're just coming home," her mother said.

"I'm getting too old for this shit. When I was a young man, I would've taken this as a challenge, but

I'm getting older now. If they don't want us here, we'll leave them to their backward ways. I could've brought jobs, education, commerce…"

"Some people don't want that," Mallory said, knowing her honesty might upset him. "I imagine the native people around there have lived without Western ways for centuries. They might not even understand what you're trying to do."

Her father just sighed.

"Your father has plenty of options back at home. We just have to handle a few last details here, and soon, we'll be packing."

Mallory thought that her mother was probably relieved. She hadn't been thrilled with the idea of living in the jungle for months. Her father had supposedly built some kind of structure for them, not just a tent. But she was used to the finer things. Her mother hadn't been a socialite, but she was from a wealthy family. How she wound up falling for her blue-collar dad was still a mystery.

"Oh, I should let you guys know, I have a serious boyfriend. His name is Dante Fierro, and he's a firefighter."

"Oh! That's great, honey," her mother said. "Is he good to you?"

"Of course he's good to her," her father said. "It's a new relationship. She won't see his bad side for a few more months."

"I don't think he has a bad side," Mallory said.

"Ha. We'll see about that."

"You never know," her mother said. "Sometimes people surprise you."

"Are you talking about me?"

Mallory could picture the smile on his face as he teased her mom and vice versa.

"Well, let's just say you surprised a lot of people. My parents in particular."

He laughed.

"We can talk more about that later. We just called to find out if you were all right," her dad said. "Now I'm going to go and say a few words to the employees who stuck by me."

"We miss you," her mother said.

"I miss you too. When do you think you'll be back?"

"I'd say by the end of the week. There isn't a lot of packing to do since we never accumulated very much. I was able to cancel most of my interior design orders."

"Well, let me know if you want a ride from the airport."

"Did you buy a car?"

"No, but Dante has one. I'm sure he'd be happy to come and get you."

"That's sweet, but we'll probably just call a cab. I think we'd like to freshen up first and meet your young man when we're rested and relaxed. Maybe we can all go out to dinner."

"That sounds good."

Now she had to prepare the love of her life for the people who thought nothing in her life was out of the ordinary.

~~~

Kizzy called her dad. "I found it! I found the other book!"

"Seriously? Where is it?"

"I'm at Noah's house in South Boston. He thought it was a book of alchemy, and it is! Unfortunately, without the other book or books, he couldn't have created gold from the ingredients alone. And we couldn't perform some of our spells without the ingredients he has listed here."

"How big is this book?"

"Not as large as ours, but it's got about 150 recipes. I'm not really able to give you exact numbers, because they didn't put any on the pages."

"So, Noah had it. Where did he get it? How do you know you can trust him?"

Kizzy was annoyed her father would even ask that question. But if she bristled at him, he would just figure she was covering something up. "Here, why don't you ask him yourself?" She hit the speaker button.

"Uh… Hello, sir. This is Noah Fierro. I guess you have a question for me?"

"I have several questions for you, young man. First of all, where did you get that book?"

"I found it in an old bookstore on Cambridge Street."

Silence met their ears. At last, the elder Dr. Samuels said, "I know the place. I wonder how it got there?"

"I don't know, sir. Sometimes old books are found at estate sales. It could've come from one of those."

"Yes, that would make sense, if someone had the book and didn't guard it closely, then died without heirs—or perhaps the relatives had no idea what it was. Either way, he or she should've had someone clued in… By the way, how are you feeling about all this?"

"Sir?"

"I assume my daughter told you. We're not exactly a normal family."

"Yeah. I understand, and I'm perfectly okay with it."

"Wow. Just like that?"

"I admit it was a bit of a surprise. But it's okay. I trust your daughter. In fact, I love your daughter."

"I see. And if something happens between you two, are you going to tell anyone about us?"

"Absolutely not."

There was a quiet moment on the other end of the line. Kizzy knew what her father was thinking. Now that Noah knew, breaking them up would *not* be a good idea. She was quite happy with that turn of events.

"Guard that book with your life." Dr. Samuels hadn't addressed the comment to anyone in particular, but she knew he was speaking to Noah.

"I will. It may not have been passed down to me, but Kizzy has let me in on some of the secrets it might hold, and I recognize the importance of it."

"Not everyone is as lucky as we are, Dad," Kizzy said. "There are three of us. And someday, there may be more. Each generation has someone to pass it down to, usually."

"Until they don't." Dr. Samuels sighed. "Well, I would like to see this book for myself. But I don't want either of you to take it outside where it's vulnerable."

"You're welcome to come here, sir."

"You can stop calling me sir. Why don't you call me Aaron?"

Noah visibly relaxed. "Thank you, sir. I mean Aaron. Why don't I give you the address?"

"Yes, please do that."

"It's 40B L Street, in South Boston. We're on the second floor."

"Thanks. I'll be there with Nick Wolfensen as soon as possible."

"Dad?" Kizzy asked. "Is it a good idea to let anyone else in on this? I don't know Mr. Wolfensen that well. Do you?"

"I don't see how we can keep this to ourselves completely. I may need Mr. Wolfensen's strength and *other abilities* to get there safely."

Kizzy knew what those other abilities were. He might need an attack wolf. Her father didn't have the same powers. In fact, his hands were tied, in a way. He had taken the Hippocratic oath. However, even though they were both healers, Kizzy was the stronger one when it came to protection. For some reason, the females received a little more power in certain decidedly female traits: Ruth's psychic abilities, and Kizzy's matriarchal protective instincts. Her father's male protectiveness was more of a human trait. And he wasn't allowed to destroy anyone. Not that he would. She hoped.

Kizzy worried her lip. "Okay. Do whatever you have to do to feel safe, but I don't know if it's a good idea to put the books together."

"Exactly. I was thinking the same thing, so we'll have ours in its locked and warded room for now, but I'd really feel better if I could see this new book for myself first before we decide anything."

"I understand. Noah and I will wait for you. Meanwhile, I'll cast a few wards that only you and Mr. Wolfensen can get through."

"Good thinking."

"Wait a minute," Noah said. "I have a roommate. My brother. He's not due home for another hour or so, but I certainly don't want to lock him out."

"It will only be temporary," Kizzy said.

"If he comes home early, he won't get zapped trying to open the door or anything, will he?"

Both Kizzy and her father chuckled. "No. The door just wouldn't open. I don't zap unsuspecting strangers."

"Okay then. Ward away."

Aaron chuckled. "See you in a few minutes."

He hung up the phone, and Kizzy disconnected on her end. Then she set the phone on Noah's kitchen counter and draped her arms around his neck. "I think that went well. Don't you?"

Noah let out a deep breath. "Better than I thought it would."

"I love you, Noah."

"You should probably tell your dad that."

"Oh, he knows. Trust me. He knows."

~~~

What seemed like only a minute later, Noah heard a knock at his door. "I wonder who that is?"

"Can you see who's at the door by looking out the window?" Kizzy asked.

"No. Can you see through the door?"

She laughed. "Who do you think I am? Supergirl?"

He inwardly laughed at himself. "Well, if you're not, I'll just have to open the door and see who's there. There's no peephole in some of these old homes—including this one." He tucked the book in a kitchen cabinet among a couple of cookbooks.

When he got to the door, he took a deep breath before opening it. He was shocked to see Nick and Dr. Samuels there already, and they had a redheaded woman with them. "Come in."

The woman stepped inside ahead of the two men.

Noah shut the door. "How did you get here so fast?"

"Can he be trusted?" Nick asked Aaron.

"My daughter trusts him. She's a pretty good judge of character."

Kizzy entered the room. "Pretty good? I'd say I'm very good."

The woman smiled. "Except where love is concerned. Then things like judgment and trust can get very confusing."

"Spoken like someone who knows," Nick said and smiled at her.

Noah's patience for all this cryptic conversation was wearing thin. He folded his arms. "Is anyone going to introduce us?"

"Oh! I'm sorry, Noah. This is Nick Wolfensen's wife, Brandee," Kizzy said.

"How did you get here so quickly?"

Brandee shrugged. "I'm a good driver. I know how to avoid traffic."

Noah narrowed his eyes at her.

"It's okay," Aaron said. "He knows."

Brandee placed her hand over her heart. "Whew, I was afraid we were going to have to come up with some kind of bizarre explanation for my being able to change time and transport physical matter through the ether."

Noah raised his eyebrows.

"I don't think he knew all that!" Aaron said.

"Actually, I'm familiar with a deity who can do all that, and more."

This time, Brandee's eyebrows shot up. "It sounds like you're talking about my boss."

"If her name is Gaia, then yes."

Brandee grinned. "Oh, my paranormal family. How the heck do you know her?"

"It's a long story. One I'd rather not get into right now." He glanced at Kizzy.

"I agree. Dad, you wanted to see the book. Is it okay to bring it out to the living room and show everyone, Noah?"

"I don't see why not. The only one I don't know is Brandee, and Nick can vouch for her. What do you say, Nick? Can your wife be trusted with a secret?"

Nick laughed. "Absolutely. She didn't divulge mine even when she thought I was... Never mind. It's a long story too."

"Okay," Noah said. "I'll go get the book." He went into the kitchen and took it out of the cabinet where he'd stashed it. He hoped showing it to them would help somehow. He wasn't quite ready to surrender it though. He had everything set up in his lab, but having the right words would really help. Kizzy might be willing to divulge the information he needed later.

Taking the book to the living room, he handed it to Aaron.

"I'll be damned. That's it." He didn't even study it. Just a quick perusal of the cover and contents made him smile as he scanned.

Aaron turned to Brandee and nodded. Noah wondered what that was about. Suddenly, everyone disappeared except the redhead he'd just met.

———∿∿∿———

"Son of a monkey's butt!"

"Kizzy! Language!" her father said, horrified.

"I didn't swear. None of those words are swears."

"But would you say them in the ER?"

"Probably not. Sorry. But how do you expect me to react to this a-hat behavior?"

"I expect you to be on your best behavior—at all times," her father said.

"So suddenly, here I am with you and Nick. Where is Brandee?"

Nick and Aaron glanced at each other. "She's with Noah. She has to get a friend to help wipe his memory of the book."

"A friend? Who? And why?"

"There's no way we can let anyone who doesn't absolutely need to know in on this. It's for his own safety, Kizzy."

She sagged. "I understand, but how much of his memory is Brandee's friend going to wipe?" She narrowed her eyes at her father.

Her father straightened his spine. "What are you implying?"

Kizzy shrugged. "I know you don't like him. Maybe you want her to wipe his mind of my existence?"

Her father looked hurt. "I would never do that. Your love life is your own. Your mistakes are your own. I don't want to be responsible for making those decisions for you."

"And yet you tried to talk me out of seeing him."

He shrugged. "I never said I couldn't express an opinion."

"You did more than that. You told me to break up with him."

"I'm sorry. I shouldn't have."

She was tempted to make a crack about how maybe he was finally seeing her as an adult or mellowing but didn't think this was the time. "I appreciate your opinions, but not your interference." Before he could respond, she held up her hand. "I really do love Noah. And I know he loves me. I trust you wouldn't ruin that, even if you didn't approve."

Kizzy went to the refrigerator and poured herself a glass of ice water. "So, Nick. How much of Noah's memory is Brandee's friend going to erase?"

He shrugged. "Not much. We have a friend with the power to mesmerize. Ruxandra can erase memories as well as replace them with new ones. And she'll ask her to only erase his memory of the book. He won't know about its existence. That's all."

She couldn't help being suspicious. How would she pull that information out and leave everything else alone?

Brandee popped into the room. "I'm sorry it took so long. I had a nice chat with your young man before Ruxandra erased his memory—with his permission."

"Seriously?" Kizzy asked. "He agreed to it?"

"Yes. He's a good guy, Kizzy."

"I know that." She eyed her father. "I wish everyone did."

"Honey…"

"Stop. I understand. You just want what's best for me. The thing is, Noah *is* what's best for me. I've never known anyone so selfless. Maybe it will work out. Maybe it won't. But for now, he's the only true friend I have outside this family."

"I understand that now. There's no doubt in my mind

that you two could be good for each other. Of course, I'll need to wait and see."

Kizzy let out a deep sigh. "Yeah. I have to expect that. I imagine it's the same with every parent who thinks no one is good enough for their baby."

"You'll find out," Brandee said. Her bright-blue eyes twinkled.

Both Kizzy and her father looked at her in surprise.

"Oops. I guess I should've yelled, 'Spoiler alert!'"

"Wait—you can't mean Kizzy's…"

"Not yet. Sorry," Brandee said.

Kizzy smiled, and it grew into a grin. "Just knowing that I'll have children eventually makes me happy." Then she turned to her father and said, "Mazel tov, Grandpa."

Aaron groaned. "Grandpa? Already?"

Kizzy laughed. "It's not like you've got a lot of time to get used to the idea. I may not be pregnant, but Ruth is."

Suddenly, she remembered she and Noah hadn't used anything other than magical protection—and she'd never tried it out before. Maybe she was pregnant! Nah… She didn't feel any different. Still, she'd better keep that little tidbit to herself.

~~~

Dante walked into the house and hung up his jacket. "Hi, honey, I'm home."

Noah wandered into the living room, scratching his head. "I just found something, and I'm hoping you can tell me what it is."

Dante took in the strange look on his brother's face and grew alarmed. "What is it? Some kind of new bug crawling on our food or something? I told you to put everything in airtight containers."

"Come with me." Noah strode toward the back of the hall and veered left into the spare bedroom. He indicated the amateur chem lab with a sweep of his arm. "This. What's all this?"

Dante gaped at his brother with concern. "Your lab? You set the whole thing up but don't recognize it? You don't know what experiment you're doing in here?" Dante strolled up to his brother and felt his forehead. It was no warmer than usual. "Are you feeling all right?"

Noah stepped away from him. "I feel fine. Look, I'm just confused—and concerned. All of this equipment... these ingredients... This stuff is *extremely volatile*, and it's ready to go. One wrong move and *kerblooey*! I obviously know some of this stuff is mine, but who set it up? If I did, why don't I remember it?"

Dante took a step back. "Are you telling me you forgot about the alchemy experiment?"

"What alchemy experiment?"

"You can't remember you're doing an alchemy experiment? Did you inhale something you shouldn't have?"

Noah threw his hands in the air. "I don't know what's going on. If I did inhale something, it was an accident. You know I wouldn't do anything like that on purpose." He rubbed his forehead. "At least you know more than I do. What can you tell me about the alchemy thing?"

"Where's the book?" Dante hurried to the closet where he thought Noah was keeping it. He looked through the shelves, and there was nothing even remotely like it. He even looked in and picked up boxes, in case it had slipped into or behind something. "I don't see it. Did you take it somewhere?"

Noah shrugged. "I don't know what you're talking about. What book?"

Dante was becoming more and more concerned. "Come on, Bro. If you're joking, I don't appreciate the prank."

"I'm not joking."

"I believe you. You're not that good of an actor." Now he was downright worried about his brother and his state of mind. What was going on with him? "Let's go check around the kitchen and see if we can find it there."

"Okay. But I don't know what I'm looking for." Noah followed him to the kitchen.

Dante began opening cabinets and drawers while Noah just watched. Finally, when Dante didn't see the book anywhere, he turned and said, "I don't think it's here. I'll look in my own room, even though you never go in there." Then he stopped in his tracks. "You don't, do you?"

"Of course not. Why would I?"

Dante strode off to his bedroom and did a quick survey of the area. There wasn't a lot to see. He checked his dresser drawers, his closet, under his bed, but there was nothing that looked like the ancient book Noah had brought home.

What the heck could've happened to my brother? That was what was really bothering him. He went back to find Noah searching his own bedroom.

"I wish I knew what I was looking for. I guess there's some kind of book that doesn't just contain the usual science experiments." He held up a chemistry 101 textbook from high school.

"Yeah, that's not it. You said you found it at an old book shop on Cambridge Street. It's leather-bound. The pages are all yellow, and some of the edges look a little crispy. You showed it to me because it's in Latin, and you thought I could translate it. Translating it was kind of weird. It just seemed like a recipe book."

Noah stood tall and turned toward him. "Like a cook-book? Why would I get a recipe book in Latin?"

"Damned if I know. Maybe you were just curious about it. Knowing you, buying a book that intrigued you for no apparent reason isn't out of the realm of possibility."

He *might* pull a joke on Noah like this, but Noah would never do it to him. Even if he was trying to be a wiseass, he'd have given it up by now. "Come on, buddy. I think you should lie down for a bit in the living room."

"You mean I'm losing my mind, apparently."

"Maybe you're just thinking too hard. Go relax, and I'll get you a beer."

"Okay…" Noah strolled off to the living room with a blank stare on his face.

What the hell could have happened to him?

Dante returned to the kitchen and grabbed that beer while looking in places he might've missed the first time. Maybe his brother had a minor stroke, or maybe this was a symptom of early-onset Alzheimer's. He didn't even know if phoenixes could suffer from things like that. But there was no other explanation. He checked the oven and slid out the drawer below it, thinking maybe it was an absent-minded professor thing. The whole situation had him vexed.

Dante returned to the living room with two beers. Noah was on the couch with his feet stretched out on top of the coffee table. Dante handed him his beer without telling him to get his feet off the table. The guy deserved a break, *if he hadn't already had one of some kind*.

Dante took a seat in the adjacent chair, took a swig of his beer, and watched as Noah seemed to prod his brain for some kind of information. If this was a joke, he was staying in character.

"I wish I knew what happened." Noah shook his head.

"Me too." Dante leaned back and asked, "Is there *anything* else you can remember about today?"

"Like what? Like what I've had to eat?"

"Sure. Anything. Anything at all. You never know what might be a hint."

Noah leaned back and said, "I woke up in my room. Went to the kitchen and poured a bowl of that Engine 2 cereal. Got the milk out of the fridge…"

Dante was tempted to tell him to hurry it up, but he didn't dare. He might miss a critical step, so he let his brother drone on about every possible event he could remember, from getting dressed to brushing his teeth to having a phone call from… *And there it is*.

"Kizzy? She called you?"

"No. I called her. I wanted to see how she was doing. She wanted to come over, but instead, I went to see her. Then something happened… It's kind of foggy."

Dante realized something had triggered this. And perhaps that something was Kizzy. "Where is Kizzy now?"

Noah looked around as if expecting to see her. "I don't know. She was here a few minutes ago."

"Here? Here in our apartment?"

"Yeah." Noah set his beer on the coffee table and froze. "She was here along with a few other people. Her father, his friend Nick, and Nick's wife…and someone else. I don't remember who the other woman was. She was only here for a short time."

"I thought her father didn't like you."

"Yeah, I didn't think so either. But I feel like something—changed." Noah rose and took different spots in the living room as if standing in different people's shoes. At last, he shook his head. "I'm sorry. I just can't make any sense of it."

Maybe he got a bump on the head. "Do you feel well, physically? I was just thinking you may have gotten hit on the head or something."

Noah patted his head, his jaw, his shoulders, and looked at his hands and wrists. Then he stretched his legs, bent his knees, and swiveled his ankles. "Everything checks out. No pain. Everything works."

"Except your memory."

Noah let out a frustrated breath. "I'd hate to call Kizzy and say, 'Hey, can you fill me in on the last two hours? I've completely misplaced them.'"

Dante smiled sadly. If he had to say something like that to Mallory, he knew she would understand. Even if she didn't, they'd shared enough weirdness that it wouldn't even be creepy. She'd just try to help him. But would Kizzy be that understanding? He didn't think they had the same kind of easy relationship. "Maybe it will come back to you later."

"I don't know. It's not like I just forgot a name or address. It feels more like a dream, and the further I get from it, the more it disappears."

"Maybe you should call in sick tonight."

Noah stared at him. "And do what? Just rattle around

the apartment, hoping something will come back to me? I might never remember this rumored book or experiment. But I do remember how to fight fires. I think that would help me more than anything right now. Not that I wish for a fire… I'd never do that. I'd just like to feel normal."

Dante wasn't going to call him on the fact that the book wasn't a rumor. He had seen it with his own eyes. But if he was in the same situation… Yeah, Noah needed to get his mind on something else besides questioning his own sanity.

"I get it. So you'd better clean up and put on your uniform." Dante checked his watch. "We have another forty-five minutes before we have to leave, but we should get moving."

As he walked to the bathroom to grab a shower, he couldn't help wondering what the hell had happened to his brother and how to deal with it. Would just ignoring it make it go away?

Did he have the right to question his brother's girl-friend, who seemed to have something to do with this? Listening briefly to his own heart, his inner wisdom quoted his mother. *If you don't know what to do, don't do anything.*

But if some sort of solution didn't present itself soon, he might talk to their dad. That's what he was there for. The head of the family always listened and was the last word on problems any of them faced.

He might not like it, but if Noah didn't regain his memory, that's what Dante would do.

Chapter 13

A CRASH FROM THE LIVING ROOM MET NOAH'S EARS. HALF-dressed, he popped out of his bedroom and saw their front door in pieces and two strangers standing inside—only they weren't strangers. Here in his living room were the two guys from Kizzy's backyard. That was something he hadn't remembered until now. These two guys had been after something...and Kizzy had stopped them. With magic.

"What the hell do you want?"

The older of the two strode right up to him. "Where's the book?"

"Goddammit. Everyone's asking me about a book. I don't know anything about it. What book are you talking about? I have textbooks. I have cookbooks..." With a sweep of his hand, he gestured to their bookshelves. "I have all kinds of fiction, but I don't know what book you're talking about."

"You know exactly what we're talking about. And it isn't fiction. You were holding one of the books this morning at your girlfriend's house."

Noah tried to remember holding any kind of book this morning, but he couldn't. He saw in his mind these two armed and dangerous thugs, coming after Kizzy. He had tried to block her, then she had done something behind his back that resulted in the two guys flying backward. They had been holding guns but dropped them. Then

Kizzy had just extended her arms, and the weapons flew into her hands. She was a witch. He remembered that. He remembered teasing her about being a witch doctor.

Okay. He was getting some context, at last. So what the heck did these guys want with him? Were they after a book she had, thinking she'd given it to him?

The younger one leaned around Noah and asked, "Is there someone else here?"

"Yeah. My brother's taking a shower."

"Tell him to get dressed. Unless you can just hand us the book. Then we can be gone without his even seeing us or knowing we were here. That would be best for him."

"What the hell do you mean by that? How did you find me, anyhow?"

The guy had a sinister smile. "I think you know."

Noah had no idea, but he had to concentrate on getting them to leave. Maybe Kizzy knew how they learned his address. He'd ask her later. "As I recall, you lost your guns. I don't know why you're threatening me in my own home. It seems like you're at a disadvantage here."

"No. *You're* at the disadvantage," the elder one said. "You don't know what else I might have at my disposal."

Noah shrugged. "And you don't know what I have at mine. I think you should go."

At that moment, Dante exited the bathroom with a towel around his middle. He glanced at the living room. "Whoa. I didn't know we had company."

"I wouldn't exactly call them company. They broke in here."

The two strangers laughed. "Instead of making introductions, which would just be worse for you later, why

don't we just get to it? Where. Is. The. Book?" the older
one demanded again.

Dante glanced at Noah. Noah said with firm conviction, "I don't know what book you're talking about.
Seriously. I don't."

The intruders turned their gazes on Dante. The
younger criminal said, "You know though, don't you,
towel boy?"

Dante scrunched the towel tighter. "No, I don't. You
want a book? What kind of book?"

The older one stomped his foot. "*The* book!
Goddammit, the ancient book! It's in Latin. It looks
as if it's leather-bound. Actually, it's bound in skin.
Human skin."

"Gross." Dante wrinkled his nose.

Noah had the same reaction. "Human skin? Why?
Why would anyone bind a book in human *skin*?"

The two guys just laughed.

"Look, guys. We're getting ready for work. We have
to be there in less than half an hour. We'll be missed if
we're not there. I have to go put on my uniform now."
Dante turned and strode down the hall.

"I'm coming with you," the younger one said.

"Keep an eye on him," the elder man ordered. "He
knows something. I can tell." Then the guy whirled on
Noah and demanded, "If you want to keep your brother
safe, you'll hand over the book right now."

Noah stared at the ceiling and tried counting to ten.
This whole thing was frustrating as hell.

The older man decided to take a stroll through their
apartment, and Noah followed him. "What the hell do
you think you're doing? Get out."

"Not yet."

Noah didn't like violence. He didn't want to get into a fist fight, but these two guys weren't giving him much of a choice. He followed the man into the kitchen. The guy spotted his phone on the kitchen counter and grabbed it.

"Hey. Give that to me."

The bastard smiled wickedly. "I don't think so. I think there's something on here you don't want me to see. Maybe you had the book digitized?"

"Unless it's an ebook, I don't have it on there. I've never had a book digitized, and may I remind you, I don't know what the fucking book is," Noah yelled.

"Open this!" the man demanded.

They stared each other down for several moments. Sick of this idiot making demands, Noah said, "I've had enough of your shit. Get out, or I'll escort you out."

At that moment Dante appeared, cinching up his belt. The younger guy followed close on his heels.

"I'm telling you to get out," Noah yelled.

"Interesting. He didn't get riled until I picked up his phone." The blond man, speaking evenly, as if noting the results of an experiment, tipped the phone back and forth in his hand.

"I think anybody would feel that way about a phone they kept their contacts in," Dante said. "I'll bet you wouldn't want us calling any of your friends."

The guy tucked Noah's phone in his inner jacket pocket. "I'll just keep this. Unless you want to use it to call that girlfriend of yours. She knows where the book is."

Dante looked at him imploringly. "Is this something Kizzy could tell them over the phone?"

"I'm not sure."

"Yes," the older one said. "Call your girlfriend, and ask her where the book is. If she can tell us, then maybe we can avoid harming you two."

Dante laughed. "How are you going to harm us? I haven't seen a weapon."

The guy pulled something out of his boot. "Oh? You mean this?"

He had some kind of pistol with a long, thin black barrel, and now it was pointed at Noah.

"Don't tell him anything, Bro," Noah said. "I don't know what the fuck he's talking about, and Kizzy probably doesn't either. Leave her out of this."

The younger guy looked surprised. "You were there this morning! She had the book and tossed it to you. How are you claiming neither of you know where nor even what the book is? Liars!"

Dante looked from the pistol to Noah and back. "I don't know, Bro. I think you'd better tell them something. Or get Kizzy on the phone. Maybe she knows enough to get them off our backs."

Noah noticed the guy who wasn't holding the pistol moving toward Dante. Unfortunately, a wooden block with a butcher knife was closer to the guy than to his brother.

"Listen to your brother. He's making sense," the elder one said.

"Fine. I'll call my girlfriend. But let's all leave the kitchen."

"Okay." The older guy nodded to the younger.

The young guy lunged for the knife and grabbed it before Dante could. Then he moved behind Dante and, with the blade pointing at his back, said, "March!"

—⁓⁓—

"Kizzy? It's Noah."

She was glad to hear his voice, but something was wrong. It was higher pitched and seemed to tremble a bit. "Noah? Are you okay?"

"Not really. There are some guys here that claim I have some kind of book that belongs to them. I don't think I do, but they won't leave without some kind of explanation. They think *you* might know more about it."

"Oh shit…"

"Kizzy!" Her father had heard her swear.

She strode toward his voice and pressed the speaker button on the phone at the same time. When she saw him in the living room, she held her finger in front of her lips, showing him he needed to be quiet.

"Who are these guys, Noah?"

"I don't know." After a brief pause, he answered, "They said to call them 'the entity.'"

Kizzy's eyes widened, and her father's face fell. "Oh no. Please let me speak to them."

Her father reached for the phone, and she swiveled at the waist, keeping it away from him.

"Hang on," Noah said. "I'm putting you on speaker."

A familiar voice said, "Hello again. Kizzy, is it? That's an odd name for an odd girl."

Damn. It was one of the brutes from that morning. She shouldn't have let them get away.

"If I'd known you'd be bothering my boyfriend for something he doesn't have, I wouldn't have let you run off—like cowards."

"Oh? And what would you have done instead?"

"Why should I tell you? I might still want to do it."

The guy laughed. "I don't think you will. You see, I have hostages. I have a gun trained on your boyfriend, and my partner is holding a knife to his brother's neck. It's a big knife too. I've seen him use one like it on animals and reptiles—he has sliced living things in half, all the way through and down the middle, without blinking. He's quite deadly."

"Noah?" she said, her voice suddenly an octave higher. "Is he telling the truth? Are they holding you at gun and knifepoint?"

"Yes, but don't let that influence you."

She almost dropped the phone. "Don't let…"

Her father grabbed for it again. She got herself under control and stayed out of his reach. He *wouldn't* negotiate with these guys. He'd tell them to go ahead and do anything they wanted to the Fierros.

"Look, I'll cooperate. Don't hurt them. They're completely innocent. They know nothing about any books. Noah just happened to be visiting me this morning. He still doesn't know about—anything."

"Kizzy," Noah's voice announced. "Don't give him what he wants. My brother and I know how to get out of this."

Both members of the entity laughed. "Your boyfriend is very much at a disadvantage. I think he's trying to be a hero. You won't let him sacrifice himself though, will you?"

"Of course I won't." Kizzy managed to click the speaker function off before her father could answer for her. He took off into the next room. Maybe he was getting Nick, but there was nothing a PI could do that she couldn't. She strode back into the kitchen. "Now, let's talk terms."

Suddenly, Kizzy heard a loud explosion over the phone, and then silence. She gasped. "Noah?"

When she was met with no sound at all, she cried louder, "Noah!"

Nick rushed into the room with Brandee. She grabbed Kizzy's hand. "Let's go!"

Kizzy found herself floating in a cool, hazy place, still holding onto Brandee. Everything was surreal. She seemed to be staring at the immediate aftermath of a giant explosion. Flames leapt from pieces of wood, which were tumbling everywhere, like matchsticks falling to earth. Sparks and smoke flew upward from a dark cloud.

Strangely, out of that, two birds appeared. They were glowing white, but as they flew, they turned brown with the exception of their tails. Almost like the fire they had flown out of, the long feathers were orange, yellow, and red.

"What... Where are the Fierros?" she asked the minor goddess.

Brandee just nodded toward the birds.

"That's them? Noah and Dante? Are they all right?"

"Yes. They will be."

She breathed a sigh of relief, then realized he was much smaller than earlier when he'd shown her his bird form. "He looks different than he did when he shifted before."

"He was full grown. He's a baby bird again. They both are. They're flying home."

"Home? Where is that?"

"The family home in the South End. I'm not at liberty to share anything more."

"That's all right. As long as I know they're okay." She let out a breath in a whoosh. "I know where to find them. Thank you."

Brandee nodded, and they reappeared in an unfamiliar kitchen.

"Where are we? Is this their parents' house?"

"No, it's mine. I want you to see where the other book is hidden now." With a flick of her head, she indicated that Kizzy should follow her. "Since we all agreed the books are safer kept apart, Nick and I are guarding it with our very long lives, right here in our own home on Beacon Hill."

In what looked like a library, Brandee pulled a certain book's spine, like a lever. A hidden door sprang open, revealing a small panic room.

"My husband built it before we got together. Now that he has me, he doesn't really need it, but we have it to use for a sort of paranormal underground railroad or, when necessary, when the kids need a time-out."

Kizzy's brows shot up.

Brandee burst out laughing. "Kidding! They don't even know it exists."

"That's wonderful. I'm grateful to you, but I also really want to see Noah. I have to know he's all right."

"Yes, you should explain events—to the best of your ability—to their parents. Leave out the part about the books, of course. The Fierros will know what to do for them, but I imagine they'd like to know something about what happened to their sons."

"Can't the guys shift back and explain it themselves?"

"Not for a few months."

"Months!"

"Well, several weeks, at least. I'm not sure exactly how it works, but the Fierros can fill you in. Do you have their contact information?"

"I was supposed to go there this weekend for Sunday dinner. I guess I can look them up online."

"Good. Then I'll leave you to it."

In the blink of an eye, Kizzy was in her own kitchen again.

Mallory hadn't been able to reach Dante all afternoon. Maybe his phone's battery needed to be charged. She had hoped to talk to him before he went in to work at six. She hated to call him at the station, but she really wanted to talk about her parents coming home and let him know what he should and shouldn't say to them. She probably had a few days, it wasn't an emergency… But she didn't know how many days he would be on duty.

"Shoot. I really wanted to talk to him." Who else could she talk to? Maybe Mrs. Fierro—er, Gabriella, Dante's mother? Would she understand? She certainly knew what it was like to be a parent of someone with a paranormal secret. Maybe she'd be the perfect person to talk to.

She took a deep breath, remembering that Dante programmed their phone number into her contacts as well as his own and Noah's personal numbers. Maybe she should call Noah. No. He was on the same schedule.

Don't be a chickenshit, Mallory. Call Gabriella. She brought up her name and connected.

"Hello?" Gabriella answered in a musical voice.

"Hi, Mrs.—I mean Gabriella," Mallory said. "I was just wondering if you were busy."

"Well…"

The long pause concerned her. Mallory began to back-pedal. "If you're tied up right now, it's okay. I can wait."

"No, darling. You don't need to wait. In fact, it might be a good idea for you to come over."

"Come over? I was just thinking we could chat on the phone."

"Oh? Are *you* busy? If you only have time for a phone call, that's fine, but I have something to show you… something important. It may take a while to explain. Can you come for dinner?"

Dinner. She hadn't even thought about dinner yet. It would be nice to have a home-cooked meal, other than her own crappy cooking, and talk face-to-face about paranormal things.

"Yeah, I'd like to come to dinner if it's really okay. I didn't mean to invite myself over."

"You didn't." Gabriella chuckled. "I invited you. Just now."

Mallory giggled. "I guess you did. I'll just need a few minutes to get there. When are you planning on having dinner?"

"Whenever you get here. I have some leftover mani-cotti I can reheat. Antonio will be out with his old fire-fighting buddies for the evening, so it will just be the two of us. They're going to a Red Sox night game. I'd like the company."

Mallory felt better knowing that she wasn't an imposition. Also, it sounded like they'd get some privacy. "Thanks. I'll see you in thirty or forty minutes, probably."

"Great. I'm looking forward to it."

Gabriella hung up the phone and turned to her husband, who was placing bits of raw meat into the birdcage.

"What time are you leaving for that game?"

He turned, a surprised look on his face. "Are you trying to get rid of me?"

"No, it's just that Mallory is coming over, and it sounded like she needed to talk. Just in case it's girl talk, I thought it might be easier if you weren't here."

The little bird that was Dante hopped up and down and chirped at the sound of Mallory's name.

"That would be Dante's young lady, correct?"

"Yes. I can feed the boys."

"I thought you wanted Kizzy here too. Since they both need the same information, I didn't think you wanted to go through it twice."

"It would be easier for me to get the whole explanation out at once, it's true, and it might be nice for them to have each other to sympathize with, but Mallory — well, she seemed a little nervous at even the mention of Kizzy's name when she was here for Luca's graduation dinner. Did you notice that? I think there's something between those two. Noah and Dante denied any rivalry with each other, but something was clearly going on."

Dante hopped up to the edge of the cage as if he were listening intently.

"And you're sure you don't want me here?"

"You can stay if you want to, but it sounded like maybe Mallory wanted to talk to me alone. I don't mind going through it again with Kizzy."

At that moment, the doorbell rang.

"Coming," Gabriella sang out. She walked to the door, and upon opening it, she saw the beautiful brunette she had met at the basketball game. "Kizzy! Please come in."

She held the door open wide for the young doctor and shot a questioning glance at Antonio.

Kizzy seemed hesitant but entered and held out her hand as if to shake Gabriella's.

"Oh, we can't have that. No handshakes here," she said and grasped the girl around her back. Both of them were petite, so it was a treat for Gabriella to hold someone her own size.

"Thanks, Gabriella. I needed that."

"I'll bet you did." She took Kizzy's hand and led her into the dining area where the birdcage was. Her son, the baby bird Noah, hopped up and down and flapped his wings.

Antonio strode over and stuck out his hand for a handshake. Kizzy looked confused but took his hand and shook it. He laughed, then pulled her into a hug. "It's nice to see you again, Kizzy. Apparently, I'm on my way out to a night game at Fenway."

"Apparently?"

"Well, that was the plan five minutes ago."

"Oh. Aren't you curious about what happened?" She pointed to the cage. "That's what I came to tell you."

"I certainly am." He looked at Gabriella. "Are you sure you want me gone for the evening? I'd really like to stay. I can go to a game anytime. That's what season tickets are for."

Gabriella smiled. "Of course you can stay. It's your

house. If we need some privacy for girl talk later, we can just move to the man cave and turn it into a woman cave." She winked.

"Or I can lock myself in my man cave and let you have the whole rest of the house."

Gabriella giggled. "That would probably be better. Let me put on some tea, and we can all get comfortable while you tell us what you know, Kizzy. Or would you rather wait for Mallory?"

"Mallory is coming?"

"Yes. She called a few minutes ago. She'll be here for dinner in thirty or forty minutes. I hope you can stay for dinner too."

"If it's no imposition… I'd like to get to know Mallory better—oh, and you two, of course!"

"Wonderful! Have a seat. I'll be right back with some tea."

Kizzy and Antonio sat at the dining room table while Gabriella filled the electric teapot and plugged it in. Wishing she had something fancier on hand, she settled for putting some cheese and crackers on a plate and brought that over first.

"I'm afraid we only have one type of tea in the house. Good old Lipton. Is that all right?"

"Perfect," Kizzy said.

Gabriella put a teabag right in each cup and set them on a tray on the kitchen counter.

Before she sat down with the two of them, Gabriella heard Antonio ask, "Would you like to feed the boys?"

She peeked around the corner as Antonio passed the little Tupperware container with a few strips of beef to Kizzy.

She took it and held up one strip of meat. "Is this what they eat?"

"Yes. You can hold it in your fingers. They won't bite you."

"Do they know who I am?"

"They have some of their memories, even though their maturity is in question. Well, not in question so much as just not there yet. They have to grow up all over again in bird form before they can shift back. At least that's the quickest way to do it. Every time they're in bird form, they age faster. In human form, they age much more slowly."

Kizzy took a strip of meat and poked it through the cage. One of the little birds hopped up to her, chirped, then opened his mouth wide. She dropped the meat, and he swallowed it whole.

"Was that Noah?"

"Yes, I believe it was."

"How can you tell them apart?"

Antonio shrugged. "I'm not the one to ask. Gabriella could tell you for sure."

Gabriella smiled. "Yes, that was Noah. A mother just knows. So what happened to them?"

Kizzy sighed. "It's a long story, but you deserve to hear it first. I'll start with the fact that there may be things I have to leave out, but I'll tell you what I can."

"We understand," Antonio said. "You don't know us that well yet, but you'll learn you can trust us."

"I'm counting on it. I'm a good judge of character, so I've been told."

The whistle on the teakettle blew, so Gabriella unplugged it, set it on the tray, then brought everything to the table. As soon as she sat down, Kizzy began her story.

"So, here goes…"

Over the next half hour, Kizzy explained about her family having something that a group in South America wanted. She called the group "the entity" and said she would tell the Fierros what she knew about the group, but that was limited, because she didn't know much. When she got to the part about a big battle in her backyard and how she and Noah went back to his apartment afterward, she stopped and blushed.

"Oh?" Gabriella tipped her head, smiling. She hoped Kizzy would feel comfortable enough to elaborate on her relationship with Noah, but she probably wouldn't. Actually, she didn't have to. The look on her face said it all.

"Noah revealed his other form to me. He didn't have much time to tell me about phoenix shifters, but I'm glad I knew what he was. That's the only reason I wasn't totally confused and shocked by…this." She indicated the cage with a sweep of her hand.

Gabriella was delighted. Her boys didn't reveal themselves to a woman unless the relationship was serious. Noah seemed to have met the lady love who would understand his paranormal secret.

Kizzy continued. "So, an hour or so later, I called my father. He and a couple of his friends showed up, and that's when I was transported home—against my will, I might say. A few minutes later, the phone rang, and it was Noah. Dante had come home by then, and they were being held hostage by the entity."

Gabriella was curious about her father and friends and what she meant by "transported against her will" but didn't want to interrupt her. They could ask questions later.

"Noah sounded kind of scared, and when he said a couple of guys calling themselves the entity were there, I got scared too. Very scared. These guys think nothing of skinning people alive to get what they want, and both Dante and Noah were innocents caught in the middle."

She worried her lip as if remembering the moment. "One of the entity said he had a gun pointed at Noah and his cohort had Dante at knifepoint. I would have done anything to save them. I was just beginning to negotiate when Noah called out not to tell them anything and said he and Dante knew how to get out of it.

"A few moments later, I heard an explosion."

—~~~—

Mallory jogged up the steps, looking forward to seeing the Fierros again. Upon knocking, Gabriella opened the door.

"Mallory! Come in!" Gabriella took her hand and led her into the dining room.

When she saw Kizzy, she froze.

Gabriella tightened her grip on her right hand.

"Now, girls. We've sensed there's something going on between you two. It's none of our business, of course, except if it affects our sons. I don't think anyone wants to come between them, knowing how close they are."

Mallory's posture deflated, as did her fear. "I'm sorry. It's probably my fault. Kizzy? You remember that day…when we almost met but didn't. You know the day I mean?"

Kizzy seem to understand. "It's okay, Mallory. I'm not judging. If anything, I need understanding too."

Mallory gazed at her and saw some sort of sympathy

coming back...no, not sympathy. It wasn't sympathy. Maybe hope?

Gabriella pulled Mallory to the dining room table and said, "Please. Have a seat. We're just having some tea and appetizers before dinner." Then Gabriella placed her other arm around her and gave her a friendly squeeze. "I hope you know how welcome you are. We want to get to know both of you better. We know you're important to our sons."

A little bird in the cage she hadn't noticed before chirped and hopped up and down, flapping its wings.

"I don't know if you've met Dante in his other form," Antonio said.

Mallory wandered over to the cage, openmouthed. "That's him? He was bigger last time I saw him in bird form. Is he still a phoenix or some kind of sparrow?"

Gabriella laughed. "If he could speak, he'd let you know he's no sparrow. Yes, my boys are smaller but growing up again in phoenix form. If they shifted now, they'd revert to infants, complete with the amnesia that happens when human souls return. It's just faster and better if they grow up in bird form."

"I see they're still roommates. How did they get this way?"

"Kizzy can explain what happened."

Gabriella let go of Mallory's arms, and now that she was more curious than scared, she finally sat down at the table.

Kizzy reached across the table, offering Mallory her hand. She took it, and they shared a sympathetic squeeze.

"Mallory, what happened might be a little upsetting. Do you really want to know?"

"Absolutely. I'm *not* fragile, despite what some people may think." She may have said that a little too emphatically.

Kizzy let go of her hand. "I know you're not. I just wanted to make sure you wanted the whole story. Like I said, it could come as a shock to anybody."

Mallory nodded.

"Well, the short explanation is they blew themselves up."

Mallory would have liked to hide her shock, but she was sure her eyes must be bugging out of her head. "They what?"

Kizzy grimaced. "I'm sorry if that was blunt. They wouldn't have done it if it weren't absolutely necessary. Basically, they were being held hostage, and it was my fault." She hung her head.

"Oh. I'm sorry. I don't think I know anything about this. Hostage? How?"

"No, you probably don't. Noah was sworn to secrecy, and he's good to his word. I don't know how much Dante knew about it. Noah probably didn't even tell him."

"That would make sense. Noah seems like a very trustworthy person."

"He is," Gabriella said. "All my boys are."

"And so are we," Antonio added.

"I know. You're a very special family," Mallory said. And she meant it. Not many people would witness her turn into a spider monkey and not bat an eyelash.

"Now, getting back to the situation that led up to this."

"There's not a lot I can say," Kizzy said. "But that's because I've been sworn to secrecy too. If we… Never mind."

"Say what you were going to say," Mallory prompted.

Kizzy shook her head. "It's too soon."

Gabriella cleared her throat. "If I may be so bold, and I don't know if this is what Kizzy was going to say, but *I'm* going to say it, if you two become part of this family, there will be no more secrets. We will trust each other completely. If you can't do that, say something right now."

The girls glanced at each other across the table and then at Gabriella.

Kizzy spoke up first. "Are you psychic too?"

Antonio burst out laughing. "Our sons think she is, but her only superpower is she's a mom! And her women's intuition is scarily accurate."

"Well, yes, that's sort of what I was alluding to," Kizzy said. "But I don't know where we are relationship-wise. Mallory and Dante seem a lot further along than Noah and I. We were just getting close. I'm guessing you and Dante are—serious."

One of the little birds jumped up and down and chirped. Gabriella chuckled. "That was Dante. I think he was affirming your assumption."

"So, you can't understand bird language?"

"No. Antonio is a little better at guessing than I am. Plus we've come up with a way to get yes or no responses. If you ask them a yes or no question, and they look at you with their right eye, it means yes. If they look at you with their left eye, it means no."

Mallory smiled at the little bird. "Well, then, in answer to Kizzy's question about if we're serious... I'd say yes."

Dante looked at her with his right eye. Encouraged

to say more, she added, "We're in love. I wish I could throw my arms around him right now and give him a hug and kiss, but I'm afraid I don't know how to hug or kiss a bird."

Antonio laughed. "It's probably better if you don't. Our beaks can be sharp. You *can* let them hop on you and stroke their feathers, but hugging and kissing is probably not a good idea. Oh, and if they poop on you, it means good luck!"

Gabriella gave her husband the stink eye. "He doesn't mean it, Mallory. He's just a big tease, and his sense of humor is a little warped."

Antonio feigned offense. "Warped? Me?"

Gabriella smiled at him. "Don't give me that. You know you are, but everyone loves you just the same. We are a very forgiving family, girls."

"Good thing—for me." Mallory let out a sigh of relief.

"Me too," Kizzy said. Then she focused on Mallory again and smiled. "I'm a witch."

Mallory's eyebrows shot up, then she quickly schooled her expression. "Really? A real witch, like with a wand and broom and everything?"

Kizzy laughed. "It's not like the cliché. I do cast spells, but I don't own a black cat, fly on a broom, or use a wand. I'm a healer. I can touch people and cure them. But only one per day, or else I'll deplete my own energy."

"Oh! You have the perfect job then. An ER doctor."

"Yes and no. It's hard to choose between patients. Especially if I get a serious case that *might* make it on his or her own. I never know who could come even closer to death later on in my shift."

"Do you actually save people from dying?"

Kizzy smiled. "Well, yeah. All doctors do on occasion. But I can actually pull someone back if they pass away."

"Wow! No wonder it depletes your energy. I'm glad you didn't waste your magic on me. I wasn't crazy."

"I never said you were. Which isn't to say magical healing for mental health would be a waste. It's just a lot more complicated. One doesn't know if it's nature or nurture. Curing a DNA anomaly is one thing, but trying to reverse a whole childhood of abuse or neglect—well, that's getting into strange territory."

"I was cursed."

This time, it was Kizzy who looked shocked. "Cursed? That's awful! Who would do that to you?"

"It's kind of a strange story, but here goes... My father is a real estate developer. He's in South America in a rain forest, trying to open a resort on the Amazon River. According to a wizard Dante knew, there was some kind of ritual done down there.

"I guess he ticked off the wrong people. I don't know why the curse came to me instead of him or my mother, but it did. Or maybe they were cursed too, but in a different way. There were protesters...workers quit... Eventually, they gave up and they're coming home soon."

Kizzy looked uncomfortable. "I wonder if... Um, what I'm about to tell you can't leave this room. Swear?"

Mallory raised her right hand. "I swear."

Mr. and Mrs. Fierro just nodded.

"There's a group in South America that my family considers its nemesis. We call them 'the entity.' We think they're based in Brazil near the Amazon. That's as close as our locator spell can pinpoint them. They must have wards to protect their exact location. But now, if they have to move because of development in the area, they may be risking exposure. That could be considered a threat."

Mallory was astounded. "Yes, my father is in Brazil—right on the banks of the Amazon River. This group... Are they Northern European–looking?"

"Yes. Northern European. Can you find the spot on a map?"

"I could get close, but I don't have a physical map. Could pulling one up on my phone work?"

"We have one," Gabriella sang. She excused herself and trotted off in the direction of the stairs.

"So do you think these guys might be the same group? Your nemesis and my cursers?"

"Possibly." Kizzy worried her lip while waiting for Gabriella, who returned a little out of breath and laid a framed map of the world on the table.

"Thank you." Kizzy fell silent as she studied the map. Eventually, she lifted it so it was facing herself and Antonio only, then she touched it, drawing a small invisible circle. "Go ahead and show me where your father is." Kizzy turned the map around and laid it face up in front of Mallory.

After studying the map's topography for a moment, Mallory picked out the bend in the river her father had shown her and tapped it. "There."

Kizzy waved her hand over the map, and her invisible circle turned red, surrounding the exact place Mallory had pointed to.

Kizzy muttered, "Holy guacamole. That red area is the tightest we could narrow it down to. It's still hundreds of miles wide. You may have just pinpointed their location. The guys we're worried about are Northern Europeans somewhere in this area. I don't know about any natives working with them. I kind of thought these guys were racist."

"The wizard who tried to lift the curse said he saw one native. Maybe it's like how the Native Americans helped the Pilgrims survive in Plymouth. They needed them."

Mallory wondered if Kizzy was thinking the same thing she was—that their situations were linked…or related. If so, maybe she was cursed too! She didn't know how to ask. Kizzy looked like she was thinking hard.

The girls were silent for so long that Gabriella eventually stood up, clasped her hands, and said, "Well, I'd better get dinner ready."

Antonio rose. "And I have a thing…downstairs. I'll be gone for a few minutes, or maybe several, depending on when dinner is done."

Gabriella chuckled. "Don't worry. I'll call you the minute we're ready."

Antonio handed the container of shredded meat to Kizzy. "Would you like to give the boys the rest of their dinner?"

"I'd be happy to." Then Kizzy looked over and offered it to Mallory. "Unless you'd like to do the honors."

She smiled. "Yeah. Just show me how it's done." She rose and walked around the table, taking Antonio's seat next to the cage.

Chapter 14

ONCE EVERYONE HAD LEFT THEM ALONE, KIZZY AND Mallory took a few quiet minutes to feed the birds. At last, the shredded meat was gone, and Mallory set the container aside. Kizzy passed her a napkin to wipe her hands.

"Can I trust you, Mallory?"

"I won't breathe a word, no matter what you tell me."

"Okay. I kind of mentioned this already, but there's more to it. My whole family are supernatural witches. We're born with powers humans will never achieve, no matter how long they study magic and witchcraft. There is a book we were given to guard with our lives. It's one of three.

"Recently, another one was discovered here in Boston. Now we have two of the three, and they're hidden in different locations behind a ton of magical wards. The family's nemesis I mentioned is a scary group calling themselves 'the entity.' We think they're made up of the descendants of Nazi war criminals who were hiding in Brazil.

"As you may or may not know, there was a belief in occultism among some of the elite SS. They honestly believed they could become gods if they could purify their race. They have the third book and are looking for the others. We think they want them because it would shorten the length of time they'd need to evolve their race into gods.

"I don't know if this has anything to do with your father or not, but I wouldn't doubt it. This group is *not* made up of witches. They don't hold the same values witches do. The Witches' Rede is similar to the Hippocratic oath. It boils down to 'Harm none.' These guys don't care who they harm, as long as they get the books."

"You say they believe in the occult. Does that mean they're using occult spells or curses or whatever to find the other two books?"

"I don't doubt it."

"Up until now, I couldn't think of who could or would ever want to put a curse on me. Dante was the one who thought of finding out if my symptoms might be from a curse or wayward spell, and then he asked that wizard he knew to lift it. He was able to remove part of the curse. I don't see dead people anymore."

"That's why you were seen talking to yourself? You were actually talking to spirits?"

"Yes. And I haven't seen any ghosts since the hex breaking. But there's another thing that didn't get lifted."

"You mean the part where you turn into a monkey?" Kizzy asked innocently.

Mallory's eyes widened. "You know about that?"

"I know that the monkey at the basketball game was wearing your cute white pin-tucked blouse and carrying your JanSport crossbody bag."

"You thought my blouse was cute?"

Kizzy burst out laughing. "That's what you took away from that?"

Mallory giggled. "I was trying to lighten the moment."

Kizzy smiled. "I'm glad we're having this conversation. I really want us to get along."

"Me too. So what can *I* do to help your family protect the books from the entity?"

"Nothing. We've done all we can. There are wards around both places and people to reinforce them if necessary. All you can do is keep this completely to yourself and help us find that exact location."

Mallory fidgeted in her seat until Kizzy noticed her discomfort.

"What's the matter? Are you afraid you might not be able to keep this secret?"

"It's not that. My parents are coming home. I don't know what to tell them. I mean, about me. I would never mention anything about your family or the books you have—unless you wanted me to."

Kizzy breathed a sigh of relief. "Thank goodness. Can you imagine the implications if word gets out that these books lead to unlimited power?" *Hell, I shouldn't have told her anything.* Then she corrected her inner language. *Heck—I mean heck.* "What have you told them already?"

"Nothing at all. I was hoping I could get this all resolved before they came home. I'm an only child. They worry about me enough as it is. I had to reassure them a million times that I'd be all right on my own. I'm twenty-five years old, for heaven's sake."

"I understand, but all parents worry. I'm not an only child, and I'm older than you are. My father is still overprotective. So what do you feel you should tell them? I mean since you could turn into a monkey right in front of their faces. It doesn't seem like something you can control if you get nervous."

"You're right. I can't. I don't know what to tell

them." Mallory dropped her head into her hands. "I'm screwed."

Kizzy wrapped her arm around her new friend's back. "Would you like me to get rid of that particular problem for you?"

Mallory's gaze snapped to hers. "Can you? Even if you don't know how I got this way?"

"I think so. Sometimes, I have no idea why something is happening to a patient, but it doesn't seem to matter. I just want to help them, and that seems to be enough."

"So, does that mean you want to help me?"

Kizzy smiled. "If you want my help, I'd be happy to give it."

"Yes, please."

Kizzy closed her eyes and channeled her energy into Mallory.

"So, can you do it?"

"It's already done."

Tears streamed down Mallory's cheeks. "Thank you, thank you! I don't know how I can ever repay you, but I'll be forever in your debt."

Kizzy laughed. "Nobody repays me. There is no debt. This is my destiny."

Mallory gazed at her openmouthed. "That's quite a destiny. I don't know what mine is. Just to make the world more interesting, I guess." Her cheeks pinked.

Kizzy still had an arm around her and gave her a side hug. "That's a valid destiny too."

Gabriella entered the room and smiled. "I'm glad you girls are getting along. Dinner will be ready soon. Which one of you would like to set the table?"

Mallory looked at her hands. "I just had meat juice

all over my fingers. I'll have to wash up, and then I'd be glad to help."

"Same here," Kizzy said.

The birds chirped as if to say, "Thanks for all the meat."

"Follow me, girls. I'll show you where I keep the silverware and dishes right after you wash your hands."

––––––ᴘ––––––

Mallory met her parents at the airport by the luggage carousel. She was genuinely happy to see them, and they each gave her a strong, warm hug. "I'm so glad to see you, honey," her mother said. "We missed you."

"Same here. You too, Dad. Did you have a good flight?"

Her father groaned. "It's been a challenging few days, but I think the flight was the most relaxing part of it, even with the turbulence." He laughed.

"I'm surprised you're in a good mood. I thought you'd be very upset about your project not panning out."

Mr. Summers sagged. "Well, I've been trying to be philosophical about it. It was a good idea, but maybe it wasn't meant to be. I hit roadblocks everywhere—not literal ones, although the damn protesters did their best to keep the construction crew out. It was just too stressful."

"I was worried about his health."

Alarmed, Mallory asked, "Are you okay? Did you have chest pain or anything?"

"No, but it might have been a matter of time. I had to throw in the towel and admit it was just not worth it. Sometimes, you have to let things go."

She hugged him. "I'm glad you're able to take it philosophically." She had never known him to be that way. Maybe he'd been changed by the experience, in which case all was not wasted. "You're right, and sometimes things don't work out, but it's the best thing that could've happened to you."

Her mother smiled. "Is that coming from experience, dear?"

"Maybe. I never would've believed it if it hadn't happened to me. I really like my new job."

"You'll have to tell us more about that later," her father said. "I'm exhausted."

"Where's your young man?" Her mother glanced around the airport.

"Oh, Dante couldn't be here. You'll meet him... sometime."

Her father, Nigel, asked, "Is he working? Or did he just not want to meet your parents?" He laughed. "Not that I want to meet anyone right now either."

"No, he wanted to meet you, but something else took precedence. He...uh...he had to fly somewhere at the last minute. A family member died. He might be away for a while."

"Oh, that's a shame," her mother said. "We were looking forward to meeting him."

Before they could get any further into it, Mallory said, "So where are your bags? Let's get you home. I know how cruddy I feel after a long flight."

Her father smiled. "I can't wait for a nice hot shower."

Her mother leaned toward her, side-whispering, "And a glass of brandy wouldn't hurt."

Mallory's father didn't have a drinking problem, but he had one to relax after a tough day, and those seemed to be fairly frequent. But this must've been the mother of all bad days. All the stress of the job must have been awful.

They got the bags and wheeled, carried, or rolled them to the cab. Mallory wanted to get help, but her father insisted they didn't need it.

"Wow, you had a lot of stuff. I thought you didn't."

Her father laughed. "You never know how much crap you have until you have to pack it all up and move it."

Her mother rolled her eyes. "So, it sounds as if you started your new job and it's going well..." She was a master of changing the subject.

"I've been learning a lot. It's on-the-job training, so to speak. I can have a great idea, but it doesn't always translate the way I see it in my head. Of course, that can happen with a painting too. I'm just more invested in getting things exactly right. I need a few days to get everything just the way I want it. There are differences between working on a canvas and working on a computer. It takes a while to get used to it."

When they reached the taxi stand, the driver popped the trunk open. As he loaded the trunk, Mallory wondered if they shouldn't have asked for a van.

"How much stuff did you bring home anyway?"

Her mother laughed. "There were so many wonderful things there, and I just couldn't leave them. I took a few of the smaller items and packed up some of the bigger ones to be shipped later."

Mallory stared at her. "You mean there's more?"

She giggled. "I bought a few things for your town house. How is it working out, by the way?"

"It's working out just fine," her father snapped. "I don't build junk."

"I never said you did, dear. I just wondered how Mallory was adjusting to living on her own in her own home."

So, her father's good mood lasted about ten minutes. That was some kind of a record. It didn't take long to find a hot button and push it. At least she wasn't the one who had set him off this time.

Kizzy's father was intrigued when she brought home the map with the red circle on it and told him about Mallory. She'd had her make a blue ink mark as close to the exact location of her father's construction project as she could. It was almost dead center. If one moved the dot to the other side of the river, it would indeed be the exact midpoint.

"So, how did you meet this girl?"

"She's Dante's girlfriend. Dante is Noah's brother."

"I see. So, where is Noah anyhow? I haven't heard about him for a while. He didn't forget you when they wiped his mind, correct?"

She forced a laugh. "Of course not." Kizzy didn't know whether or not Nick or Brandee had explained what had happened to him. Apparently not. Her father could have discovered the house in South Boston was now a pile of kindling, but maybe he didn't care enough to check. That made it easier. She really didn't want to say a firefighter blew up his own home.

She still wasn't quite sure about the how. It happened so fast… She suspected it might have had something to do with his lab, but she didn't know what he had already set up. Maybe a combination of chemicals that were dangerous when mixed were close at hand.

"I saw him the other day. He's fine. Just, you know… doing his thing." *Yeah, growing up all over again.*

"Ruthie said she hasn't sensed any threats recently. I wonder if the entity gave up? That doesn't seem like them."

Kizzy wished she could tell him Noah was the one responsible for eliminating the threat. But until and unless she had permission to share her knowledge of Noah's paranormal side, she wouldn't be able to tell her father about the reincarnation. So she just had to hope Noah returned to full-grown human before he found out that her boyfriend had blown himself to smithereens — in the ultimate heroic sacrifice.

"It looks like I'll be able to go back to work," Kizzy said.

"They'll be happy to have you. I hear it's been busy down there in the ER. People have asked me how you are."

"Yeah, I can't wait to tell them I had hysterical blindness, but now I seem to be fine." She rolled her eyes.

"It could happen to anyone, Kizz."

"Sure. I just don't think they're going to believe it happened to me. And in a way, I hope they don't. It's a psychiatric problem."

"Well, they believed me. And since I already made excuses to HR for you, that's the story we need to go with. They'll keep the reason to themselves, and when you're ready, they'll clear you. As long as you behave professionally, nobody will think you don't belong back at work. Your supervisor will know, of course, but you shouldn't have to say anything to your coworkers except 'Hey, it's great to be back.'"

"I'll keep that in mind."

Kizzy wouldn't blame them if they made her see a shrink before she went back. Hysterical blindness was pretty uncommon. The newer diagnosis, known as conversion disorder, was made when someone presented with neurological symptoms like numbness, blindness, or paralysis not due to a well-established organic cause.

She would never expect to experience it based on the reports of Freud and a few of his neurologist colleagues. They believed many women suffered from what they termed "hysteria." Later on, it was discovered that many of these cases stemmed from sexual abuse, but the doctors covered for their wealthy patrons. The main thing Freud did right was to give the symptoms credibility and take it out of the "faking it" or malingering category.

She figured whatever condition presented as hysteria, it had to cause significant distress, and eventually, it could be traced back to a psychological trigger. She certainly had one of those she could weave into her story. Likely seeing someone hit by a train could remind her of witnessing her mother's and grandmother's sudden deaths. But had anyone been hit by a train recently? It didn't matter. She could have seen it in a movie or on TV or something.

Just to be sure she had her story straight, she grabbed the nearest psychiatric diagnostic manual off the shelf of their library. She was glad she did. Apparently, they'd kept the main category of conversion disorder but had also given her little excuse a subtitle called functional neurological symptom disorder. The new criteria covered the same range of symptoms but removed the requirement of a psychological stressor. *Well, okay. That doesn't sound quite so bad.*

She could do this.

Returning to the hospital meant everything to her. She wanted to help the people she had helped before. Not only those at death's door due to horrendous accidents or heart attacks, but even the usual sniffles and scrapes. Even though it had only been a few days, she missed it terribly.

"Well, Kizz, we both need to get to work," Aaron said. "But I want to talk about this map more later."

That was just perfect for her, because she needed to talk to Mallory and get their stories straight first. She wanted no mention of houses blowing up, boyfriends growing up, or monkeys showing up. Mallory would understand that last one, for sure.

<hr />

Antonio had called a family meeting. This usually entailed every son and his spouse, but he decided to let Ryan and Chloe off the hook this time. They were in Ireland and really didn't know what was going on with their younger brothers and the girlfriends. Nor did they need to.

Antonio sat at the head of the table, with his sons Jayce and Miguel and their wives Kristine and Sandra on one side, then on the other side Gabe and Misty, who was holding their baby, Tony, and Luca. Gabriella was gathering items for snacks in the kitchen.

"I'm glad you're all here," Antonio said. "This is a delicate situation, but we believe it must be dealt with. As you can see, two of your brothers are here too—sort of." He indicated the cage with the two phoenixes who were probably in their bird teens now.

Gabe asked, "What's going on, Dad?"

"Here's what we've been able to get from your brothers' girlfriends. Dante is dating Mallory Summers. Noah is dating Kizzy Samuels. They were here the other day, and Kizzy explained what happened. It's not the usual thing."

"It certainly isn't." Gabriella came in from the other room with a tray holding a big carafe of coffee, cream, and sugar, plus a plate of cookies. Fresh-baked biscotti, if Antonio wasn't mistaken. Gabriella always made her own.

After she had placed the tray in front of Antonio, she gathered coffee mugs from the hutch nearby and set them in front of each son and daughter-in-law.

"What's so unusual about this one?" Jayce asked. "Did they not die in a fire?"

"That's correct." Antonio pinched the bridge of his nose. "Apparently, they blew themselves up."

The young men all stared at the cage. The birds looked down and then turned to face away from the large group as if in shame.

Gabriella jammed a hand on her hip. "It's not what it sounds like, for heaven's sake. They didn't do it on purpose. Or even if they did, it was necessary at the time."

"I'm confused," Miguel said. "What would make it necessary for two of my younger brothers to blow themselves up?"

"Let me explain the best I can," Antonio said. "Kizzy told us they had been taken hostage. Apparently, she and Noah had something the kidnappers wanted."

"Although they didn't really kidnap the boys." Gabriella took a deep breath and sighed. "They were in their own home. Someone broke in and threatened them. Noah had just given the item, whatever it was, to Kizzy. And Kizzy had taken it home.

"He was forced to call Kizzy, but he didn't really want her to bring the item they wanted back. When she was negotiating for their safety, Noah yelled, 'Don't do it. My brother and I know how to get out of this.' Then she heard a loud explosion."

"Okay," Jayce interrupted. "It *does* sound like the explosion was done purposely, as a way of dealing with the problem. Whatever Kizzy had must've been important for them to resort to that, or they didn't think they'd make it out alive any other way."

"Does anyone know what happened to the kidnappers, for lack of a better term?" Misty asked.

Antonio frowned. "Why don't we call them what they were? Criminals."

"Were?" Misty asked. "Are you sure they're…"

"Dead?" Gabe had put his hands over little Tony's ears as he finished Misty's sentence for her. She looked up at him gratefully.

"I would imagine so," Antonio said. "I visited the spot where their house used to be. It's a foundation and charred rubble now."

"Shit," Jayce muttered. "Did anyone else get hurt?"

Gabriella smiled sadly. "No, thank goodness. They had downstairs neighbors up until about a month ago, but they moved out."

"So what excuse did you give the chief this time?" Miguel asked his father.

Antonio groaned. "We used up most of the usual ones. Ryan supposedly died, and because it was on the

job, we had to go through a big public funeral. There
was no way around it. That could have caused all kinds
of problems if anyone had discovered the casket was
empty. Ryan still can't show his face in the city. Not
for a century or so. And Jayce, you supposedly were in
a coma. We were just lucky you were visiting your girlfriend at the time and Kristine lived in New York. That
kept your buddies from trying to drop in to visit you."

Gabriella looked sheepish. "We decided to give the
chief a happy explanation this time."

"You decided," Antonio corrected.

"Well, people are beginning to feel sorry for us and
wondering if, with so many accidents, having several
sons in the fire service is a good idea."

"That's one fatality out of seven," Gabe said. "I didn't
die. I was burned over fifty percent of my body. We told
everyone I had to go away to Rio for their experts in
plastic surgery. And Miguel has never been hurt in a
fire at all."

Gabriella sighed. "It's only the bad things people
remember. But they will forgive and forget a couple of
brothers who won a trip around the world."

"What?" at least three people exclaimed at the same
time.

Antonio laughed. "It was the best your mother could
come up with at the moment. She was cornered at the
grocery store. Apparently, Noah's captain was just stopping on his way home for bread and milk and wondered
why Noah didn't show up for work. And he didn't
receive so much as a phone call. That's not like him."

"Not at all," Jayce said.

"Of course, Dante's captain knew it was their house

that was blown to smithereens. It was his firehouse that had to respond."

"Didn't he wonder what had happened?"

"Fortunately, that captain is a friend of the chief. When the chief arrived, he said he'd call me. I had to give him the same cockamamie story, of course."

Kristine, also a BFD captain, said, "So, I guess we all have to get on the same page in case anyone asks about them."

"You said they went on a world tour?" Sandra asked. "How did you explain their sudden departure?"

"I just said it was a now or never thing. They won and had to go right away—or forfeit the trip."

"That's bizarre, Mom," Luca said. "But I guess it could happen."

"It could, and with luck, people will believe it did."

"Now we need to ask one of our daughters-in-law if she can use her muse powers and figure out a way to go back in time and make this contest a reality," Antonio said.

"You don't ask for much, do you?" Gabe said. "Misty is still new at this."

"I don't know how to do something that complicated. I can go on my own world tour and drop postcards from them in the mail. Can anyone fake their handwriting?"

"I can probably do that with a sample," Antonio said. "How about you, Kristine? Do you know how to go back in time and invent a whole contest?"

Kristine shook her head. "I'm afraid not. I'm still learning my muse role too. I can manipulate time a little bit, but that's all."

"Damn. Then we're screwed," Antonio said.

"No, you're not. I'm more experienced, and sure'n I can come up with somethin'." Chloe's voice came from the ether, and then she stepped out of thin air.

"You didn't think you were going to have a family meeting without us, did you?" Ryan stepped out of the same rift in the air, holding Chloe's hand.

The whole family rose to greet them. Hugs and slaps on the back were given all around.

"Let me set more places!" Gabriella hurried to the hutch to find more plates and mugs.

"It looks like you're going to need to buy more dishware," Luca said and laughed. "And silverware, and napkins..."

"And maybe another leaf in the table," Antonio said. "Especially if the new girlfriends become more than that."

"True. It sounds like Noah was ready to sacrifice himself for this Kizzy girl. Is that her real name, by the way?" Miguel asked.

"Yup. At least that's what Noah said. We spoke to him after he introduced her to us. And we've gotten to know her better recently."

"Is Dante just as serious about Mallory?" Gabe asked.

"Even more so," Gabriella said. "And I couldn't be happier for them. Both girls are absolutely lovely." As she poured Antonio's coffee and began walking around the table, pouring a cup for everyone who didn't place their hand over their mug, she added, "Dante was talking about moving in with Mallory."

"That was supposed to be kept confidential," Antonio said.

"Your father was sworn to secrecy, but *I* wasn't," she sang.

The family laughed.

"Okay then. What do you need us to do?" Jayce asked. "I'm assuming there's more to the story. You could've just texted us and told us the excuse you'd come up with."

Antonio cleared his throat. "You're right. There's more to the story. A lot more. Apparently, there are some scary people down in Brazil, and they're giving Kizzy's family a run for their money. Or whatever it is they want from them."

"It's got to be more than money," Kristine said. "Goddess knows there are wealthy people a lot closer to these enemies in Brazil."

"Yes." Antonio folded his hands on top of the table. "As you know, we have some distant relatives in the Amazon rain forest."

"It sounds like you're ready to get involved and include some distant relatives, Dad, but you don't even know what this group wants? That's not like you," Jayce said.

"You're right. It isn't, usually. Or it wasn't until you and your brothers defied me to help Kristine down in New York."

She smiled. "And thank goodness you did. Without all of you, Jayce couldn't have kept me from revealing my dragon form to half of Manhattan, and I couldn't have rescued my mother without him."

"And we're glad you all did what you decided to do too," Gabriella said.

Antonio gave them all the hairy eyeball, one by one around the table. "But don't ever defy me again. We really have to pick our battles."

"So you're giving the okay for this one," Jayce said.

"I'm glad. If our brothers need us, we're going to be there for them, no matter what."

Antonio nodded. "That's how I raised you to be. Even the fire service reinforces it."

"So let's summarize what we know so far," Jayce said. "There's a scary group in South America. We have relatives in South America. Are we going to involve them?"

"Only by asking them to house us for however long it takes. I'm hoping it won't be long, but we need a base of operations that's off the grid."

"And how are we going to get involved ourselves?" Miguel asked.

"That's what I hope you'll all figure out before you leave," Gabriella said.

Antonio held up one hand. "If any of you have reservations about this, you're not obligated to go. We can't fly that far that fast, so we'll need to take a plane to Brazil, then meet up with our relatives. From there, we'll go hunting for this group."

"I'm in," Ryan said.

"So am I," Jayce said.

"And me."

"Ditto."

One more yes would make it unanimous.

"So I guess we're going to Brazil," Luca said. "Cool. I'd love to see the beaches near Rio. Oh, but it will be my graduation gift, right?"

Antonio chuckled. "Don't worry. No one has to pay for this trip. It's on me. Noah can pay me back later, with installment plans."

The two birds hopped up and down in their cage, squawking.

"I don't think Noah's objecting to your payment plan. I think the two of them want to go with us," Gabe observed.

"And that would be fine if they were fully mature," Antonio said. "But they're about fourteen right now. Not a good age if restraint is needed." As if to illustrate the point, Noah squawked loudly and flapped his wings. Dante flew over him and pecked him on the head until he stopped.

"See what I mean?"

"I do," Gabe said. "At fifteen, I made a stupid mistake that messed me up for about a decade."

Then Dante squawked as if to disagree. Noah began hopping up and down again.

"Knock it off, you two. You're staying here with your mother, and that's final." Antonio huffed. "Now, does anyone know how to reach this Kizzy Samuels?"

Chapter 15

KIZZY HAD ENJOYED HER FIRST DAY BACK AT WORK. As expected, a couple of coworkers hinted they would like to know what had happened to her so suddenly. She just smiled and changed the subject.

On her way home with Ruth, her phone rang.

"Hello?"

"Is this Kizzy Samuels?"

She didn't recognize the phone number or the voice. "May I ask who's calling?"

"Yes. It's Noah's father, Antonio. I think we need to talk."

"Oh. Is Noah all right?"

Ruth glanced over at her, concern written on her face. Kizzy looked to her for any hint of trouble in her psychic senses. Ruth shrugged her shoulders while keeping her hands on the wheel.

"Noah is fine. We're just concerned about that problem of yours and thought we might be able to help."

Kizzy was tempted to ask which problem, but she didn't want to give them the impression that she had several. Besides, she was pretty sure she knew what he meant. "Are you talking about the entity?"

"Yes. We may be able to help you find them. As phoenixes, we blend in with the colorful birds of the Amazon. We can soar above, pick out the exact location, get an idea of how many there are, if they're armed…anything to help Noah and Dante have nice, peaceful lives after this. What to do with the information is up to you and your family."

Kizzy was excited. "Is it all right if I talk to my father about this? He'll want to be involved, I'm sure."

"Absolutely. I'd be happy to talk with him too. Is he a witch, like you?"

"Yes." Kizzy was overwhelmed by their offer. She swallowed around a lump in her throat as she thanked him and promised to have her father call him.

As soon as she disconnected the call, she turned to Ruth and excitedly explained the other half of the conversation. Ruth's eyes widened. "They can find them? And then what do we do? You're a doctor, and as a doctor, you can't kill them. Or you could…but then you'd just have to turn around and save their lives again."

Kizzy's posture sagged. "You're right, but they offered to help. Maybe… I don't know. It's a lot to ask."

"You'd better not be talking about asking the Fierros to kill them."

"No, of course not." Kizzy rubbed her forehead, feeling a headache coming on. "Dad will know what to do. I sure as hell don't."

"Kizzy! You said 'hell.'"

Kizzy laughed. "Yes, I did, and I might do it again."

Ruth grinned as she drove into their father's driveway.

Energized, Kizzy got out of the car and jogged up the steps to the side door. Throwing it open, she called out "Dad! Where are you? I have some exciting news."

Aaron met her in the kitchen. "What's going on?"

As soon as Ruth followed her through the side door and shut it behind her, Kizzy spoke freely.

"Only the answer to a prayer. Noah's family has given me permission to talk to you about their paranormal status. And even more exciting, their willingness to help us root out the entity!"

Aaron took a step backward. "Paranormal status? What…is he?"

"It's a good thing, Dad. They're all phoenixes. Shapeshifters. Well, all the boys and Mr. Fierro are. His name is Antonio, by the way. And he would like to speak with you. He said they'd do anything they could to help."

"Phoenixes? I never heard of any paranormal phoenixes. Are you sure they aren't just pulling your leg?"

"No, Dad. I've seen them with my own eyes. Noah shifted, flew around the room, and shifted back."

"So, they're shape-shifters. I never thought the phoenix was anything other than legend."

Kizzy shrugged. "Apparently there are a few pockets of them around the world. One group is in the Amazon. They're distant relatives of the Fierros, but Antonio knows them well enough to get them involved if need be."

"And what can they do?" Dr. Samuels asked. "Burn down the place and rise from the ashes?"

"Yes, although I'd never ask them to do that. It's complicated. Phoenixes aren't just a myth. They are real. As firefighters, they're able to reincarnate if the worst happens."

Aaron stroked his bearded chin.

"I can tell you something in confidence, Dad, right?"

"Of course."

"I thought you didn't want me dating a firefighter because he didn't make enough money. He thought so too."

Aaron's posture straightened. "What? No. Of course not. I'd like any boyfriend of yours to have steady employment, but whatever his salary is isn't an issue. You've seen plenty of burn victims. And many fire-fighters inhale toxic gases too. I imagine you'd be worried sick about him. But this…immortality, this changes things."

"Yes, it does. And the possibility of getting rid of the entity, maybe even retrieving the last book, well, that changes everything!" She went to the refrigerator and grabbed a bottle of wine. "Would you like a glass?"

Aaron reached for the bottle. "I think we all might need one for the rest of this conversation. Thanks."

"I'll give you Antonio's phone number. When you're ready, you can call him."

"I'm ready right now. Just dial the number and hand me the phone."

"Kizzy! How's it going?" Mallory said.

"It's going weird. I wouldn't bother you, but my father and Mr. Fierro thought we should talk. Your dad was doing some construction in Brazil, and my family's nemesis is hiding out there, probably in the same area."

"Uh-huh. I remember the map thingy we did."

"The Fierros are going to try to help us find their exact location. Since our situations are probably con-nected, you could pinpoint where they should start their search."

"I thought you knew the exact spot from scrying."

"No. Just the general area. Having them fly overhead and find it from a logical starting point could save a lot of time. How would you like to help put a stop to the jerks who put a curse on you?"

"*If* it's the same group, you mean."

"I'm pretty sure it is. Not many people would curse a total stranger. But these horrible asshats would."

Mallory couldn't help getting excited. She'd love to know who cursed her and why. More crucially, she'd like to be sure they wouldn't do it again! "But I don't know the exact location. I mean, I think it's near a certain bend in the river, but I'm not *exactly* sure. Should I ask my father? He's the one who could give precise coordinates, but he might ask why I need to know."

"I talked to Mr. Fierro and my dad. They said if you didn't know, they would approach your father. It's tricky, because they don't know him, and I assume he's human?"

Mallory chuckled. "Sometimes I wonder, but yes. As far as I know, he's human."

"They said if he asks questions and they feel they can trust him, they might reveal their paranormal status."

"Dante made me think they weren't supposed to reveal themselves to humans."

"Yes. And if he freaks out, they have friends who can erase his memory."

Mallory took a deep breath. "Is that safe?"

"Yes. They did it to Noah. I wouldn't have let them if they hadn't assured me they could do it completely safely."

An upside would be that Mallory could share the whole monkey fiasco with her father. They had been getting closer lately. An even greater upside would be making sure these asshats couldn't curse anyone else.

"I'm in!"

———

Five phoenixes glided over the Amazon River, their colorful tail feathers reflected in the slow-moving water. Aaron and Antonio sat in lounge chairs on the torn-up shore, mesmerized by the beautiful birds.

Mallory's father, Nigel, exited a shack, bringing over a tray with a pitcher of lemonade and three empty glasses on it. He set everything on a rustic-looking coffee table. "I've never seen anything like them."

Antonio smiled. "They're pretty magnificent, right?"

"Magnificent indeed," Aaron said. "I still wonder why you wanted to help us. It's not your problem."

"From what I understand, my sons are getting serious about your girls. If they become part of our family, we *all* have a problem. But together, we're a solution."

Aaron's brows shot up. "A solution? You have a plan?"

"Wait," Nigel said. "Before we get to that… Nothing has been said or decided yet, right? You seem to think Mallory will be joining your family."

"Yes. My Gabriella thinks she will, and she's never been wrong. That woman can spot a daughter-in-law at thirty paces." He laughed. "I know this is more for Kizzy's sake, but if Mallory ever needs anything, we're here for her too. We'd do anything for family."

"Thank you."

Aaron looked thoughtful. At last, he spoke. "If Noah makes Kizzy happy, and she has trusted you with her secret and you have trusted her with yours, I don't see anything wrong with joining our families."

Antonio leaned toward him. "Thanks. Gabriella

thinks he's found 'the one.' They speak the same language. He's an EMT with ambitions to go on and become a paramedic—maybe someday a doctor. Meanwhile, if he ever gets hurt in a fire, we can heal him. She can heal the rest of the world. Together, they'd make a pretty powerful couple."

Nigel chuckled. "I never knew all this stuff existed. Thank you for trusting me with your secrets. Now that I know my construction troubles could have been fueled by magic and hidden agendas, I feel oddly better."

"You understand how important it is to keep everything between the three of us, right?" Aaron asked.

"Who would believe me? Besides, after all my daughter finally told us, I understand it was your daughter and the Fierro family who were looking out for her. If I'd had any idea, I'd never have started this stupid project."

Antonio glanced around the chained-off area that had been cleared. "Oh, I don't know if I'd call it stupid. The idea was probably a good one. Most people never get to see this remote part of the world. To take them on tours could be a good thing—as long as you coupled it with a healthy respect for the environment and talks about the interdependence of the plant and animal life along the river."

Nigel smiled. "Exactly. I'm glad someone appreciates what I was trying to do. It wasn't about a five-star hotel experience as my daughter thought. That would be an impossible feat to pull off in this part of the world. I'm glad I could be here to explain my vision."

The birds took a sudden turn and flew over the tops of the trees until they could no longer be seen.

Antonio sat up. "They've seen something."

"Let's hope so," Nigel said. "How are you going to rid the world of this menace?"

"We have a plan. I know it may seem strange that I can't give you details, but together with some friends who prefer to remain anonymous, I think we can manage to do this without killing anyone."

"I hope it's foolproof," Aaron said. "I can't get over all the wonderful people you know, willing to do whatever it takes to help one another."

Antonio smiled. "Neither can I, Aaron. Neither can I."

———

After scoping out the area and gathering intel, the phoenixes landed in the backyard of a modest house. It was very private. They shifted and dressed in the track suits they had left on the picnic bench there. Then they met their third cousins at a large truck with a cage over the back and a canvas covering, the kind of thing that would transport soldiers.

"Let me do the talking when we get there," Jayce said.

"You'll have to. We don't know what's going on." It was the first time Jayce had met these cousins, but they seemed like old friends, immediately wanting to help.

"It's probably better to keep it that way."

There were only two of them here, Marco and José. The other relatives lived closer to town and blended in with the locals. Jayce climbed into the back of the truck with the rest of his brothers. They started up and jolted over the rough terrain. They weren't far from the area where they would meet up with their father and the two men he said were Mallory's and Kizzy's fathers—and very likely Dante's and Noah's future fathers-in-law.

As the truck rumbled along, Miguel asked, "So now that we know where they are, what are we going to do about them?"

Jayce shrugged. "That's up to Dad. He says he has a plan, but he won't let anyone in on the nitty-gritty details. Not yet anyway. He said he had to get a few other people involved and get their permission."

"Permission to do what?"

Jayce reclined against the rustic bench. "I'm not at liberty to say."

When they reached the cleared land along the shore of the Amazon, they all jumped out of the back and waved goodbye to their cousins.

The elder Fierro strolled over to meet them. "So, boys, what did you find out?"

"Are you ever going to stop thinking of us as boys?" Luca asked.

"Nope." Antonio folded his arms and waited.

As soon as the truck was out of sight, Jayce turned to his father.

"There's a compound. A fairly sizable one. Fifteen buildings on about four acres. We saw at least twenty men of various ages. A few women and children."

"Damn," one of the men said as he strolled up beside Antonio. "If I had known there were that many assholes across the river, I probably wouldn't have chosen this build site."

"They're more than just assholes," the other unfamiliar man said. "They're dangerous. Extremely dangerous." Then he looked to Jayce, stepping forward and extending his hand. "I'm Kizzy's father, Aaron Samuels, by the way. I assume you're the one called Jayce?"

Jayce shook his hand. "Yes. I'll be the new leader of the family when my father retires."

"I didn't know you were still working, Antonio," Aaron said. "I thought you had retired a while ago."

"You're right. I retired from the fire service several years ago. But now I want to retire from the family service. My boys are all grown, as my youngest will tell you, and they can take care of themselves. But I insist on leaving someone in charge. Actually, even Jayce has a backup. His brother Miguel will co-lead. We have unique problems, and somebody needs to be the final decision maker." Antonio turned to his sons. "Did you see anyone armed?"

"Yes. There were a couple of guards carrying rifles. One on each side of the compound."

Aaron nodded. "I would expect as much."

"Is there any way to sneak in?"

"There's a small tributary bordering it. A fairly steep bank could hide someone."

"Can you give us exact coordinates?" Mallory's father asked. He pulled a map from his back pocket and opened it. Then he carried it to the coffee table, spread it out, and smoothed it.

Antonio said, "We don't have built-in GPS, but Jayce's sense of direction can certainly guide my next guests to where they need to be."

"Next guests?" Aaron prompted.

"It's time for phase two." Antonio nodded to Jayce and said, "You know what to do."

Jayce closed his eyes. "Kristine? Can you hear me?"

His beautiful wife appeared next to him. "I could hear you better if you took your shirt off." She waggled her eyebrows.

The guys laughed.

"Is that all I am to you? A sex object?" Jayce teased.

"No. You're much more than an object. So, how are we going to do this?"

Jayce shrugged. "I have no idea. It's been you and my dad cooking up this whole thing."

"Antonio? Do I have your permission to share the plan with everyone?"

"Why don't I share it?" he said. "You just go and get the people we need."

"Okay. I'll be back in a jiffy."

Kristine disappeared.

"We belong to a paranormal club in the city, which is where I found certain people to help. And that was my daughter-in-law, Kristine. We can all visit later, but I don't think we should delay in case anyone on the other side of the river gets suspicious and leaves the compound."

He didn't have a chance to say more before two people appeared with Kristine, all holding hands.

"Thanks for the lift," a guy with a short military haircut said.

Kristine let go and stepped away, joining Jayce.

Antonio introduced them briefly. "This is Kurt and his wife, Ruxandra. We need their help to end this thing. It's going to take some doing. My boys will be in the trees watching in case anything goes wrong. Kristine will transport these two over the river, following Jayce.

"The rest of the plan is fairly simple. Kurt is a wizard and can freeze time briefly. Ruxandra has the ability to erase minds and replace memories with new ones."

Ruxandra, a gorgeous blonde in a red dress, said, "I'm

a vampire and can mesmerize these idiots and convince them they are, and always have been, simple farmers."

"Wait," Aaron said. "They have a book we need. Before they lose their memories of it, you need to find that book."

"Boy, you don't ask for much, do you?" Kurt said. "How many people do I have to hold frozen in time at once?"

"I'd estimate at least thirty-five or forty," Jayce said.

"Can you do that?" Luca asked. "Freeze people then thaw them out one at a time for your wife to mesmerize?"

Kurt grinned. "With any luck. And it's not so much thawing them out as it is allowing time to advance in one place and not another. It's very complicated, and I hope I can do it without my head exploding."

Kristine's jaw dropped. "You mean you're not sure you can do this without harming yourself? I can help turn time back a bit, but I have no idea how to manipulate it in one spot and not another—at least not by myself. I'd need several of my muse sisters for that."

"Don't worry. I should be okay. And if not, I understand there's a doctor here?"

Aaron stepped forward. "Yes. I'm a doctor. And you're...human?"

"One hundred percent. I've studied magic all my life, but I have no supernatural powers."

Aaron set his hands on his hips. "Manipulating time? That sounds pretty darn supernatural to me."

Kurt shrugged. "What can I say? It's possible I have some kind of paranormal power, but as far as I know, I'm just damn talented."

"Well, whatever it is, we're just grateful you're

here," Antonio said. "My bunch of phoenixes wouldn't be able to do more than set fires and put them out. And that really rubs us the wrong way."

"And if I harmed anyone, I'd be violating not only my Hippocratic oath, but the Witches' Rede too," Aaron said.

Jayce stepped forward and shook Kurt's hand. "Thanks, man. This is above and beyond."

"Well, I'm a nice guy and all that."

Ruxandra looked shocked. "I thought you said they were paying us."

Kurt put an arm around her. "They are, hon. Don't worry. You'll get that honeymoon we never took."

"Oh, good."

Antonio withdrew his wallet and took out a check. "I have it right here. You already received the other half up front, correct?"

"I paid them. Don't worry," Aaron said.

Ruxandra focused on the third man and said, "How about you? Do you leave the tip?"

Nigel's jaw dropped, and he was silent for a moment. "Sure. If you're successful and our families are completely out of danger forever, you can have this land you're standing on."

She looked satisfied and nodded once. "Fine. We can honeymoon right here." She turned to her husband and said, "Kurt, honey? You can conjure up a building and some staff and a pool, right?"

Kurt laughed. "I love you, my diva wife. And you know I can't refuse you anything. Your wish is my command."

Ruxandra smiled and kissed him on the cheek.

Then she turned to the three men and rubbed her hands together. "Let's get this shitshow on the road."

———~~~———

Jayce led the way. Kristine held the hands of the vampire and wizard, and all three of them remained in the ether as she followed her husband's lead.

The guards didn't look too "on guard," so to speak. In fact, they seemed pretty lackadaisical.

Ruxandra and Kurt walked out of the ether, appearing to have come out of thin air. Kristine watched from within. She could jump into the scene and turn back time by a few minutes. Just enough to send a bullet back to its chamber, if necessary.

Ruxandra strode boldly, catching the guard's eye. His jaw went slack, and he didn't move. *Damn, she's good.* Kristine made a note of that for the future.

She couldn't hear what was said, but the guard handed over his weapon. Suddenly, the other guard came charging across the length of two football fields, shouting. All eyes turned to the vampire.

"Aw, crap." Kristine was about to step in when the wizard drew an arc in the air. Everyone froze in place. He then went from person to person with his wife, unfreezing and refreezing each person in turn.

Kristine was almost mesmerized herself by the amazing feat they were pulling off…until a couple of men armed with pistols came running out of the nearby building. Time to snap out of it.

She stepped out of the ether and froze them. Then she backed up time a bit. Unfortunately, that undid the wizard's work on the last women he'd frozen.

"Damn it," she muttered. "I hadn't counted on that."

Kurt raised his hand and called over to her. "It's okay. We'll just start with the buildings first." As soon as he and Ruxandra were inside, with a snap of his fingers the women who were hanging damp laundry resumed their work.

Back in the ether, Kristine followed them inside, leaving Jayce to watch over the people outside. He'd squawk if anyone was coming. She watched as Ruxandra mesmerized each of the two men inside. Then she grabbed their guns and pulled the vamp and the wizard into the ether a moment after he snapped his fingers. She paused long enough to see them looking for something—presumably farming implements.

They repeated this pattern in two of the other buildings. One was a bakery of sorts, and the other looked like a tailor's shop. A barn held some animals, but no one was in there at the moment. The rest of the buildings were either empty or only residential.

When everyone indoors had been convinced they were farmers, bakers, or tailors, they returned to the people outside.

All went smoothly with the residents outside, and when Kurt and Ruxandra were safely ensconced in the ether, Kurt unfroze the entire scene. Most people carried on with what they were doing. The two guards scratched their heads and glanced around in confusion.

"Did you tell the guards they were farmers?"

"Yes, but I may have neglected to tell them what they were supposed to be doing and hand them a hoe or something."

"Well, we can't have that." Kristine pointed at the

ground behind the men, and a hoe, rake, and seedlings appeared.

They turned around, looked like they were saying "Aha!" and started laying out the boundary of a garden.

"There! I think we're done," she said, relieved.

The three of them popped back to the American men on the banks of the river. Kristine walked the others out of the ether and dropped their hands. "I'm going back for a bit. Jayce is keeping watch, and I'll sit up in the trees with him. We'll make sure they're acting like farmers."

"Find the book, if you can," Aaron begged. "It's important they never find it again."

She saluted. "I'll do what I can to snoop around without being seen. Jayce will watch my back."

"We all will," Ryan said, stepping forward.

"No. You boys have had your fun," Antonio said. "Now it's my turn." He geared down quickly and shifted into his phoenix form. Flying slowly, more like gliding, he took off in the direction of the new farm.

Epilogue

Back in Boston, ten weeks after the little bang…

EVERYONE HAD THEIR CHAMPAGNE FLUTES FILLED, READY to toast Dante's and Noah's return from aviary life. Gabriella's excitement was as palpable as the rest.

"Are they going to be the same as we remember them?" Mallory whispered to Kizzy. The two women stood next to each other, holding hands.

"I think so. From what I understand, they'll look and act the same and have all their memories. One little oddity that shouldn't even be noticeable is now they'll be the same age."

"Oh my goodness! So, they're twins now?"

"Yeah. Fraternal twins, I guess."

"You guess right," Antonio said. He'd overheard, of course.

When would Kizzy and Mallory get used to that heightened audio ability? Gabriella smiled—she didn't always remember they had it either.

"If they stayed in bird form for another month, they'd come back a lot older. This is the right time for their ages to stay about the same," Antonio explained. "They're about twenty-five."

"Okay, so where are they?" Mallory asked.

"Shifting and getting dressed in their old room," Gabriella said. "They shared the largest room on the third floor for about twenty years. Noah moved up there when Luca was born."

"Yeah," Luca said. "I kicked him out of the nursery."

Gabriella chuckled. "That's pretty much how each of my boys got their own rooms. Each one kicked the next one upstairs."

"Then Dante moved to his own place a few months before Noah joined him," Antonio said. "That was, what…about three years ago?"

"So, they've almost always lived together," Kizzy stated.

"Pretty much," Antonio confirmed. "Dante had a roommate from his firehouse for a while, until the guy got married. Then Noah moved in."

"Well, they've been best friends all their lives, so why not twins?" Mallory asked.

Cheering started near the stairs.

"That must be them." Kizzy was shorter, so she tried to see around the crowd.

Mallory stood on tiptoes, glancing over the shoulders of the rest of the family. Dante emerged first, wearing a sombrero. Mallory handed her champagne glass to Misty, giggled, and ran to him, jumping into his arms. The hat fell back, but neither one seemed to notice. They were too busy kissing.

Then Noah walked out wearing a fez. "What a great trip! Remind me never to enter another world tour contest."

Kizzy handed her champagne off to Chloe, then ran to him and threw her arms around his waist, hugging him tight. He kissed the top of her head and hugged her back.

After lots of handshakes and pats on the shoulder, Antonio cleared his throat, then lifted his glass. "Sons, daughters, and friends, we're so glad all of you were able to be here today to welcome back Dante and Noah from their fake world tour." He smirked at Gabriella. She simply threw up her hands.

"But seriously," he continued, "if you guys don't stop this reincarnation nonsense, you're going to have to put up with sillier and sillier excuses for a two-month disappearance!"

Everyone chuckled or outright laughed.

"I know what I tell you next is going to come as a surprise—probably as much to Dante and Noah as any of you. But here it is." Antonio held up a round pellet, which glinted in the overhead light.

Dante gasped. "Is that Noah's musket ball?"

Antonio grinned and announced, "I examined the rubble that used to be your apartment and found this. Gentlemen, your brothers are alchemists! They created gold out of lead."

Noah stumbled backward. "Seriously?"

Gabriella let out a tinkling laugh. "If you ever do it again, I'll refuse to take you out of the cage until you're old men. Understand?"

"Yeah, we understand," Dante said. "But, shoot, that'll come in handy when Noah has to find a new place to live. Me? I've decided to move in with Mallory, if she'll still have me."

"Of course I will! We're going to be living together? That's my dream come true."

"We can be married, if you'd prefer."

She laughed. "I'd prefer that a whole lot!"

The two of them kissed heartily, not coming up for air and apparently not caring if anyone else was in the room while it erupted with cheers and shouts of congratulations.

When everyone had quieted down, Noah turned to Kizzy and took both of her hands in his. "Yeah. About that. I was hoping we could get a place together. Unless you're still worried about your father's disapproval."

Her jaw dropped, but she recovered quickly. "I don't think he'll disapprove at all, now that our family is out of danger, thanks to yours. And even if he did, I'd love to live with you, Noah! I love you dearly."

"I love you too. So that's a yes?"

"That's a shut-the-front-door, heck yes!"

They kissed more chastely, but to the same sounds of cheers, whistles, and catcalls. Kizzy's olive skin turned a lovely shade of rose.

"I baked a special treat to celebrate." Gabriella gathered everyone in the dining room. She had made a large sheet cake, copying the old Risk board to approximate a world map on top. "Everyone have a seat," she said.

Most of the guys and the two remaining women sat down at the very long dining table.

"Tony might have a mind of his own," Gabe said. The little boy was just learning to walk and couldn't be stopped from toddling everywhere.

"I have a solution to that." Gabriella remembered how to distract a child. She picked up her precious grandson and plopped him into a highchair. "Give him his favorite toy," she said to Gabe.

He pulled a plastic dinosaur out of a diaper bag and handed it to him. Tony chewed on it and seemed content.

Now Gabriella had her hands free to cut the cake.

Misty emerged from the kitchen carrying a tray of cups and saucers. Sandra followed with plates. Kristine was already placing napkins and silverware in front of each place.

It was amazing how much Gabriella's family had grown. As each son moved out, her heart had broken a bit. Then when they visited with a wife and even a child, her heart not only mended but grew larger to accommodate the new members. She and Antonio would have *two* new daughters very soon. And they were human. Capable of giving her more grandchildren!

Antonio winked at her. After thirty-five years together, she knew exactly what he was thinking. "Six sons settled down. One to go. Almost there."

P.S.
The third book was never found.

*Now for a special sneak peek at the next
Phoenix Brothers book!*

A PHOENIX
IS FOREVER

He was actually a cop. A real, bona fide police officer.

Luca Fierro walked out of the precinct wearing his new BPD uniform as a Boston patrolman trainee. As the new guy, he would be on the graveyard shift for a while with his more experienced field training officer, Joe.

"So, how does it feel to be a genuine cop—not a cadet?" Joe asked.

"You don't remember? How long have you been on the job?"

Joe laughed. "Fifteen fun-filled years." They paused a moment to get into their cruiser. Joe took the driver's seat. He may have carried an extra twenty or thirty pounds, but he seemed agile enough.

"Did you have a difficult adjustment?" Luca asked as he buckled his seat belt.

"Not really. My dad was a cop, so that may have helped me ease into the job."

Luca really didn't want to mention his legendary family. The Fierros were all firefighters. Some of the cops had real problems with firefighters. They called them "hose draggers" and didn't like being accused of "pillow envy," because firefighters were allowed to sleep on the night shift.

Similarly, the firefighters weren't always fond of cops. His own family called him the "blue sheep."

Instead, Luca just answered the original question. "I feel good about finally getting started on the job. I've trained long and hard for this."

Joe was quiet as he pulled out of the station's parking lot, so Luca continued. "My folks weren't in favor of my going into law enforcement, but they were okay with my studying criminal justice at Northeastern University. They thought I'd change my mind after learning what was involved. If anything, school made me want it even more."

"Oh, shit," Joe said. "You know why it's called a BS degree? You know too much to be clueless, but not enough to deal with those weird situations they didn't prepare you for. " He smirked.

"In other words, you think I know just enough to be dangerous?"

"Maybe. What did they teach you there?"

"All kinds of things. Ethics, courtroom procedures, criminal law, corrections, crime scene management, computer investigation, domestic and international terrorism… I want to be a detective someday."

Joe nodded.

Luca had to get used to one of the aspects of being a cop, and that was not giving too much away. Just answer the questions you're asked, and no more. Sometimes volunteering information just gets you into hot water.

He'd have to guard his family's secrets even more carefully.

Joe turned onto a busy street. Soon Luca would be allowed to take the wheel. Or maybe not. Different partners worked together for a while before they traded off.

"So, fifteen years… You must've seen it all."

"You've never seen it all, kid. You might hear about some crazy stuff at the bar, though. If it doesn't happen to you, it's happened to someone else."

Patrolling the city was sometimes tedious and sometimes terrifying. It was that on-and-off pace and the fact of never knowing what was around the corner that both intrigued and made most "first years" anxious, to say the least.

It wasn't long before they came across a car speeding and driving erratically. "Shit," Joe said. "I might chalk that up to a typical *Boston driver*, but the damn car almost sideswiped us."

Luca made a mental note of the vehicle's description and their approximate location. They turned on the lights and took off after it. Spotting the car climbing the ramp onto the Southeast Expressway, Joe swore.

"Dammit. I hate stopping drivers on the expressway."

"Can't you get them to pull off at the next exit?"

"We can hope." Joe went in pursuit of the black Mercedes sedan. Instead of taking the next off-ramp, the driver pulled over and stopped right on the bridge.

"Fuck. This is going to block traffic. Leave the lights on."

"Can I approach the driver?" Luca asked.

Joe opened his door. "Be my guest."

Luca crossed in front of the cruiser, noting only one person in the vehicle ahead. He knocked on the driver's window and she rolled it down. Yep, he smelled alcohol. And this woman looked almost clownlike with the amount of heavy makeup she was wearing, red hair in disarray.

"License and registration, please."

The woman heaved a heavy, vodka-laced sigh, dug through the purse on the passenger seat, and produced a wallet. She removed and handed over a current Massachusetts driver's license. Then she opened the glove compartment, found her registration, and handed that to him also.

He scanned the information and said, "Do you know why we stopped you, ma'am?"

"I have no idea."

"You've been driving erratically. Have you been drinking?"

"I am not drunk."

"Step out of the car, please."

The woman sat right where she was and folded her arms.

"You can prove you're sober with a field sobriety test, ma'am. Please step out of the car."

"I don't have to. I don't have to take a Breathalyzer and I don't have to walk a straight line. I know my rights."

"I'm sure you do, ma'am, but we'll have to take you into the station if we suspect you're drunk. I smell alcohol and you've been speeding and weaving all over the road, so you're giving me no other choice. The public's safety is at stake."

"You'll have to drag me out of this car."

"Ma'am, at this point, you're forcing me to place you under arrest. If you don't exit the car, you'll be adding a charge of resisting arrest. Is that really what you want to do?"

She blew out another vodka-heavy huff. The door flew open and Luca stepped out of the way just in time. She sluggishly moved one long leg, and a four-inch blue stiletto hit the pavement. Another one joined it. Eventually she heaved herself out of the car and rose and rose and *rose*. Soon she was leaning over him.

Luca was almost six feet tall. This woman had to be six feet two *without* the stilettos. That made her about six and a half feet…and wobbling.

He took another peek at her license. Her voice didn't sound deep and her name was Priscilla, but he didn't think she was Priscilla, Queen of the Desert. She was just a very tall woman, looking more and more pissed off by the moment.

"Turn around and put your hands on the car, please."

The woman placed her hands on her hips and looked at him defiantly.

Luca raised his voice. "Turn around and place your hands on the roof of your car. Now."

"Why? Are you going to pat me down?"

"At some point, yes. We need to know you're not carrying any concealed weapons."

By this time Joe was rolling his eyes and came over to join him. "Lady, you're going to be frisked, but that can happen later." He gave Luca a pointed look. "Cuff her up."

"You're not touching me!"

"Jesus…" Luca muttered. He gazed at Joe, hoping he would have the right words to gain her cooperation, but it didn't look like Joe had any such magic. Instead he reached out, grabbed her arm, and spun her so her torso was leaning against the car. Meanwhile he had her arm in a viselike grip behind her back.

"Owww. You're hurting me."

"Cuff her, Fierro," Joe said.

Luca took her other wrist and folded it behind her back. He had his cuffs out, but she struggled as soon as he tried to put them on her.

"Don't resist."

She struggled harder. "Leave me alone. You guys are brutalizing me. I'm going to file a complaint."

"Please do. Our dash cam will show you've been given several chances to cooperate."

At that point, she flipped around and ran across the highway, causing cars to slam on their brakes and blow their horns. Luca gave chase. He eventually had to tackle her to keep her from crossing the line into oncoming traffic. Once he had her on the ground, he was able to cuff the other wrist.

Shit. I have to learn to get the handcuffs out faster— but not too fast. There were a lot of things he could do quicker and better than a human, but he couldn't give away his paranormal abilities. He had superhuman strength and speed, but a cop wouldn't let it go if they witnessed something out of the ordinary. And he'd be in *so* much trouble with the paranormal community if he let humans know what he really was.

Joe joined him and the two of them lifted her to her feet. She immediately started kicking and screaming. They had to half lead and half drag her across the road, back to their cruiser.

"You see?" She was yelling at the cars that had

stopped. "You see the brutality? I want witness statements. I want you all to call the Boston police commissioner and tell him what you've seen."

Luca and Joe were beyond reasoning with her at this point. Joe just opened the back door of the cruiser and told her to get in.

"I don't want to. Make me."

Luca shook his head. *What the fuck do we do, now? Fold her in half and put her in there like a quesadilla?*

Apparently, pushing on her head and shoving her into the back seat, then grappling with those long legs and spiky heels was the only option.

"Knock it off, lady. Kicking a police officer with shoes like that is a felony in the Commonwealth of Massachusetts," Joe shouted.

"I don't believe you."

"We can add it to the charges, if that will convince you."

As soon as she had been stuffed into the seat and seatbelted securely, Luca slammed the door shut.

"Holy shit. That is one determined woman," he muttered.

"Yup. This one's feisty."

Joe had turned on the Mercedes's flashers so no one would accidentally plow into her car, then he jumped into the driver's seat, and Luca jogged around the car to get in on the other side.

As a car pulled up to get around them, the passenger rolled down his window and yelled out, "It took two of you to arrest a girl. Pussies!" Then he and the driver laughed and drove off.

Wonderful. Typical adolescent humor.

"I have to pee," said Priscilla from the back seat.

"We'll be at the station in a few minutes," Joe replied, glancing up at the rearview mirror, then he turned to Luca. "Officer Fierro… Would you be good enough to read our collar her rights?"

"Crap," he muttered. With all the distractions, he'd forgotten about the damn Miranda rights. What a rookie mistake. "You have the right to remain silent."

Priscilla began singing, "Silent night… Holy night…"

Luca tried raising his voice to be heard over her, but that only made her sing louder.

"Oh, for fuck's sake." Then he joined in and sang her her rights to the tune of the famous Christmas carol. *"You have the right… To an attorney… If you can't afford one… One will be appointed… If you decide to answer questions now… You have the right to stop until you talk to an attorney…"*

"All right! All right!" she yelled. "Just stop. Your voice is worse than mine."

"Great." He finished the speech in a normal voice. "So, do you understand your rights as I've explained them to you?"

"Yes."

"Are you willing to answer my questions without an attorney present?"

"No. Not until I pee, first. I'm apt to wet your back seat if I don't get to a bathroom soon."

"It wouldn't be the first time," Joe muttered. He had Luca call the station and inform them of the arrest and where the tow truck could find her car.

Their passenger was singing again. She certainly wasn't a lounge singer, but now she was crying too. Her voice wobbled and cracked as she belted out a loud rendition of "Rudolph the Red-Nosed Reindeer."

Luca glanced over at Joe and raised his eyebrows. It wasn't Christmas. It wasn't even Halloween yet. He couldn't wait to get to the station they had left only forty minutes ago.

"So, is this normal for a Monday night?" Luca asked.

"Normal?" Joe chuckled. "Fridays are usually heavy DUI nights, but nothing is 'normal.'"

"Okay. Let me rephrase. Do you deal with this often? Including this level of uncooperativeness?"

"Her? This is nothing. Just wait until you have to arrest a suspect wearing green in a rowdy crowd on St. Patrick's Day."

Coming Spring 2019

Acknowledgments

Thanks to my editor, Cat Clyne, for giving me the freedom to let the story evolve into one book about two brothers. Being best friends, roommates, and fellow firefighters, it was impossible for me to separate them in my brain.

And thanks also to Rachel Gilmer for doing great line edits and catching the mistakes I had missed. Hey, it happens to every writer. Thank goodness for a second pair of eyes to make sure our readers don't have to see those embarrassing oopsies.

As always, I want to thank my superb agent, Nicole Resciniti, for, well, everything!

I'm eternally grateful to my readers. Thanks for coming along for the ride.

About the Author

Ashlyn Chase describes herself as an Almond Joy bar: a little nutty, a little flaky, but basically sweet, wanting only to give her readers a satisfying experience.

She holds a degree in behavioral sciences, worked as a psychiatric RN for fifteen years, and spent a few more years working for the American Red Cross. She credits her sense of humor to her former careers since comedy helped preserve whatever was left of her sanity. She is a multipublished, award-winning author of humorous erotic and paranormal romances, represented by the Seymour Agency.

Ashlyn lives in beautiful New Hampshire with her true-life hero husband who looks like Hugh Jackman with a salt-and-pepper dye job, and they're owned by a spoiled brat cat.

Ashlyn loves to hear from readers! Visit ashlynchase .com to sign up for her newsletter. She's also on Facebook (AuthorAshlynChase), Twitter (@GoddessAsh), Yahoo groups (ashlynsnewbestfriends), and ask her to sign your ebook at authorgraph.com.

I DREAM OF DRAGONS

Tempers flare and sparks fly in award-winning author Ashlyn Chase's Boston Dragons series

When Rory Arish and his two fiery dragon siblings are run out of their ancestral Irish home, it seems their luck has run out—until they arrive in Boston and find a paranormal-friendly apartment building. There's only one problem: Rory's new lair has simultaneously been rented to an infuriating woman who is as stubborn as she is beautiful and will not leave "her" apartment, no matter how steamed he may be…

Holing up in their respective corners, who will be the first to blink…or give in to their off-the-charts chemistry and decide to make this unorthodox living arrangement a little more permanent?

"This story has it all: laughter, tears, magic, and sizzling heat."
—Night Owl Reviews TOP PICK, 5 Stars

For more Ashlyn Chase, visit:
sourcebooks.com

MY WILD IRISH DRAGON

One job opening, two shifters = Sparks fly

Dragon shifter Chloe Arish is hell-bent on becoming a Boston firefighter. She knows she has to work every bit as hard as a man—harder if she wants their respect.

Born into a legendary Boston firefighting family, phoenix shifter Ryan Fierro can't possibly let someone best him on the job. He'd never hear the end of it. When a feisty new recruit seems determined to do just that, Ryan plots to kick her out—until their sizzling chemistry turns explosive...

"Pure pleasure. It's like spending time with your favorite friends."

—*Night Owl Reviews* TOP PICK for *How to Date a Dragon*

For more Ashlyn Chase, visit:
sourcebooks.com

NEVER DARE A DRAGON

Dragon and phoenix shifters collide with fiery results in Ashlyn Chase's third Boston Dragons book

Lieutenant Jayce Fierro belongs to a legendary Boston firefighting family of phoenix shifters. Hiding his true form makes relationships impossible, so when he hits it off with a fellow shifter and firefighter, he's thrilled. Less thrilling? Finding out she lives in New York—three hours away.

Dragon shifter and firefighter for the NYC Fire Department Kristine Scott can't stop thinking about Jayce. She's determined to control the heat between them, but when Kristine lands herself in a blaze of trouble, Jayce will do whatever it takes to help…and prove he's worth the distance.

"A great addition to Chase's stellar library."

—RT Book Reviews, 4 Stars, for *My Wild Irish Dragon*

For more Ashlyn Chase, visit:
sourcebooks.com

HOOKED ON A PHOENIX

Locked in a bank vault together...
They might redefine the meaning of "safe" sex

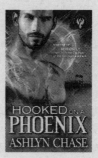

Misty Carlisle works as a bank teller in Boston's financial district. She's had more rotten luck in her life than most, except when her childhood crush shows up to cash his paycheck. Then her heart races and her mouth goes dry.

Gabe Fierro is a firefighter—and a phoenix. Like his brothers, his biggest challenge is finding a woman open-minded enough to accept a shape-shifter into his life. When his boyhood friend asks him to watch over his little sister, Misty, he reluctantly agrees. But when the bank where she works gets held up, Gabe does everything he can to protect her. The two of them end up locked in the bank's vault... where things get steamier than either of them ever imagined.

"Shapeshifting done right! This fast-paced romance is a must-read."
—RT Book Reviews, 4 Stars

For more Ashlyn Chase, visit:
sourcebooks.com

Also by Ashlyn Chase